The Adv

Sherlock Holmes

and the

Glamorous

Ghost

Book Three

Harry DeMaio

Hardcover ISBN 978-1-80424-141-7
Paperback ISBN 978-1-80424-142-4
Epub ISBN 978-1-80424-143-1
PDF ISBN 978-1-80424-144-8

Published by MX Publishing
335 Princess Park Manor, Royal Drive,
London, N11 3GX
www.mxpublishing.co.uk

Cover design Brian Belanger

Dedicated to GTP

A Most Extraordinary Bear

And to the late Ms. Woof

An Extremely Sweet

and Loving Dog

Acknowledgements

These stories have evolved over a long period of time and under a wide range of influences and circumstances. I am indebted to many people for helping to bring my versions of Holmes, Watson, Lady Juliet and Pookie to the printed and electronic page. Thanks most especially to my wife, Virginia, for her insights and clever suggestions as well as her unfailing enthusiasm for the project and patience with its author.

To Steve, Sharon and Timi Emecz for their outstanding support of my seventeen book Octavius Bear series, the Glamorous Ghost collection and my other Holmes pastiches. To Derrick and Brian Belanger for publishing The Glamorous Ghost Book One and several of my other Holmes and Solar Pons efforts. To Dan Andriacco, Amy Thomas, David Chamberlain, Jack Magan, and Gretchen Altabef for their enthusiastic encouragement. And to all of my generous Kickstarter backers.

To my sons, Mark and Andrew and their spouses, Cindy and Lorraine, for helping to make these stories more readable and audience friendly. To Cathy Hartnett, cheerleader-extraordinaire for her eagerness to see this alternate world take form.

Thanks also to Wikipedia for providing facts and specifics of Victorian England and elsewhere. And additional kudos to Brian Belanger for his wonderful illustrations and covers.

Obviously, these stories are tongue in cheek fantasies and require the reader to totally suspend disbelief. I do hope they are entertaining fun. I'm not sure what Heaven is really like but I hope to find out one day.

If, in spite of all this support, some errors or inconsistencies have crept through, the buck stops here. Needless to say, all of the characters, situations, and narratives are fictional. Some locations, devices, historical figures and events are real.

Thanks to Wikipedia for filling in historical blanks.

The Adventures of Sherlock Holmes and the Glamorous Ghost

Book Three

Table of Contents

The Adventures of Sherlock Holmes and the Glamorous Ghost

Book Three

Prologue

She's back yet again! Welcome Lady Juliet Armstrong, Baroness Crestwell once more to our pages. A former sensation of the London musical stage; a feisty member of the British nobility by marriage but recently, a most definitely *deceased* arrival at the Elysian Fields. The obstreperous noblewoman was not content to don her halo and bland heavenly garb and join the other celestial denizens in eternal bliss. She had been shot and wanted to find the blighter who did it and bring him/her to justice before going to her eternal reward. Who else to solve the mystery than Sherlock Holmes and Doctor Watson? Clad in her scarlet Parisian evening gown and wearing a chic corona fashionably tilted on her head, she persuaded the powers that be in Heaven to allow her to return to Earth and seek out Holmes' assistance. Thus began the first story in Book One of this collection of tales that takes the Glamorous Ghost, Holmes and Watson on a wild tour of crimes, personalities, situations and locations.

Holmes, no believer in ghosts, reluctantly acknowledged the noblewoman's otherworldly existence and agreed to cooperate with her in what has evolved into a series of semi-supernatural adventures. Watson followed suit.

Another ghostly and no less glamorous character aids and abets throughout. Pookie, a very clever and highly opinionated Bichon Frisé who predeceased her Baronial mistress, barks, whines and wags her way into the proceedings at every turn. Unruly as her owner, she is always instrumental in keeping the action going.

In Book Two, the Baroness and her dog continued their excursions from Paradise back to Earth with Holmes and the good Doctor. Becoming aware of the two winsome wraiths, Mrs. Hudson also linked up with the merry band. Many characters from previous Holmes and Lady Juliet stories also passed through the pages.

Now in Book Three, the madcap mystical mischief and mayhem carries on. Join us for more fantasy and tongue-in-cheek fun!

The Adventures of Sherlock Holmes and the Glamorous Ghost

Chez Paree

Prologue

"Paris! That's where Pookie and I want to go. The French theater, opera, and the fashion houses. Convince Raymond! After that insane kidnapping nonsense with the auto pageant, you owe me one." Thus ended Book Two of The Adventures of Sherlock Holmes and the Glamorous Ghost.

The Great Detective hesitated to point out that Baroness Juliet Armstrong had been amply rewarded for her performance as Rose Latour, the Goddess of Motorized Marvels at The Royal Society for the Advancement of Automotive Machinery's traveling pageant. But since she was a ghost and usually had no use for money, she was contributing most of her earnings to the Baker Street Irregulars Food Pantry administered by Major Philomena Monahan. The urchins would eat well as they continued to expand their literary and arithmetic skills under Desmond O'Reilly's tutelage. Maybe she could even get them to wear shoes.

Holmes thought, "I suppose I do owe her one. I'll speak to Raymond, the Senior Director of Paradise. He'll probably give her and the dog a few more days on Earth before they have to return heavenward. We can also see if Mrs. Hudson would like to join us in Paris."

"All right, Lady Juliet. I will contact Mr. Raymond. If he agrees, you and Pookie will have to continue your ability to change from ethereal to earthly and back again if we go to Paris."

"We? Are you coming too?"

9

"Of course. I have French forebears and have many connections with the Sûreté. And the Gallic rogues, especially gentlemen burglars, are always on the prowl. There is much for me to do in Paris. I'll see if Watson is available. If Raymond agrees to your journey, we can also invite Mrs. Hudson."

"Oh, I'm sure Martha would love to go. She travels so seldom. And she loves gourmet food. If Pookie and I are physical, we can all enjoy some of that scrumptious French cooking and wine. I'll keep a little of my earnings aside. And the Parisian musical theatre! Back to my chorus line days. Oh, the opera! I adore it. I'll sing along. Unheard, of course. Then I can flit over to the fashion boutiques and design houses and bring some ideas back to Madame Clarice at Miraculous Modes in Heaven. Such fun! I can't wait to tell Pookie. She's never been to Paris. I've only been there once and it was quite a while ago."

*****

A celestial / terrestrial conference: Holmes and Mr. Raymond had established a special communication channel during one of his adventures.

"Well, yes, Mr. Holmes, considering the excellent work she has been doing, I suppose I could look the other way if the Baroness and Pookie want to spend a few days in Paris. If necessary, I can always smooth it out with the Committee. In spite of, or maybe because of her rowdy behavior, she is a great favorite with the Almighty. They enjoy her. She's a favorite of mine too, but don't tell her that. Do try to keep her out of trouble, will you. You know what the French are like. And trouble seems to follow her and her dog around." This from Mr. Raymond, Senior Director of Paradise.

"Thank you, sir, but I make no promises. Forget the French. You know what Lady Juliet is like."

Raymond sighed, 'Yes, I do."

10

Chapter One

July 1902 - Paris: the Hôtel Regina in the Place des Pyramides, across the Rue de Rivoli from the Jardin des Tuileries, near an entrance to the Louvre. A deluxe and convenient locale from which to base one's explorations of the City of Light. From the crystal chandeliers and rich wood paneling of the reception area to the deluxe appointments of the bed chambers and drawing rooms, opulence was the "mot juste." Mrs. Hudson was awed. The view from the rooms was spectacular. In the distance the Eiffel Tower pierced the afternoon sky. A breeze ruffled the lace curtains, cooling the rooms. Thrilling!

The Baroness and Pookie flitted into the suite with Holmes, Watson and Mrs. Hudson. *"I'm glad we didn't have to join you on that awful boat train. There's a lot to be said for flitting."*

Watson chuckled, "Yes, but you have to be dead to do it."

"Touché, Doctor! This hotel is lovely. Did you see the gilded statue of Joan of Arc on horseback in the square in front? I'll have to say hello to her when I get back to Heaven."

"It's a shame we missed the 1900 Exposition Universelle but there's still plenty worth visiting. Have you heard the phrase 'Belle Epoque – the beautiful era?' I saw it in a newspaper. I have a list of places and things to see. Lady Juliet-Touriste Extraordinaire! First stop, the Louvre. It's right across the street. I guess Pookie will have to go invisible. Then we'll go to Printemps department store and look at the dome and the fashion departments. I want to ride the Metro. It's like the London Underground only it isn't. Oh, and up the Champs Elysees to the Arc de Triomphe. Come along, Martha. Time's a-wasting. You can come too, Doctor, if you wish. Holmes, you're a hopeless case. Go visit your friends at the Sûreté.

"Agreed, Baroness. We'll meet back here for dinner. I'll make reservations at the Café de la Paix. It's right by the Opera. I'll also check on what they're performing there tonight. You can do your singalong. We'll go to Maxim's tomorrow night. Two fashionable ladies and one dog accompanied by two fusty Englishmen. "

"Wonderful! Tomorrow I want to visit the fashion salons and haute couturiers, Paquin, Worth, Doucet, the Callot Sisters and bring back some ideas. My namesake, Madame Juliette Recamier is up in Heaven. She died in 1849. She won't wear those stodgy white robes, either. Like me. she's a client of Madame Clarice and her Miraculous Modes. Oh, this is merveilleux. I'm so excited. We'll order you a frock, Martha. You'll pay for it, won't you, Holmes. Of course you will. Ta, ta! We're off!"

The ghostly whirlwind headed for the door of the suite. The Great Detective shook his head and stared at Watson. "What have I unleashed?" Hearing the word 'leash,' Pookie had a brief fit of angry barking and then followed the Baroness and Mrs. Hudson. On to the Louvre.

Holmes had turned to the Doctor. "I have an appointment with Inspecteur Roget at the Sûreté. A rather unusual theft has surfaced and he wants to consult with me. After all, that's what a consulting detective does. You're welcome to join me unless you want to trudge through the Louvre or Printemps."

Watson replied, "I've seen the Venus de Milo and La Gioconda several times and I have no desire to wander around a department store. So I'll accompany you. Let's take the Metro if it goes past our destination. I want to try it."

"Sorry, Watson. The préfecture is located in the Place Louis Lépine on the Île de la Cité. Just a short walk away from our hotel.

Not far from Notre Dame Cathedral and Sainte-Chapelle. We'll take the ladies on a train ride to one of their costumiers tomorrow."

The Doctor remarked, "I have been to Paris quite a few times. In fact, I have accompanied you on several of our French adventures. Lovely city! However, the 1900 Exposition Universelle has introduced some remarkable changes in the landscape and atmosphere, mostly for the better. But if the newspapers are to be believed, there is also an undertow of strife permeating the city, indeed, the country."

"Yes, there are several incidents that blemish the outlook. I think Inspecteur Roget's little problem may be a manifestation of one of them. "Allons-y. Le jeu soit en cours!"

"Pardon? Ah, I see. Let's go. The game is afoot."

"Exactement!"

Chapter Two

The Paris Police Préfecture is a building similar in structure, style and oppressive atmosphere to law enforcement headquarters the world over. A desk gendarme led Holmes and Watson to the undersized and stifling office of Inspecteur Guillaume Roget. He rose to greet them.

Of medium height, dark hair and deep set brown eyes with a face punctuated by a carefully tended moustache, the Inspector's well-worn suit strained to cover his portly physique.

"Monsieur Holmes, Doctor Watson. Welcome to Paris! I am most pleased that you have elected to join in helping the Sûreté solve our little enigma."

"Inspecteur Roget! It is always a pleasure to renew our relationship. The Doctor and I are here both on business and pleasure. We are accompanying two ladies of our acquaintance as they tour your lovely city."

13

"Oh, ho! Cherchez les femmes, N'est-ce pas? "

"No, nothing of the sort. One is my landlady, Mrs. Hudson, whom you have met on one of your travels to London. This trip is by way of a reward for her patience in putting up with my foibles. She is the companion of a member of British nobility, Lady Juliet Armstrong, Baroness Crestwell. Both women of extreme virtue."

"Strange. I was once introduced to an English actress by that name. Can there be two?"

"I'm sure there is no relationship."

Watson coughed and smiled. They sat on chairs never meant to be comfortable.

"Now, tell me, Inspector, about this unusual theft. Another gentleman burglar?"

"It is not out of the realm of possibility but we have little evidence to support that theory. Non, this involves a missing medal insignia of a Chevalier in the Ordre National de la Legion d'honneur. It is the highest French order of merit, both military and civil. Established in 1802 by Napoleon Bonaparte. The medal belonged to Chevalier Louis Ste. Germaine."

Watson coughed again. "Forgive me, Inspector but is this an issue for the Sûreté? Is it not simply a case of a misplaced emblem? Hardly worth any of our time."

"It would be, gentlemen, were it not for the note left in its place."

Holmes' eyebrows arched. Watson said, "A note! So it <u>was</u> a theft."

"More than a theft, Doctor. It was a threat. Here is the missive."

14

A stiff white pasteboard card, unsigned, written in bold crimson script. The envelope bore no indication of origin. No watermark. It read: *(Translated)* "*Louis Ste. Germaine. You are unworthy to wear the symbol of the Legion d'honneur. You are without honor and will soon pay with your life. A Chevalier no longer. A Frenchman no longer. A mortal no longer. Adieu!*"

Watson shook his head. 'Well, that's certainly straightforward. No mistaking that message. How was it delivered?"

"A private messenger service. The sender paid in cash and gave a false name."

Holmes donned gloves and carefully took up the card. "Did you find any marks or prints that might assist in identifying the menacing individual.'

"Yes and no. The handwriting is distinctive but so far unrevealing. The messenger's fingerprints are on the envelope. There are prints on the card. As you know, gentlemen, we subscribe to Alphonse Bertillon's system of physical classification but it is of no use in this instance. We have just started to use the fingerprint system described by your Sir Francis Galton. Our file of impressions is in its infancy and thus far we have not found a match. Perhaps as we investigate further, we will come upon equivalent prints for which we know the owner."

"How did the medal disappear?"

"Ste. Germaine kept it on display locked in a glass enclosed étagère. The maid discovered it unlocked and the medal missing on the morning the note arrived. We questioned the servants but they know nothing."

"Where is Ste. Germaine now?"

"In a safe house under our protection."

"Tell us about him. What has produced this angry outburst against him?"

"Louis Ste. Germaine is an industrialist. He owns several manufactories engaged in producing weapons and war materials. He is a major supplier to the French Army although it is rumored that his companies also clandestinely support the Austro-Hungarians. There have been several investigations but no proof. He was awarded membership in the Legion d'honneur for his support of our military. There were several protests at the time but they came to nothing. Now, much later, this threat and seeming outrage occurs. As for the Legion, the Grand Chancellor, a retired general, and the Secretary General, a civilian administrator have been notified and queried. No useful information."

Holmes stared out the dirt-encrusted window of the Inspector's office. "Honor means many things to many people. Do you suppose this has nothing to do with his war-related activities. A cheated financier or business rival, perhaps or a disgruntled mistress? The husband of a despoiled wife. Stealing the medal could be a metaphoric act designed to shame as well as threaten. Perhaps something as basic as dishonesty at cards. I believe that while it has been illegal in France for years, dueling is still practiced, ironically to satisfy honor."

Roget laughed, "Yes, we thought of that but no one has emerged as a possible opponent. No second has appeared to arrange a contest. If we are to believe the card, someone simply intends to kill Louis Ste. Germaine. We believe the note and theft are all the warning he is going to get. Retribution can be a drawn out affair."

"Does Ste. Germaine have any theories?"

"None he is willing to share. He seems to be more concerned about the loss of the medal than the loss of his life. But that may all be bravado."

"He may know more than he lets on. Can you arrange an interview with him tomorrow morning?"

"Certainment! I shall meet you at your hotel at 9 o'clock."

"Merci! How have you been faring?"

"Well enough! This Dreyfus affair has the police on high alert. Riots, confrontations, vandalism."

"Could there be a connection to this problem?"

"None that I can see but who knows. Stranger things have occurred."

Chapter Three

Back at the Hôtel Regina, a breathless Martha Hudson flopped on a brocade encrusted sofa and loosened her boots. "Lady Juliet, you ghosts have no mercy on us poor mortals. We have literally flown about the sights of Paris for most of the day and I am exhausted."

Pookie, no longer used to being corporeal, was tired out and looked for a bowl of water. She found it, lapped noisily, yawned and fell into a deep snooze on a convenient pillow.

Juliet looked at the two of them and said, "Sorry, ladies. I've let my enthusiasm run away with me. Why don't you both take a short nap? (Pookie was in dreamland already.) *Remember, we have an appointment for dinner at the Cafe de la Paix with Holmes and the Doctor. He also mentioned the opera but I can flit there on my own if you're not up to it."*

Pookie greeted this with a light snore and Martha removed her footwear, leaned back, closed her eyes and drifted off.

"Well," thought the Baroness. *"Here I am by my lonesome. I wonder how Holmes is progressing with the Sûreté."*

No sooner said than the Great Detective and his literary/medical partner arrived at the suite.

Watson looked at his landlady lightly snoring and grinned. Then he realized the snores were coming from the dog sprawled in a corner. "I say, Holmes. We have two sleepy head tourists on our hands."

Juliet retorted, *"But not me, Doctor. Still full of mystical energy. Ready for an evening out. Are we on for dinner and the opera? I'm rather surprised at Pookie. She's usually as lively as they come. Flying, flitting, playing multi-dimensional fetch and tug-o-war. Paris seems to have worn her out."*

Holmes nodded. "Opera at seven. Offenbach's *La Vie Parisienne*. Dinner at ten at the neighboring Café de la Paix."

"Wonderful, Sherlock. A glorious way to end our first day in Paris. We saw some of the sights. We prowled the Louvre and then Printemps. Martha now has an evening dress. I conjured one up for myself. Pookie has her formal bow. She'll have to stay incorporeal tonight. Of course, I can't be seen with my halo. But tell me, gentlemen. What news of the Rialto or more to the point, the Sûreté?"

The detective and doctor proceeded to tell her the particulars of the Ste. Germaine episode.

"Interesting! Call it my celestial woman's intuition but I'm certain the industrialist realizes more of this than he is admitting. His concern for his stolen medal is just a ruse. I think he knows his potential killer. Although, there may be more than one candidate. When you go to see him tomorrow, I want to tag along."

"I was about to invite you. Can you forego the fashion houses for a few hours?"

"To head off a murder, of course. Madame Clarice is ahead of them all, anyway."

Mrs. Hudson woke up from her nap. "Oh, Mr. Holmes and Doctor. You're back. What have I missed?"

Watson went through the story once again.

She laughed. "I know it's not humorous. The poor man must be frightened to death but you two don't seem to be able to avoid criminal activity. I guess since you're a detective, Mr. Holmes, you don't want to avoid it. And you too, Doctor. Baroness, you are catching the crime fighting disease as well. So is Pookie. Oh dear, maybe I'm next."

*****

The splendid evening arrived. The Café de La Paix. Bustle and commotion on the Place de l'Opera. Crowded tables outside and in. In a padded booth, the Baroness sat staring at a bottle of 1900 vintage Bordeaux. *"What a pleasure to be able to sample this vintner's classic. One of the few things I miss in Heaven is the opportunity to enjoy fine earthly wines and exquisite food. Ambrosia and nectar are wonderful but worldly sustenance can be such a delight. I simply must try the mille-feuilles. Oh, and the Opera! It was not quite up to celestial standards but superb, nonetheless. Offenbach is such a rogue. I am looking forward to our venture to Maxim's tomorrow night and then a trip on the Seine in a Bateau Mouche. What do you say, Martha? Shall we go to the Folies Bergère or the Moulin Rouge. It just reopened."*

Mrs. Hudson shook her head vociferously. "I think not, Baroness. They're not respectable. Hardly places for a saint. Sorry Pookie, a pair of saints."

"Oh, Poo. You're a spoilsport, Martha Hudson."

19

She started humming an aria from La Vie Parisienne and her contralto attracted the attention of the surrounding diners. Holmes looked a bit embarrassed but Watson and Mrs. Hudson were enjoying themselves no end. An invisible Pookie came up with a series of unheard barks. She had just become corporeal long enough to snatch a dollop of pate de foie gras from the table and then disappear again.

"Tell me, Holmes. What's your theory on who is threatening Chevalier Louis Ste. Germaine?"

"Baroness, as you are aware"… *"yes, yes, I know. You never theorize but do you have an opinion?"* She giggled. Was the wine having an effect?

"Holmes, I can't wait to meet this Chevalier. With or without his medal."

"You shall, milady. You shall."

Chapter Four

Holmes did not have a theory but hoped to develop a chain of facts that would cast light on the threat against the industrialist. Promptly at 9 AM, Inspector Roget arrived at the hotel to find the detective waiting for him in the luxurious lobby. The Baroness and Pookie lurked invisible near the entrance. The dog was carefully examining the doorman's splendiferous uniform and Juliet was watching the passing parade of Parisians and Parisiennes strolling by.

Watson had elected to stay behind and accompany Mrs. Hudson on a tour of some of the churches and monuments of Paris. First stop: Sainte-Chapelle and then the glorious Notre Dame Cathedral. The Baroness had flitted there earlier that morning along with Pookie. *"Spectacular! It was probably designed by Heavenly*

Real Estate! I'm sure it's one of the Almighty's favorites." Then on to Les Invalides and Napoleon's Tomb with a stop for lunch.

The Inspector bowed in greeting, "Bonjour, Monsieur Holmes. The auto is waiting outside. Are you ready for our little excursion? It is a pension on the Left Bank the Sûreté maintains as a guarded safe house. I need hardly tell you that Chevalier Ste. Germaine is not happy with his circumstance. He refuses to take the threat to his life seriously. I am almost tempted to release him and abandon him to his fate. Almost!"

They walked out to the black Peugeot police vehicle and took up places in the rear. Juliet and Pookie, unheard, invisible and intangible, positioned themselves in the front seat next to the driver. As they moved out among the autos and horse drawn carriages, the Baroness said, *"You know, Pookie, riding about in these automajigs isn't as bad as I make it out to be. We could be flitting, of course, but unfortunately, I don't know where we're going. Whoa!! These Paris drivers are a bit reckless, aren't they. Ah, the Pont au Change! Here we go over the Seine. Rive Gauche, here we come!"* The dog whined.

They rode on and stopped in a narrow, unpretentious, cobble-stoned street. Roget opened the car door and said, "Let us walk a bit, Monsieur Holmes. Our objective is in a lane up ahead. Henri, you know where to park the auto. We shall return in less than an hour."

The Baroness and her dog flitted invisibly over the passenger door and stood, waiting for Roget to lead on. The inspector casually strolled off with Holmes, two gentlemen out for a bit of morning exercise. Unfortunately, their dress gave them away but no matter. The locals were well aware that the unassuming pension they were approaching was in fact a property of the police.

They were greeted in the foyer of the safe house by a plain clothes gendarme pretending to be a desk clerk. Pookie gave him a thorough sniffing. "Bonjour, Inspecteur. Your ward is in the master suite on the second floor. He is not at all happy with his situation. I keep telling him it's for his own protection but he is unconvinced."

Holmes and the Inspecteur, accompanied by the invisible phantoms, proceeded up the stairs and knocked on the door of the suite. Juliet and the Bichon zipped through the sealed portal. After a brief pause, the door opened a crack and an eye appeared. For someone who pretended to be more concerned about the loss of his medal than the loss of his life, the Chevalier was exhibiting extreme caution.

The Inspecteur waved at him and said, "Bonjour, Monsieur Ste. Germaine. It is I, Inspecteur Roget and my English associate, Mr. Sherlock Holmes. May we come in?"

A tall, dark-haired, mustachioed individual in his shirtsleeves peered at them. He opened the door further, looked down the hallway and stepped aside to permit the detectives to enter. The two ghosts had already settled on a sofa. "Bonjour, gentlemen. Your gendarme downstairs has persuaded me that I must be vigilant although I still believe this is all a nonsensical prank. Have you tracked down the culprit?"

Holmes replied, "Not yet! We are here to ask some questions that we hope will enable us to do exactly that."

"As I told your colleague, Mr. Holmes, I am at a loss to identify my menace. I am a rich public figure engaged in a controversial industry. It is obvious that I will have adversaries but one who wishes me dead? C'est très improbable. Mais non! C'est impossible! An affair of honneur? Pah! Such nonsense."

The Baroness chortled. *"For a supposedly astute businessman and public figure, the Chevalier is quite naïve or he'd*

22

like you to think so. We saints are quite good at detecting fabrications. He's lying, Holmes! And he's scared stiff. My money is on a disgruntled husband."

Holmes responded telepathically, *"Your feminine intuition is working overtime, Milady, but you may indeed be right."*

He looked at the Chevalier. "Have any members of your family received similar threats?"

"I am unmarried, M'sieur. Never have been. So, no wife or children. I do have an ailing father who lives with me. Problems with his heart. He is retired. I inherited his munitions business. He, too is a Chevalier of the Legion d'honneur."

Roget's eyebrows raised. "Could he be the target of the threatening note instead of you?"

"Papa? Mon Père? Non, Non! C'est ridicule!"

Holmes asked, "Why do you suppose you have received this menacing note now? What has occurred recently to motivate such animosity? Some business, political or social issue? An international incident? Are you under investigation by the authorities? Forgive me but was there an indiscretion with a lady? An irate husband or father, perhaps? A gambling loss or an unpaid debt? A personal insult or slight? Physical or financial harm inflicted on an innocent victim? A real or imagined offense."

The Chevalier's eyes widened at this catalogue of miscues and shortcomings. "I realize you do not know me, M'sieur Holmes, or you would not make such insulting suggestions. I suppose that is the way of the private enquiry agent. I am guilty of none of your accusations. Your associate from the Sûreté is aware of my excellent reputation."

Roget stared at him. "The police have no cause to question your integrity, M'sieur but it is not the police who have issued this threat. Someone does not share your opinion of your excellent reputation and wants revenge for whatever reason. It is clear from the note that this is not a case of mistaken identity unless of course, your father..."

"My father is blameless!"

Juliet interrupted telepathically. *"Holmes, does his father still have his Chevalier's medal?"*

The detective picked up on her question. "M'sieur Ste. Germaine. I assume your father still has his medal. Does he display it, as well?"

"I believe he does have it. He does not display it. He is no longer active in the Legion's affairs and has no reason to wear it. His health, you know."

Roget turned to Holmes. "We interviewed the servants and staff but M'sieur Ste. Germaine Senior was indisposed and under a doctor's care when we made our inquiries. Perhaps a return trip is in order. You can speak to the domestics and the elder Chevalier."

The industrialist was disturbed. "I do not want you to upset my father."

"I am sorry, M'sieur, but in the case of a death threat, we must pursue every avenue. We will demonstrate the utmost care and respect but your father may have some valuable evidence or opinion that will help us solve this problem. In the meantime, I must ask you to be patient a little longer and take advantage of the Sûreté's hospitality, such as it is."

The two investigators left the safe house and agreed to meet again later in the day to interview the staff at Ste. Germaine's residence in the 8th arrondissement, near the Champs-Élysées. Roget also arranged for them to meet with the patriarch, Chevalier Roland, whose health seemed to be improving. Back at the hotel,

24

the Baroness and Pookie in their bodily form joined Holmes for lunch. Doctor Watson and Mrs. Hudson had returned from their 'monument tour' and rested their weary feet as they met with the detective and the now corporeal wraiths in the fabulous Hotel Regina dining room under the crystal chandeliers. They all tucked into the culinary gems on the midday menu du jour.

Pookie was enjoying bites of charcuturie and *pâté* passed to her by the Doctor and landlady, both of whom had developed a great fondness for the fur covered imp.

Watson asked, "Well, Holmes, are you any further along in solving this 'medal mystery'?"

"The junior Chevalier vehemently denies any untoward behavior on his part that could be inspiring the theft and threat. We have an appointment to speak with the senior Chevalier and his staff later today."

Mrs. Hudson looked puzzled. "Junior, senior? Whatever do you mean, Mr. Holmes?"

Juliet intervened. *"It seems both father and son are Chevaliers, Martha. It's not certain what, if any, involvement the old gentleman has with this affair. We'll see. Meanwhile, if I am not mistaken, a trip to Maxim's is on our agenda for this evening."*

Watson replied, "Indeed it is, Baroness, your otherworldly beauty will add grace to the famous art collection. Your delightful dog will charm the jaded boulevardiers. As will you, Mrs. Hudson."

Martha and the Baroness both laughed. "You are a flatterer, Doctor, but do go on."

Holmes smiled. "Let us finish off our lunch with a lively Loire dessert wine. Then perhaps a short nap to re-energize. Watson, why don't you join us when Roget and I make our pilgrimage to the Ste. Germaine establishment at three. Lady Juliet, I assume you and Pookie will be with us in otherworldly form."

"Oh, indeed. Meanwhile, Miss Dog and I will now flit off to the fashion houses and scout out the new season's confections. Madame Clarice will be most interested." The Baroness chattered on. *"Tomorrow will be transportation day. A ride on the Metro and a luncheon trip on the Seine on a Bateau Mouche. And, oh yes, we must flit to the top of the Eiffel Tower. Preferably to watch the sun go down. It never does in Heaven, you know. I'm enjoying nights once again."* Another change of subject. *"We'll meet you back here at two thirty. I wonder if Ste. Germaine Père will shed any light on this puzzle."* She rose and departed with Pookie. They promptly disappeared.

Watson laughed. "It must be quite peaceful in Paradise with the Baroness and her dog here on Earth. How can anyone dead be so alive? She is amazing."

Martha Hudson shook her head in wonder and left. She had some knitting she wanted to finish.

Chapter Five

As the bells of the local church pealed three, the black Peugeot motor car of the Sûreté pulled up to the portico of the Ste. Germaine property. Roget and Holmes were in the back seat, Watson in the front with the driver and the Baroness and Pookie occupying no space at all.

A short, rotund butler of mature years opened the door and welcomed the trio into the ornate foyer.

(The following conversations are translated from the French.)

"Inspecteur Roget. It is good to see you again. Have you seen Chevalier Louis today? Is he well? When will he be coming back?"

"Yes, Gilbert, although he is not happy about being confined to a suite in our safe house. I hope we will have put this episode in the history books shortly and allow your employer to return to his home. Let me introduce Monsieur Sherlock Holmes and his associate Docteur John Watson. They are the English detectives I mentioned on our telephone call. We would like to interview you and the staff once again. I apologize for the intrusion and repetition. Is the Chevalier Roland also in residence?"

"He is, Inspecteur. He has seen le medecin and has been in better sprits over the last day or so although he is obviously disturbed by the events, theft and threats. I assume you wish to speak with him. But first, shall I gather the staff? There are three maids, two footmen, the housekeeper, the chef, and the masters' private secretary. Each of the gentlemen has a valet and of course, there is me. Do you wish to speak to us individually or as a group?"

Roget looked at Holmes for guidance. The detective replied in flawless French. "I think we can deal with the household staff as a group but I would like to interview your good self, the housekeeper, the valets and the secretary individually. And oh, yes. Which of the maids discovered the medal was missing? I'd like to question her. "

"Certainment. That would be Louise. I'll call the domestics together."

The Baroness had invoked the universal linguistic gift all celestials share and was listening to the dialogue 'en Française.' She murmured to Holmes, *"Watch the housekeeper, too. I have suspicions about her."*

Holmes nodded. "Gilbert, may we have a moment with your housekeeper?"

"That is Madame DeVries. Here she comes with the domestics. "Madame, ladies and gentlemen. You remember

27

Inspecteur Roget. Allow me to introduce M'sieur Sherlock Holmes and his associate, Docteur John Watson. They are assisting the Inspecteur in his inquiries into the Chevalier's missing medal and the threats to his life. I'm sure you will be most cooperative in answering their questions."

He introduced the two valets, Claude and Joseph. They nodded. A dark haired but otherwise colorless slight individual with large spectacles and a pronounced stoop, the secretary, Maître Jerome, bowed to the lawmen.

The chef, like many of his kind, was temperamental. "I have a dinner to prepare. Chevalier Ste. Germaine Senior is most meticulous about his meals. I have already answered all of the police's questions. I have no time for missing medals. I'm going back to my kitchen." He stalked off.

Gilbert shrugged. "Alphonse considers himself a gastronomic genius and the old gentleman caters to his every whim. So does the current master. He is a culinary artiste but something of a trial. Louise, it was you who discovered the medal was missing. What can you tell these gentlemen?"

The bird-like maid gulped, stared at her co-workers and blurted. "I was doing my daily dusting. I found the étagère unlocked. As you all know, the medal usually occupies a place of honor on a velvet pedestal." The domestics all nodded agreement. "The shelf was empty. The pedestal was there but no medal. I ran to report it to Madame DeVries. I did not take it. I am an honest woman. Tell them, Madame. What would I do with a medal? Wear it? Sell it? Oh, I am desolée."

The housekeeper patted the maid on the shoulder. "Messieurs, Louise has been with us for ages. We have no reason to mistrust her. As she says, she is an honest woman."

Juliet said, *"I believe her. That medal wasn't stolen for profit. It was an act of revenge and warning. Remember the threatening note. A house maid wouldn't invent something like that. Maybe a housekeeper, a valet, butler or secretary bearing a grudge but not a maid. I doubt it's the chef. He's a prima donna but not a killer."*

Watson and Holmes concurred with the ghost's assessment. "Inspecteur Roget, I think we can safely dismiss the maids and footmen. I doubt if we will learn anything more than you have already discovered in questioning them. Shall we interview Madame DeVries first? Gilbert, Madame, is there a room we can use?"

The butler directed them to the library. Watson took a side chair near a bookstack. The Inspecteur and Holmes sat at one side of a reading table and the housekeeper sat opposite. Unseen, Juliet and Pookie took up places on a sideboard. Roget got up and closed the door.

Before any of the men could pose a query, Madame DeVries had a question of her own. "Do you gentlemen have any idea why someone is threatening the Chevalier?"

Holmes smiled. "That is a matter we are here to inquire about, Madame. If I am correct, you have been with this household for quite some time. You must have seen and heard all there is to know about the personal affairs of both Monsieur Ste. Germaine Senior and Junior. I eagerly await your answer to your own question."

She looked perplexed. "I really don't know. I doubt any of this household is responsible. I certainly am not. I trust Gilbert implicitly. The old gentleman can be a bit of a trial and occasionally tests the patience of his valet, Claude. But Joseph and master Louis get along quite well."

29

Watson asked. "How about Maître Jerome. Is he secretary to both the Chevaliers?"

"Yes, he is, but he does very little for the old gentleman now that he is totally retired and in declining health. Claude and Gilbert take care of his needs. Maître Jerome is kept quite busy with the personal affairs of Monsieur Louis. The young Chevalier has a large number of outside interests as you might expect. He is quite active in several social and political clubs and the Legion d'honneur. His business dealings are handled by his staff of assistants at the manufactories. Gilbert and Maître Jerome can tell you more."

Roget looked at her. "So you can shed no light on who our culprit is?"

"Other than to exclude the members of the household, no, I cannot. A burglar perhaps."

"Since the medal was taken from the locked and unbroken etagere and followed by a threatening note, I find it difficult to agree with you that it was stolen by an opportunistic sneak thief."

She made no reply.

Holmes smiled and said, "Thank you, Madame. Unless you have something you wish to add, I believe we are finished. You have been most helpful. You may return to your duties. Will you ask Gilbert to step in."

The Baroness had been listening carefully as she and the dog perched invisibly on the sideboard. *"She has her suspicions, Holmes. She's covering up for someone."*

"I agree, Milady. The question is 'who'. Here is the butler."

Gilbert entered the room and took the seat the housekeeper had vacated.

Roget looked at him and said, "I realize we have been through this inquiry process already, Gilbert, but M'sieur Holmes brings his own methods, viewpoints and perceptions to each situation he encounters. He is here at the request of the Sûreté. Please answer his questions fully and to the best of your ability."

"But of course, Inspecteur. How may I assist, M'sieur Holmes?"

"Madame DeVries is convinced of the innocence of this entire household and believes, in spite of some clear evidence to the contrary, the theft was what we would call 'an outside job.' Do you concur?"

He replied. "Correct me if I am in error but Inspecteur Roget and his men found no signs of a break in and the etagere door was not forced. Whoever sent the note knew the Chevalier, so no, I do not believe it was, as you say, an outside job by a common robber. The medal would be unsalable and its metal and jewel content hardly worth melting or destroying. There are many other things in this house that would be of far greater interest to a cat burglar. I believe the perpetrator is among us with specific designs on harming the Chevalier. Let me hasten to add, it's not me." (Smiling)

"You are quite astute, Gilbert."

"I have Doctor Watson here and you to thank for that, M'sieur Holmes. I have read every one of the Doctor's stories of your adventures. At least those translated into French. I wonder, Doctor, would you sign several copies for me?"

Watson fought hard to keep back a laugh as he looked at the frown on Holmes' face. "Of course. I will be happy to."

"Oh, good! I shall bring them to you. Now, what else can I tell you gentlemen?"

"How long have Claude, Joseph and Maître Jerome been in the Chevalier's employ?"

"I have been here for eight years and the two valets were in place before I arrived. Maître Jerome made a more recent appearance. The old gentleman fired his predecessor. He can be quite touchy. Since his illness, he has reduced his social interactions. He no longer has need of a full time secretary so Maître Jerome devotes most of his time to the non-business affairs of Chevalier Louis."

"Thank you. That agrees with what Madame DeVries told us. Now, have there been any recent conflicts between M'sieur Louis and any of the staff?"

"Not to my knowledge, M'sieur Holmes but I am not privy to the Chevalier's interactions with his valet. I do know that Maître Jerome is a somewhat moody and sensitive individual but no specific incidents come to mind. Of course, when it comes to sensitivity, our chef Alphonse is a prima donna but this household eats and drinks extremely well."

"Alphonse is also your sommelier?"

"Yes and an excellent one. Our cellar is among the finest in Paris."

"I envy you. That is a very high standard."

"Indeed, the Ste. Germaine's have highly discriminating culinary taste."

"What occupies the Senior Chevalier's time now that he is retired?"

"I am not sure any longer. A former member of the military, he was engaged in dictating his memoirs to Maître Jerome but with his increasing illness, he has abandoned that effort. The Maître now devotes most of his time and activities to Chevalier Louis' requirements."

"I assume that you and Madame DeVries between you manage this household."

"If you mean that the Chevaliers leave the day-to-day conduct of the affairs of this establishment to us, I would agree. I suspect you would get minority reports on that point from the valets and Alphonse who believe they exert major influence in the running of the house and its occupants. Maître Jerome is above all of that sort of thing. He is absorbed in his own world."

"Thank you, Gilbert. I should now like to speak with Joseph, Chevalier Louis' valet."

The butler left and Holmes looked at Roget. "Any new information?"

"Not yet. Let us see what we uncover with the valets and the moody Maître. Then on to Ste. Germaine Senior."

The Baroness, who had been relatively quiet up to this point telepathically said to Holmes and the Doctor. *"Woman's intuition, gentlemen but I'll bet the old man in not as out of it as he would like you to believe."*

"You may be right, Baroness but let's see what the valets and secretary have to say. Here is Joseph."

The valet entered the room and ignoring Holmes and Watson, immediately turned his attention to Roget. "Inspecteur, I protest. I should be at this safe house or whatever you call it, serving Chevalier Ste. Germaine. I am sitting here, useless. A valet without his master. A master without his valet."

Roget responded, "I appreciate your sensitivities, Joseph but the harsh realities of this state of affairs take precedence. I'm sorry, mon ami, but you along with all of the household staff are suspects in this threat situation and the purpose of a safe house is to isolate the potential victim from exposure. I am sure you are offended by the prospect but that is the nature of things." He laughed. "You may wish to take up a hobby to while away the hours."

The valet turned to Holmes and Watson. "Do you two English gentlemen have any influence in restoring the world to its proper order?"

"I'm afraid not, Joseph. The history and literature of crime is full of valets who turned against their employers. No doubt, you are not in their number but I must agree with Inspecteur Roget's decision to be cautious until we find the true culprit. Is there any information you can give us about the missing medal or the threatening note?"

"I was with M'sieur Louis when he received the note. The medal had already disappeared. Although he made light of it, the note did upset the Chevalier. At first, he made to burn it but changed his mind. He said something like, 'The fool is revealing himself.' He told Gilbert to pass it on to the police."

"Do you have any idea whom he was referring to?"

"No sir, I suggest you ask him yourself."

"We will. Thank you Joseph. You may go. Please send in Claude."

"Claude is with Monsieur Ste. Germaine Senior at the moment, Inspecteur."

"Well then, ask Maître Jerome to join us."

Once again Juliet intervened. *"Aha, the Junior Chevalier knows who sent the note and probably who stole the medal. Is anybody here telling the truth?"*

"A good question, milady. After we finish here we will return to the safe house."

"Don't forget we have a date for dinner at Maxim's. Martha is looking forward to it."

"And you are not? How could I possibly forget?"

A knock on the door and the slight, dark haired, pale secretary, Maître Jerome, entered. Straightening his habitual stoop, he crossed the room, sat and adjusted his spectacles. He said nothing but gazed vacantly past Roget and then Holmes and Watson.

The Baroness giggled. *"Isn't he a dynamo?"*

The Inspecteur broke the silence. "Maître, thank you for coming to see me again. You have been introduced to M'sieur Holmes and Docteur Watson, investigators from England. As you know, we are engaged in trying to ferret out the truth about the theft of Chevalier Louis' medal and the menacing note he received. We understand you are kept quite busy with his personal affairs."

The secretary finally broke his own silence and answered in a near whisper. "Yes I am. At one point, I was occupied with transcribing the memoirs of the elder Chevalier but since his increased illness, I have been almost exclusively engaged with the activities of his son. The younger Chevalier has a large number of outside interests as you might expect. He is very active in several social and political clubs and, of course, the Legion d'honneur. I do not handle his business dealings. Those are the responsibilities of his staff of assistants at the manufactories."

Juliet said, *"Well, that checks out with Gilbert's and Madame's description. Perhaps there is some truth-telling here, after all."*

"What can you tell us about the missing medal and the note?"

"Nothing, I am afraid. I became aware of the theft when I heard the maid's cries. And I have not seen the note. I'm not even sure where it is."

"It is safely stored away in an evidence box at the Sûreté. We are analyzing it for handwriting and fingerprints."

This revelation by Roget didn't arouse any reaction from the Maître other than a slightly raised eyebrow.

Watson intervened, "How long have you been in the Chevalier's employ?"

"A little over a year. I was hired to replace another secretary who worked for the Senior Chevalier. He was fired by the old gentleman for reasons I do not know. As I told you, I now have very little to do with M'sieur Roland."

"Did your predecessor work for both parties?"

"Yes, he did but mostly the elder Chevalier. Based on some remarks he has made, I don't believe young M'sieur Louis and he got along all that well. When I first came into the household, there was a substantial logjam of filing and unanswered correspondence that needed taking care of.

Holmes asked, "What is his name? Where is he? Inspecteur Roget, have you interviewed him?"

The policeman replied, "Armand Duclos. He is here in Paris on the Left Bank. No, we saw no need but now that you mention it, I suppose he could be holding a grudge from his dismissal. However, it was over a year ago. Maître, can you comment?"

"No, M'sieur, except to repeat my statement about the clerical backlog. I never met the man. Perhaps Gilbert or Madame can shed some light."

Juliet snorted in a most unladylike fashion, *"Your friend, the Inspecteur, missed on that one, Holmes."*

36

"Agreed!"

"Inspecteur, I think we must interview this Armand Duclos. Can you arrange that?"

"Certainment!"

"Meanwhile, let us continue here. I believe we can let you go, Maître. Except! One more question. You live here in the mansion?"

"Yes, I do. I have a room and an office."

"Thank you. Could you see if Claude is available? He is Chevalier Roland's valet, is he not?"

"Yes, he is. I'll find him."

Roget got up from the table and went to the door. "I'll arrange for us to meet with Armand Duclos as soon as he is available. We only have Claude and Ste. Germaine Senior to interview here." He left.

The Baroness ruffled Pookie's invisible ears. *"What do you think, Miss Dog? Who is the medal thief? Is the note real or a red herring?"* The Bichon yawned and wagged her tail.

With the Inspecteur out of the room, Holmes felt free to speak openly to Lady Juliet. *"What do you mean, Milady?"*

"Oh, it occurred to me that this whole thing is just a bit too mysterious and melodramatic. Forgive me, my theatrical background is showing."

Before she could say any more, there was a knock on the door and a tall, greying, clean shaven, figure immaculately dressed in formal morning clothes poked his head in tentatively. "Pardon, M'sieur Holmes. I am Claude. Did you wish to speak with me?"

"Yes, I do, Claude. Please enter. Thank you for coming. Inspecteur Roget just stepped out for a moment. He'll be right back. I understand you are Chevalier Roland's valet."

He walked in and took the seat Holmes indicated to him. "Indeed, sir. I have been in service to the master for eleven years now. I have the honor of being the longest serving member of the household except for Madame DeVries. Of course, the Chevalier has retired from his businesses but is still quite alert and physically active."

Roget returned, nodded at Holmes and said, "It is arranged for tomorrow morning." He turned to the valet and extended his hand. "Claude, we have met several times."

"Yes, Inspecteur. My pleasure. I hope you and M'sieur Holmes are on your way to settling this affair."

"We progress. Is there any more information you can give us about the missing medal or the threatening note?"

"Nothing I have not already shared with you, Inspecteur.'

"Would you please repeat what you told me for M'sieur Holmes' benefit."

"Certainment! It is not much. I see to the old gentleman's needs with a little assistance from Gilbert and Madame."

"Does Maître Jerome support the Chevalier?"

"No longer! When the Chevalier's health began to worsen, he set aside his plans for dictating his memoirs and the Maître's services were no longer needed except for some minor correspondence.'

"If you don't mind revealing it, what is the problem with the Chevalier's physical condition?"

"The Docteur has detected a murmur of the heart and of course, he is getting on in years. You would not believe it to see or talk with him. Lately, he has been quite vital. He has been taking several medicines which seem to be restoring his energy. Perhaps he may pick up his memoirs again"

Holmes commented to the Doctor. "Watson, you should speak with the Chevalier's physician and also observe him yourself. Perhaps we should reschedule our interview until tomorrow and meet this doctor at the same time."

"Sounds like a good idea. What about this Duclos chap?"

He looked at the valet. "I assume you were familiar with Armand Duclos."

Claude frowned, "Yes, I was. He was the old gentleman's secretary until the Chevalier dismissed him and hired Maître Jerome."

Roget pounced on this. "Why was he dismissed?"

"I couldn't say. Perhaps you should ask the Chevalier."

Holmes took out his hunter-case pocket watch, opened the lid and remarked. "The hour is getting late. Might we postpone our meeting with the Chevalier until tomorrow? I should like my colleague here to meet him as well. It would be ideal if the old gentleman's physician could be here."

"As it turns out, Docteur Valentin will be calling at lunchtime tomorrow. He and Chevalier Roland are good friends. If you wish, with his permission, I will ask Gilbert and Madame to arrange additional seats for three more. I'm sure Alphonse would welcome the opportunity to display his culinary skills to a wider audience, although he will probably complain about it."

The Great Detective smiled, "That would be most enjoyable. I understand both the kitchen and cellars of the Ste. Germaine estate are quite enviable. Would that fit your schedule, Inspecteur Roget?"

"Yes. Quite satisfactory!"

The valet rose. "I'll speak to the Chevalier immediately. If you'll wait here. Is there anyone else you wish to interview."

"No. perhaps tomorrow we could have a little private time with Chevalier Roland after lunch as well."

"I'll ask."

Lady Juliet pouted, *"Oh, you and Watson get a wonderful lunch tomorrow while Pookie and I starve. We'll take Martha Hudson someplace interesting. You'll have to be especially generous at Maxim's this evening to make up for it."*

"I wasn't aware of your serious mistreatment. Milady. I thought you planned a lunch trip on a Bateau Mouche for tomorrow and a ride on the Metro."

"Oh, so I did. Martha should like eating and riding up and down the Seine at your expense."

"At the Sûreté's expense. They are paying me a fee but their resources are not unlimited. Nor are mine. Ah, here comes Claude."

"M'sieur Holmes. The Chevalier will be delighted to accommodate you, the Inspecteur and your colleague at luncheon tomorrow and he can spare some additional time afterwards. Doctor Valentin will also be there. I shall inform Gilbert, Madame and Alphonse. He eats precisely at noon."

"Thank you, Claude. I look forward to it."

Chapter Six

Roget let Holmes *(as well as Juliet and Pookie)* off at the Hotel Regina with an understanding that he would meet him and Watson in the morning for their ten o'clock interview with Armand Duclos. Then on to a noontime lunch and discussion with Chevalier Roland Ste. Germaine and his doctor. They also planned a return to the Sûreté safe house and another meeting with Chevalier Louis.

Meanwhile, the Baroness, her dog and Mrs. Hudson after riding the Metro, would be steaming up and down the Seine on a Bateau Mouche sharing a splendid waterborne lunch. These boats that were so popular during the Paris Exposition Universelle 1900 had remained favorites of the tourists that thronged the City of Lights ever since. Tomorrow!

But, this evening's event was still in the offing. Dinner at Maxim's! In the flesh, Juliet whirled around the suite, magically changing her costume as she flew. Pookie scampered along at her side. She burst into song:

> "I'm off to Chez Maxim
> To join the whirling stream.
> For one brief hour entrancing
> The moments fly romancing.
>
> At Maxim's once again
> I swim in pink champagne.
> When people ask what bliss is
> I simply answer, "This is!"

She collapsed onto the brocade sofa, laughing. Martha and Watson joined in the hilarity. Holmes allowed a grin to lighten his face.

Mrs. Hudson said, "Oh, how jolly! What was that?"

41

Catching her breath, Juliet replied, "It's 'You'll Find Me at Maxim's' from *Die Lustige Witwe The Merry Widow Operetta* by Franz Lehar."

The Doctor said, "I say, Baroness. I've never heard that song before or that operetta."

"And you won't, Doctor. Lehar hasn't written it yet. Not until 1905. At the Saintly Spectaculars, we perform music yet to come. It's a wonderful gift for us singers."

Eyebrows went up all around the room. "You foresee songs before they are written?"

"Yes, it's such fun to predict what will be the next sensation. Lehar gets my vote. Ah, Maxim's! I am so looking forward to the gorgeous gowns and the handsome men. You two gentlemen will no doubt be the object of much speculation by the Parisienne beauties. Don't let it go to your heads."

Watson laughed, "And with your appearance you will cause consternation among those same jeune filles and not-so-jeune Mesdames."

"All in an evening's work, Doctor. I'm used to it. I understand the restaurant is building a collection of Belle Epoque Art Nouveau. I'm a great fan. Speaking of fans, I must conjure one up."

As she left the room, she asked, "Holmes, is Maxim's food and champagne really that good? Pookie wants to know."

The detective chuckled, "Fear not, Milady and Miss Dog. You will be more than satisfied. Come Watson. We must plan our activities. I hope you will be joining Roget and me tomorrow at lunch. As you know, the senior Chevalier's physician, Doctor Valentin will be there. You can form your own conclusions as to Roland Ste. Germaine's condition.

Watson nodded, "I'll be there. His recovery is noteworthy."

Holmes agreed, "Of course, earlier in the morning, we have an appointment with the old gentleman's former secretary, Armand Duclos. I am eager to find out why he was dismissed and whether he has sufficient rancor against the Ste. Germaine's to be the thief and note writer."

Watson shook his head. "If he felt an injustice was committed against him, why would he wait over a year and why aim his revenge at the junior Chevalier when the senior sacked him. It doesn't make sense."

"You're probably right but he may be able to shed a little more light on the situation and relationships in the Ste. Germaine establishment. Something doesn't smell right at that mansion."

Chapter Seven

No. 3 Rue Royale in the 8th arrondissement! Maxim's! Well on its way to becoming one of the most famous restaurants in the world thanks to the 1900 *Exposition Universelle.* Mrs. Hudson, entering through the revolving doors and through the bar, had to work hard to keep her eyes from popping and her jaw from dropping as she gazed at the lights, the tables covered in snowy cloths, the Art Nouveau ceiling and décor, and most of all. the glamorous diners. Men in white tie and tails and women in the height of Parisian fashion. Liveried waiters gliding between the tables, taking orders and delivering succulent food and champagne, champagne, champagne.

Hugo, the Maître d', inspired by Holmes' generous gratuity, bowed and led them to a central banquette where the quartet took up their seats. Pookie, resplendent in her bright red bow sat on the floor next to Lady Juliet. *(Dogs were allowed in the dining room and a few pets could be found among the patrons – surprisingly well behaved, except for a somewhat feral cat who periodically howled and hissed. Pookie ignored him.)*

Many a jealous female eye was focused on the Baroness as she sat down opulently bejeweled and most stylishly clad in a signature scarlet creation from Madame Clarice. Diners of both genders paid special attention to the ascetic figure seated next to her and the obviously ex-military gentleman sitting opposite. Mrs. Hudson, handsomely attired in her new evening dress, was noticed as well.

Music from a quintet joined the chattering conversations and incessant laughter to fill her ears. She had been impressed by the Café de la Paix. Here, she was thrilled. She giggled at the popping cork of the magnum of pink champagne and the bubbling fizz as the waiter filled the crystal flutes. Holmes lifted his drink and proposed a toast. "To beauty in all of its manifestations." They raised their glasses, drank and set about ordering from the impressive menu. Pookie lapped at a bowl of the sparkling wine and was looking forward to an array of gourmet table scraps. An Epicurean Canine.

As was her wont, Lady Juliet hummed along with the piano, increasing the volume of her contralto with each sip of champagne. Much to her surprise, she was greeted with applause and urged by the surrounding tables to rise and sing in full voice. Her own tablemates joined in encouragement. Blushing a bit *(It was uncertain whether from winsomeness or wine)* she stood and sang a popular love song in French. The entire restaurant was mesmerized and when she concluded, gave her a major ovation. *(Except for a few musical actresses who jealously sat on their hands.)* She bowed, laughed coyly and sat down to enjoy the first course which she and Mrs. Hudson shared with Pookie. The dog then turned her attention to Watson who became her very best friend as he fed her delicious tidbits. Holmes was spared doggy attention.

A splendidly dressed, short, balding individual with a rudimentary moustache approached the table. "Mesdames and Messieurs, Welcome to Maxim's. We are thrilled to have you here. I am Gustav Cornuche, the proprietor of this establishment."

Before the Baroness could respond, Holmes intervened. "M'sieur Cornuche. I am Sigerson. Allow me to congratulate you on your wonderful café. It is a marvel. Let me introduce you to our group. We are from England here on a short holiday. This is Madame Rose LaTour who entertained you all a few moments ago. Her companion is Madame Hughson, a lady of property in London. This gentleman is Madame Rose's physician, Doctor Woolrush and this little fur covered hoyden is Mamselle Pookie." The dog barked softly and wagged her tail furiously.

"I am ecstatic to meet you all. I am especially delighted to meet you, Madame Rose. Enchanté. "

Lady Juliet produced a sparkling smile, reached out and touched the man on his arm. "Moi aussi, M'sieur. "

"You can tell by their reaction how excited our usually jaded customers were by your brief performance. I have come to enquire whether you can be persuaded to become a featured artiste here at Maxim's. You would be a sensation."

Holmes once again intruded. "I am afraid I did not adequately introduce myself, M'sieur Cornuche. I am Madame Rose's theatrical agent. We are most grateful for your interest but helas, Madame is under an exclusive long term contract with Richard D'Oyly Carte in London. She is taking her holiday here in Paris before embarking on the Fall Season with the Company."

"Quel dommage! Ah, well!" He snapped his fingers at the Maître d' and said "Hugo, another magnum of champagne and there will be no bill for this table. My thanks for your heavenly singing."

(Little did he know.)

As Cornuche walked away somewhat downcast, Lady Juliet turned to Holmes. "Sigerson indeed! Spoilsport! It might have been fun."

Holmes frowned, "Milady, may I remind you of your transitory condition. Madame Rose LaTour is a charming and talented figment as is your dog."

"Oh, Poo!"

And so the evening progressed. Music, laughter, dancing, gourmet food and bubbly champagne. Mrs. Hudson was enchanted. The Baroness was enchanting. Pookie was overfed. Watson was more than sated and Holmes, being Holmes was caught up in his own mental exercises.

Chapter Eight

Next morning, a bit worse for wear after the Lucullan feast at Maxim's, Holmes and Watson worked their way through a small breakfast punctuated by a large supply of coffee. The Doctor sniffed, "I assume the ladies will be lying in for a bit before going off on their jaunts on the Metro and Seine river boats. As we both know, Lady Juliet is indeed an original. Her performance last night was amazing. I wish I could find a wife like her. Perhaps I will. "

He continued, "Don't expect Mrs. Hudson to revert to her sedate self after her Parisian adventures. She's already primed for investigating crimes after her stint with the Mystics of Evil and her night on the town with the Baroness and Pookie. *(Book Two)* Speaking of Pookie, that dog is a Canine Wonder. Clever well beyond expectations, physically astounding with no end of talent. She's a Heavenly Top Gun. However, she has an emotional makeup that perfectly matches Lady Juliet's. We have our hands full."

Holmes listened to this little analytical lecture with typical resignation. He had his own opinions but as usual kept them to himself. "Come. It is time to meet Inspecteur Roget. The game is once more afoot. Let us see what Armand Duclos has to say for himself. I am amazed that the Inspecteur didn't see fit to interview him. He certainly has motive and possibly means. I don't know whether he had opportunity to steal the medal and write the note."

The Police Peugeot was waiting at the door to the hotel. Roget waved to the detective and the doctor and they climbed aboard, Once more onto and through the Ile de la Cite, over the Pont au Change and into the streets of the Left Bank. On to the Latin Quarter.

Watson asked, "What does Duclos do now that he is no longer secretary to the Ste. Germaine's?

Roget laughed, "He teaches at the Sorbonne. Law and Political Science, would you believe! We are meeting him there."

Holmes frowned. "That may explain a few things." He explained nothing.

47 rue des Écoles, in the Latin Quarter. The address of the *"Sorbonne Université, creators of futures since 1257."* The car pulled up into a courtyard and they proceeded into an impressive building of indeterminate age. Students, faculty and an army of unidentified and unidentifiable individuals rushed here and there, no doubt on their way to lectures, seminars, meetings and the like. Roget led them through a warren of corridors until they came to an office door, identical in all respects to a parade of other portals but distinguished by a number 756, and a name 'Loi et Science Politique', the domain of Armand Duclos.

A knock on the door was answered by a clean shaven, middle-aged man of startling stature, taller than Holmes. Clad in an academic gown too short for his height, he wore a set of tweeds that would have been at home at Oxford or Cambridge. His smile was

47

Gallic, however, and his dark unkempt hair and deep brown eyes screamed 'French.'

Roget introduced himself and his two colleagues. "Professeur Duclos, bonjour. Allow me to identify myself and my associates. I am Inspecteur Roget of the Sûreté. We spoke yesterday on the telephone. Thank you for agreeing to see us. May I present Mr. Sherlock Holmes and Docteur John Watson, the famous British detectives. They are assisting me in untangling a puzzle involving the Ste. Germanies."

At the mention of the Chevaliers, a cloud passed over Duclos' face. It quickly disappeared and the smile reestablished itself. He snickered. "Past history, Inspecteur. I doubt if I can be of any assistance in solving your current problem, whatever it is."

Holmes responded, "Perhaps not, Professeur, but sometimes memories can spark a very useful line of inquiry. If I am not being insensitive, what caused you and the Chevaliers to part ways?"

"How polite, Mr. Holmes! The truth is I was dismissed by Chevalier Roland. I had no issue with Chevalier Louis."

"That is interesting. We were given to understand that you had problems with both of them."

"No, in fact, I keep up correspondence with the younger Chevalier. It was his father who dispensed with my services."

"May I ask why?"

"Mr. Holmes, Doctor. How familiar are you with 'L'affaire Dreyfus'? I'm sure Inspecteur Roget is well aware of the situation."

"Even in England, we are aware of the conflict but we are not living through it as the people of France are."

Duclos smiled again. He switched into professorial lecture mode. "D'accord! 'L'affaire', as it is known, has come to symbolize modern injustice in the French speaking world. It is a classic example of miscarriage of justice and antisemitism.

"The scandal began in December 1894 when Captain Alfred Dreyfus was convicted of treason. Dreyfus is an Alsatian French artillery officer of Jewish descent. He was falsely convicted and sentenced to life imprisonment for communicating French military secrets to the German Embassy in Paris, and was imprisoned on Devil's Island in French Guiana, where he spent nearly five years."

"In 1896, evidence first came to light—which identified the real culprit as a French Army major named Ferdinand Esterhazy. But when high-ranking antisemitic military officials suppressed the new evidence, a military court unanimously acquitted Esterhazy after a trial lasting only two days. The Army laid additional charges against Dreyfus, based on forged documents."

"Emile Zola's open letter *J' Accuse...!* appeared in the newspaper *L'Aurore* accusing the army top brass of conspiracy and trial-fixing. It created a growing movement of support for Dreyfus, putting pressure on the government to reopen the case. In 1898, Zola was convicted of libel but he fled France for England. He has since returned and I am an associate of his."

"In 1899, Dreyfus was returned to France for another trial. The intense political and judicial scandal that ensued has divided French society between those who supported Dreyfus called 'Dreyfusards' and those who condemned him the "anti-Dreyfusards." The new trial resulted in another conviction and a 10-year sentence, but Dreyfus was pardoned and released in 1899. At the time he stated, 'Liberty to me is nothing without Honour. From this day forward I shall continue to seek amends for the shocking judicial wrong of which I am still the victim.' Today in 1902, he fights on."

Holmes interrupted (as usual) and said. "Thank you for your concise summation of 'L'affaire' but it does not answer my question. "Why were you dismissed by the senior Chevalier?"

"Several reasons: The Chevalier is a rabid antisemite and I am Jewish. It took him a long time to make that discovery but when he did, he acted swiftly and summarily. Reason number two: I am a staunch Dreyfusard and have been quite vocal and active in my support of the Captain's rehabilitation. Three: Chevalier Roland is a former officer in the military power elite and an owner of a large manufactory producing weapons for the Armed Forces. His bias is intense. Finally: I am an associate of Emile Zola's. Take your pick or all of the above! Oh, I forgot. I am also friends with Chevalier Louis and have persuaded him to take up Captain Dreyfus' cause."

This last point rang a loud bell in Sherlock Holmes' brain.

"You have been most helpful, Professeur. Two last questions. Have you had any recent contact with Chevalier Louis and if so, has he spoken to you of his missing medal and the threatening note he has received."

"Two answers: No and no! But, Mon Dieu, Louis been threatened?"

Roget answered. "Yes. It is that which we are investigating along with the mysterious disappearance of his medal of the Legion d'honneur."

"Ah, now your visit makes more sense. Let me assure you, gentlemen. I know nothing of any errant medal or threat. I am certainly not responsible. Please express my concern to Louis when you see him next. Given his father's disapproval of me, we do not meet often. We do correspond, however."

Roget shook his head. "For the moment, the Chevalier is in a Police safe house. Hopefully, we can release him shortly."

"Give him my best. I hope the threat turns out to be a hoax."

"As do we, Professeur. As do we."

They got up and left. Roget's driver was at the door.

*(**Note to Reader:** Emil Zola died on September 29.1902 from carbon monoxide from a stuffed chimney. Many found this suspicious. His funeral was attended by a crowd of over 50.000 including Alfred Dreyfus. Dreyfus was completely rehabilitated in 1906. His rank was restored to Major and ironically for our story, he was named as a Chevalier of the Ordre National de la Legion d'honneur.)*

Chapter Nine

Once outside, Watson, who had been quietly observing all this, said, "I say Holmes. this casts a rather formidable shadow on this whole situation. It puts the Senior Chevalier in a delicate position. "

"It does indeed, Watson. I'm glad you will be with us when we meet this Doctor Valentin. We also have to ensure Claude is with us. If the father is at the bottom of this, Claude may well be a co-conspirator. What say you, Roget?"

"It is difficult for me to imagine the old man threatening his son but stranger things have happened. Well, we have a lunch appointment. Let's depart."

On the way to the Ste. Germaine mansion, Watson queried Inspecteur Roget further. "What can you tell me about this Docteur Valentin?"

"Georges Valentin is a highly respected physician who is affiliated with the Paris School of Medicine. He is a specialist in afflictions of the heart. He is a good friend of Chevalier Roland and has been treating him and his illness for several years."

"I'm looking forward to consulting with him. As a general practitioner, I have treated numerous cases of cardiac ailments, usually with limited results. The symptoms can be dramatic. There is little that can be done to actually cure the sickness. Most physicians are constrained to just mitigating the warning signs and pains and trying to make the patient more comfortable. Unfortunately, death is all too prevalent."

Holmes remarked, "I wonder how serious the Chevalier's condition really is. We shall see."

They reached their destination at thirty minutes past eleven. They were welcomed once again by Gilbert, the butler. "Good morning, gentlemen, you are early. Lunch is scheduled for noon. The Chevalier is a stickler for exact timing. Doctor Valentin is here. He has been attending the Chevalier and will be joining you shortly. Please follow me to the anteroom. May I offer you some pe-luncheon refreshment? We have an excellent sherry that should please your English palates. You too, Inspecteur."

Watson accepted. Holmes refrained and Roget said he could not while on duty although he would enjoy a glass of wine with the meal. Holmes enquired, "How is the Chevalier, this morning?"

"Claude said the old gentleman had a relapse and restless and painful night. He administered laudanum according to the doctor's instructions. That seems to have some calming effect although recently he has experienced extreme mood swings. He as always been moody and touchy but now he is also quite euphoric. A strange combination. Claude is concerned."

Watson pondered, "That could be the laudanum. It is highly addictive, based as it is on opium and can impact the personality."

Gilbert shook his head and then looked up. "Ah, here is the Docteur now."

A tall, slender man with a short dark beard and full head of hair entered the room. He was clad in professional morning clothes. He removed his pince-nez and greeted the trio. "Georges Valentin at your service. I know you, Inspecteur Roget. May I assume that your companions are the famous English detectives, Sherlock Holmes and Doctor John Watson?"

Holmes replied. "We are indeed, Doctor. I am Sherlock Holmes and this gentleman is my highly trusted associate, Doctor Watson. A physician like yourself."

"Delighted to meet you both. Gilbert, is it too early for a glass of Alphonse's splendid sherry?"

"Not at all, sir. I was about to fetch one for Doctor Watson. Excuse me."

Valentin blew out his cheeks. "A difficult morning. The Chevalier has had another attack of angina pectoris. I tried to persuade him to cancel this lunch conference but he insisted on meeting with the three of you. He is in one of his extreme moods. I cannot predict how he will behave. I hope you will bear with him if he becomes, shall I say, unconventional."

Watson replied, "I understand that you are dosing him with laudanum to relieve his pains."

"Not a favored choice, Doctor but the lesser of two evils. Extreme pain or addictive reactions. I am not optimistic about the outcome in either case."

Holmes asked. "How long has he been suffering from this condition?"

"As best I can tell, his heart has always been weak. He retired from the military because of it but he ran his businesses and began his memoirs in spite of it. Now, all of that has changed. The formerly active Chevalier is becoming quite feeble and erratic. But he is still consumed with rage over a number of issues, especially the Dreyfus affair. Are you familiar with it?

They nodded affirmatively.

"As you might expect, as a former Army General Staff officer, he is a staunch and vocal anti-Dreyfusard. Please do not mention Emil Zola in his presence. He is also a virulent antisemite. Have you met Professeur Duclos, his former secretary. Yes? The Chevalier became violent when he discovered Duclos was Jewish. Had him physically removed from the house. Ah, thank you, Gilbert. This will calm my nerves." He took the sherry as did Watson.

"Gentlemen, Chevalier Roland is ready to receive you at lunch."

He opened the door to a splendid dining room. Oak paneling trimmed with gold. The table, covered with snowy linen, was set with obviously valuable silver utensils and glassware The old gentleman was already seated with his valet Claude standing behind him. With his white hair and mutton chop beard, rheumy eyes and shrunken frame he had certainly seen better days. Although clearly in poor health, he still evinced signs of a strong military presence. He was dressed in a now ill-fitting colonel's uniform and wore the medal of the Ordre National de la Legion d'honneur around his neck. He no doubt intended to impress his guests.

He waved in their general direction. "Gentlemen, please be seated." Two footmen were strategically placed behind large ornate chairs and helped the quartet take their places. Alphonse entered the room and with Gilbert's help poured a white wine for each of them. He then snapped his fingers and the footmen exited and returned with tureens of consommé. The Chevalier raised his glass. "To the confusion of our enemies." He broke out into a gale of raspy laughter. "Drink up! Eat up!" He slurped a large spoonful of the soup, sighed, looked at the chef who had remained in the room and said, "Splendid as usual, Alphonse. My compliments"

A few more slurps and he turned to Roget "So, Inspecteur. I assume these two are the English detectives you have imported to find my son's medal and find out who is threatening him. Is the Sûreté corrupted so badly that French policemen cannot solve a simple puzzle? For shame!"

Before Roget could respond, Holmes interjected. "No, mon colonel, the puzzle has been solved long since. We are just waiting for the culprit to reveal himself. Incidentally, I am Sherlock Holmes and this is my associate, Doctor John Watson."

"Another doctor! Come Valentin! Are you going to allow these minions of perfidious Albion to usurp your position as my all-knowledgeable physician? What is France coming to? The treacherous Jews undermining all of our precious values. Treasonous Dreyfusards attacking the integrity of our military. That snake Zola and his preposterous accusations. My former secretary spewing his vicious Hebrew nonsense at the Sorbonne to all who will listen to him including my own son. Louis, a traitor to his country and to his father. It is too much to countenance. I can no longer bear it."

During this tirade, he had turned a deep shade of red and began coughing. He gripped his chest and murmured, "Claude, Valentin! Au secours!" He passed out before they could reach him. Both of the footmen grabbed him and the physician rushed to his side. "Take him to his room. I shall attend to him."

The valet was about to exit with them when Holmes seized his arm. "Before you leave, Claude. Where have you hidden Chevalier Louis' medal? Did you write that threatening note or did Chevalier Roland?"

"Let me go, damn you. The medal is hidden in a vase in the drawing room. Those stupid flics never bothered to look in there and no, I did not write the note. My master did. He was enraged at his son. As am I. He betrayed his father and all of France. Now, release me. I must go to him."

Holmes freed him and looked at Watson and Roget, "Our mystery is solved. Inspecteur, you may wish to inform Chevalier Louis and escort him from the safe house back here to his home. I assume he will want to return."

Watson stared at Roget. "Are you going to charge the old gentleman?"

"I suppose we could accuse him of theft and extortion but it would cause a major scandal. Unfortunately, unlike the English, the French penal code does not include wasting police time as one of its punishable violations. I would have liked to slap Claude with that one. His confession and the old man's ranting should be enough to close the book on this incident."

Holmes shrugged. "I suspect you will have to add another chapter."

He was correct. That evening, Roland Ste. Germaine, industrialist, retired Colonel of the French Army High Command, Chevalier of the Ordre National de la Legion d'honneur and antisemite fanatic passed away as a result of a severe heart attack. His valet, Claude Fontaine, overcome by grief and guilt. committed suicide.

Epilogue

A light supper in the Regina Hotel dining room for Lady Juliet, Mrs. Hudson, Holmes and Watson. And of course, Pookie.

"So while Martha, Pookie and I were lunching on the Seine, you two were being feted at the home of the senior Chevalier."

Watson smiled at the Baroness. "We got no further than the soup, although it was delicious. Chevalier Roland worked himself up into a incensed state and profound heart attack which proved to be fatal. It was he who stole his son's medal and wrote the threatening note."

Holmes corrected him, "He and his valet, Claude who has committed suicide as a result of the demise of his master."

"Why would a father threaten his son in such a way?"

"Milady, history is awash with cases of filicide. Remember Abraham and Isaac."

"But God stopped that sacrifice. Do you think Roland actually intended to kill Louis? You say he was terribly frail."

"Impossible to say. Perhaps Claude would have done his dirty work for him. As to why, I suspect his frequent use of laudanum for his angina shattered his mind. He was wildly unreasonable. The man was a rabid antisemite. The Dreyfus affair enraged him beyond rational limits and the thought of his son supporting the disgraced Captain pushed him over the edge. He regarded Louis as a traitor to his country and himself, no longer fit to be a Chevalier."

"It's tragic."

"Indeed! Louis is back at his home supervising the funeral rites for his father and the valet. Roget has closed the case and has been exuberant in his gratitude to us. Between my connections with the owners of this hotel and the fees paid to us by the Sûreté, this Parisian adventure has cost next to nothing. I hope you have enjoyed it."

"Oh, indeed! But Raymond has called Pookie and me back to Heaven. Rose LaTour will mysteriously disappear but not before we two flit to the top of the Eiffel Tower. An excellent take off point for our journey home. Au revoir, Doctor, Martha and Holmes. Perhaps we will yet conspire again. It has been thrilling chez Paree." They vanished.

The Adventures of Sherlock Holmes and the Glamorous Ghost

Chez Paree

The End

The Adventures of Sherlock Holmes and the Glamorous Ghost

Where's Charley?

The following letter was delivered to Sherlock Holmes' rooms by messenger on a balmy Summer morning after their return from Paris. He opened it with his jack-knife and after perusing the contents, passed it to Doctor Watson.

Carlotta & Sebastian
Gaiety Musical Theatre
Brighton Pier, England

Mr. Sherlock Holmes   20 August 1902
221B Baker Street
London, England

Dear Mr. Holmes:
        My name is Sebastian Fordyce, of the world famous quick-change team of Carlotta and Sebastian. Carlotta (Charley O'Hara) has been my partner for over six years and we have travelled the world, entertaining and thrilling audiences with our split second costume changes and disappearing act. We have played for royalty and nobility on the Continent, Russia and the Mediterranean. We have been called the premiere performers of our type by the international theatrical press. While other performers do quick-change, none also add the vanishing turn with which we end our performance.

        We have been playing to capacity audiences at the Brighton Gaiety for close to a year, perfecting our routines in preparation for another world tour. We have ten more months in our agreement before setting out once again. This time we are booked for an

59

extensive engagement in the United States. We've added more "magical" costumes and several props to better support our change and vanishing feats. The effect is indeed startling when Charley disappears.

The trouble is that now Charley has truly vanished! She has been missing for seven days, causing the theatre to temporarily cancel our act. Needless to say, the Gaiety owner, George Capstone, is mightily upset and is threatening to sue us for breach of contract. She has never gone astray before and I am extremely worried about her well-being. She shares rooms with Leila Vance, a singer who is a headliner here at the Music Hall. Leila claims she has not seen or heard from Charley since the 13th. She did not leave a note and her clothing, costumes and some personal materials are all intact in her room.

I have been to the Brighton Police but they refuse to take the situation seriously. A publicity stunt or a performers' or lovers' spat, they say. Charley and I are both unmarried and not romantically involved with each other or as far as I know, anyone else. We have been too taken up with our theatrical work.

She is an incredibly attractive, tall brunette with a willowy figure and gorgeous blue eyes. In the course of our routine, she alters her outfits a number of times at lightning speed. Some would-be lotharios take this as an indication that she is a woman of loose morals. Nothing further from the truth. She has been subjected to several offensive approaches by "stage-door-johnnies." I have had to quite forcibly and physically insist that a few of them cease and desist. Did one or more go too far? Has she been the victim of violence, assault or kidnapping?

In the absence of Police cooperation, I am approaching you for assistance. I have had the pleasure of meeting your associate, Doctor Watson, several times. He is a music hall enthusiast and we have had occasion to talk about your adventures. He has met

Charley. He has spoken so highly of your skills that I feel my best alternative to the Police is to seek you out and ask for your help in finding my partner.

I hope you will be willing to take on the case and solve this puzzling problem posthaste. I can be reached at the Gaiety or the Actors' Hotel here in Brighton. Thank you for your attention and please give my best regards to Doctor Watson.

Best wishes,

Sebastian Fordyce

*****

"What say you, Watson.? Do you recognize this Sebastian Fordyce and his charming co-star?"

"Oh, indeed Holmes, I have seen them perform several times. Their quick change act is amazing, especially when she totally disappears from the stage and immediately reappears at the back of the house. She is a dazzling creature."

"It seems she has vanished permanently leaving Mr. Fordyce in the lurch and George Capstone enraged."

"Are you going to take the case?"

"Yes, I am fascinated by life imitating art. Is Charley O'Hara nowhere to be found? Speaking of missing persons, what has become of the Baroness? Did she return to the Heavenly Elysian Fields after leaving the Eiffel Tower? Has it occurred to you, Watson, that she would be the perfect substitute for Miss O'Hara. Her attractive looks are highly similar. She can change outfits in a trice and disappear and reappear at will. Of course, she cannot admit to being a ghost."

"No, I can't! Lady Juliet had returned to earth and had invisibly been listening to their conversation. *"Hello, Holmes, Watson! Raymond has allowed me to come back to England after*

Paris. He's such a sweetheart. Is this a show business assignment for Pookie and me? It is? Goody!"

"Yes, Milady! Welcome! On to Brighton and the Gaiety Theatre. Watson, wire Fordyce! We're coming."

Capstone's Gaiety Musical Theatre
Brighton Pier, England

Holmes and Watson were ushered into an office decorated with theatrical posters, exotic costumes and extravagant props. The invisible Baroness and Bichon floated in and proceeded to examine the elaborate décor. Overcome by nostalgia, she sighed. They needed to return to Paradise and play once more in the Saintly Spectaculars. Once a thespian, always a thespian. But this adventure might turn out to be fun and they needed to find the elusive Charley.

They were greeted by a tall, dark haired, mustachioed and very slick looking individual dressed in a pearl grey formal coat. Watson's suspicions were immediately aroused. The Baroness was reminded of a number of theatrical bad 'uns from her mortal days. Pookie let out an ethereal growl. Holmes remained his impassive self.

"Mr. Holmes and Doctor, allow me to introduce myself: Impresario George Capstone of Capstone's Gaiety Musical Theatre at your service. I have been given to understand by Sebastian Fordyce that you have agreed to investigate the mysterious disappearance of his partner Carlotta. (or Charley O'Hara, as we all know her.) Thank you!"

"I cannot begin to describe what a blow her absence has been to the bill at the Gaiety. I have had to temporarily replace them with Captain Billy's Acrobatic Dogs. The canines hardly fill the seats and ticket sales are seriously down. *(Incidentally, I am willing to contribute to your fee to see the quick-change act rapidly restored to our stage.)*"

He paused to take a breath and smiled unctuously.

"Please do not think me mercenary or uncaring. I am genuinely concerned for Charley's welfare. I would not for the world wish to see any harm come to that lovely lady. I have worried in the past when it seemed she and Sebastian were seriously at odds. They are both temperamental artists. She strongly objected to some of her new costumes and the escape mechanisms they were testing for their disappearing act. She once sat out a performance to register her displeasure. To my knowledge, they have never come to blows but close…close. I hope nothing of the sort has happened this time."

"Leila Vance, her roommate, has confided in me that Charley has been unhappy for some time with Sebastian and has considered teaming up with Claude Wainwright, an adequate but second tier performer. Leila believes Sebastian is aware of this and is furious about it. He feels that he has been the making of "Carlotta" and that she is a "selfish ingrate.""

"Knowing that Charley was not all that keen on another world tour, especially across the Atlantic, I have made overtures for them to extend their contract here and at several of my other properties in England, including London's West End. So far, they have not responded. Sebastian seems set on going to North America. and perhaps even back to the Continent."

"Of course, he is the technical genius who devises the costumes, curtains, trap doors, enclosures, illusions, music and dances. But it is the beautiful Charley who keeps bringing back the customers. If, and I hope it is not the case, she has indeed vanished, Sebastian will be hard pressed to find an equally attractive partner. But I insist that he try and have told him to start a search for understudies immediately. Under no circumstances will I release them from their current contract. She must return and they must play out their obligations. No compromise."

Holmes smiled and said "I think we may have temporarily solved that requirement, Mr. Capstone. We are shortly meeting a train bringing a lady who should be Miss O'Hara's perfect substitute. Madame Rose LaTour, who bears an uncanny resemblance to Baroness Juliet Armstrong, the late, lamented star of the musical stage, is briefly available. As soon as we leave here, we will join her and take her to meet Mr. Fordyce. If they are found to be compatible, we will introduce her to you. Unfortunately, she is committed to return to the continent in short order. Hopefully, we will have found Miss O'Hara safe and sound by that time. I understand you are currently employing acrobatic dogs. Madame LaTour works with a highly talented Bichon Frisé who I'm sure will also delight your audiences. Not to take anything away from Captain Billy's Canine Acrobats, of course."

Lady Juliet had recently played the part of Madame Rose LaTour, Goddess of Motorized Marvels at the national pageant of the Royal Society for the Advancement of Automotive Machinery. *(Book Two)* Among her several roles, she was to be kidnapped by a group of Neo-Luddites, a fictitious gang dedicated to upsetting the use and progress of automotive vehicles. This was the brainchild of the pageant's producer/director who wanted to scuttle the event to avoid personal bankruptcy. She, of course, escaped, leaving the villains confounded. She hoped she would not have to be kidnapped again while tracking down Carlotta. She looked at the ethereal dog. *"Oh drat, Pookie, Where's Charley."* They flitted from Capstone's office where they had been silently and undetectably listening and prepared to meet Sebastian Fordyce, quick change artist.

Holmes and Watson met her outside the theatre *where she and the dog had converted to their physical states. She gave a most unladylike snort. "Oh, Holmes, you've done it again. I wouldn't trust Capstone as far as I could throw him...if I could throw him. I think he's a liar. Pookie wanted to bite him. By the way, let's let Pookie keep her proper name. She got confused during the automotive pageant when she was called Speedy. Doctor Watson, you've met this Fordyce. What's he like?"*

Watson laughed, *"I'm afraid Capstone, though a liar, had it right. Sebastian Fordyce is a Class A flamboyant artiste. Temperamental genius, devoted to his performances and techniques. I'm sure he and Miss O'Hara have their differences. But they worked beautifully together. You should be used to theatrical histrionics. I suspect you demonstrated quite a bit before your saintly transition."*

"Oh yes! So did Pookie. But now we are all sweetness and light. I suppose I could call up some volatility on command, however."

On Stage

Capstone's Gaiety Musical Theatre

Brighton Pier, England

They met at center stage. "Mr. Fordyce, I am Sherlock Holmes. You already know my associate, Doctor John Watson. This lovely lady is Madame Rose LaTour. We believe she may prove to be an excellent substitute until we locate and restore Carlotta to your act."

Sebastian smiled, "Gentlemen, thanks for responding to my letter. Good to see you again, Doctor. I wish it was under better circumstances. Madame, thank you for coming. You are most attractive and not unlike my partner in appearance but I'm afraid Charley's, that is, Carlotta's, performance calls for a unique combination of timing, speed, illusion, movement and attitude that took a long time, much rehearsal, effort and stagecraft to develop. I

65

doubt you will be able to simply step into her role in time to restore our routines. I'm sorry!"

Juliet, who was an expert in male psychology, looked at him and said. "Oh, that's quite alright, Mr. Fordyce. May I call you Sebastian? I am Rose. I enjoyed the train ride down from London. *(She flitted. She hated trains.)* I've always wanted to enjoy an ice cream on the pier and go for a donkey ride. All the charming little shops and pavilions. Brighton is a wonderland. C'est la vie! It was good to meet you. Thank you for your consideration. Shall we go, gentlemen? Come Pookie!" As she turned to leave, her scarlet gown changed shape and color to a forest green frock. Holmes and Watson stifled grins.

Fordyce stared at her. "Wait! How did you do that?"

"How did I do what, Sebastian?" Her voice echoed down from the Royal Box where she now stood in an elaborate orange and white evening dress topped off with a feathered boa, ornate chapeau and sparkling jewels. "Oh this old thing. Something I just threw together."

Fordyce was slack-jawed. " I don't understand!"

"And you won't, Sebastian dear. You have your secrets. I have mine. Now, can we put together a performance that will amaze the punters or shall I go in search of that donkey ride. I think Pookie needs to go out, don't you, dear."

"Yes. Let's work something out right now. I'll tell Capstone. He'll want to see this.

She laughed. "Let him wait until we have our act perfected. It shouldn't take long. We're both professionals. So is my dog."

Holmes chuckled. "I shall leave you two to your discussions and rehearsals. When Miss O'Hara hears from her roommate that you have another partner, she will no doubt swiftly return to the fold. Unless, of course, she has suffered an untoward event. I hope not. I am on my way to consult with Inspector Evans of the Brighton Police. He may have news."

The Metropolitan Police Station
Brighton England

"Mr. Holmes, Doctor Watson, I'm Inspector Clive Evans, Welcome to our patch. I am told that you have been hired by Sebastian Fordyce and George Capstone to conduct a search for Miss Carlotta (Charley) O'Hara who has been missing since the 13th of June."

"At first, it was our opinion that she left the rooms where she was staying during her theatrical engagement at the Gaiety Music Hall and voluntarily vanished. Since her act consisted of quick-change costume substitutions and disappearances, we suspected a publicity stunt was at play. The local press picked up on her absence and gave it coverage."

"However, this morning, the body of an unidentified woman answering Miss O'Hara's general description was found floating beneath the Brighton Pier. She had been in the water for several days. The effects of the sea, tides and fish have made precise identification extremely difficult. We believe the death may have been a suicide but nothing definitive has been determined. Neither Mr. Fordyce nor Mr. Capstone could say conclusively that the body was Miss O'Hara's. We asked Leila Vance, Charley O'Hara's roommate, to also identify the corpse. She was doubtful it was the actress."

"The cadaver is currently in the Brighton Morgue and is being examined by the Coroner's office. We are actively searching for further identification. No one has stepped forward to enquire about a missing woman except of course, Miss O'Hara. You may enquire at the Coroner's office for further information."

The Grand Brighton Hotel

"I say, Holmes. I've been to Brighton a number of times but I never realized what an opulent pile this hotel is. I'm especially intrigued by these hydraulic lifts. My war weary limbs appreciate not having to climb stairs to reach our rooms. And what rooms! How are you affording this?"

The Great Detective chuckled. "I have called in a few favors I've performed for the hotel's owners. We are staying, dining and drinking 'on the house' as they say."

"Splendid! Will the Baroness require accommodations?"

"Madame LaTour in her earthly manifestation, has a suite at her disposal. She and her dog will be well cared for. Let us test the hotel's brandy and then return to the theatre. I'm eager to see how the quick change act is working out."

Back Stage at Capstone's Gaiety Musical Theatre

"Mr. Holmes, Doctor, welcome! I am greatly relieved to tell you that the Police just called to tell us the body discovered floating under the Brighton Pier was identified as a Mrs. Lucinda Paterson of Birmingham. The Inspector said the unfortunate lady had indeed committed suicide after a love affair gone awry. However, the Inspector is still without any worthwhile clues as to Charley's whereabouts. I hope you will be more successful."

"I have not yet told George Capstone that I have a temporary replacement for "Carlotta." We plan to appear this evening. Madame LaTour is a wonder. Astounding! She performs miracles."

Juliet bowed and Holmes and Watson chuckled. "Little does he know."

68

"Her dog is a charmer. We have included her in our routine. Captain Billy stopped by and wanted to sign Pookie up. It's a shame you two must return to the Continent."

"I am sorry, Sebastian but 'needs must.' Show business, you know. I'll leave it to you to tell Mr. Capstone. Will he be willing to let us go on tonight?"

"Wait till he sees us. He will be pressuring you to stay on."

"Impossible!"

"Capstone can be very persuasive."

Juliet murmured to herself. "Let him just try!"

Fordyce continued. "I have enquired of Leila Vance and our few mutual friends and acquaintances in the hope they could shed some light on Charley's current status and location. No help! I sincerely hope she has not met with foul play but my fears are certainly aroused. It's not like her to just disappear except, of course, during the conclusion of our act. She is a beautiful woman but not the brightest and is easily taken advantage of. She is quite willful and capable of doing foolish things."

"No one has come to get her belongings in her theatre dressing room and that leads further to my concerns. Has she left the area or even the country? Has she been kidnapped, spirited away or worse? There have been no demands for ransom or similar threats that I am aware of. George Capstone claims he has not been approached. I am close to despair. Is Charley still alive? The mystery gets more intense with each passing day."

"Mr. Holmes, I realize that you are taken up with a number of cases and can only devote limited time to this problem. However, I would greatly appreciate hearing any information, theories or conclusions you would care to share. If there is any way I can assist you please call on me immediately. Madame Rose will be a lifesaver. But I must find a permanent solution. Meanwhile my time will be taken up auditioning women who I hope on Charley's return, will simply be understudies."

Capstone's Gaiety Musical Theatre
Madame Rose and Sebastian
The Performance

On stage, everyone! A briefing for the Master of Ceremonies and rapid replacement of posters announced the new bill and a change of schedule with Captain Billy's dogs leading up to the entrance of Madame Rose and Sebastian. A clever transition was worked out with Pookie first performing with the dogs, hanging back as they left and then bringing on Madame Rose (Juliet). As she strolled from the left across the stage, the Bichon did back flips by her side. At each flip, her gown and hat changed form and color. The audience collapsed in gales of laughter and amazement. Sebastian entered, waved his arms and both dog and actress vanished only to reappear in the stage right box. More applause. Another arm wave and he disappeared. He was replaced by the lady and her dog onstage. They looked up to the stage right box in time to see Sebastian lean over the railing and wave at the crowd. This was followed by more quick changes by Madame Rose with Sebastian reappearing at center stage where he, too, went through a series of costume alterations. Finally, the trio responded to the prolonged applause, bowed *(yes, the dog did too)* and with a startling explosion of sound and light, vanished. An ovation greeted the now empty stage.

George Capstone was floored. He was at a loss to explain what he saw but he had to ensure that act stayed at the Gaiety. Madame LaTour must be persuaded to stay in Brighton. The old reliable routine – a private little champagne supper with the lady where he could exercise his formidable charm – was called for.

(Capstone is a well-known Lothario. Singer Leila Vance, Charley's roommate, calls him randy George, the Brighton lecher. Seduction is his specialty.)

Holmes and Watson had been watching the act from the wings, aware of how these miracles were taking place even if Sebastian hadn't quite figured it out. "Watson, let us locate Lady Juliet. I have a strong suspicion as to what has happened to Charley O'Hara and I would like the Baroness to do a little more acting and confirm my feeling. I think we will find her with Pookie back in her suite at the Grand Hotel. We must congratulate her on her outstanding performance. The dog, too."

The Doctor concurred. Back at the hotel, the Baroness, still in her physical state, was stretched out on an ornate settee, shoes off and a glass of sherry in her hand. "It's not nectar, Pookie but it will have to do." The Bichon looked up from demolishing her Heavenly Chewy *(Juliet kept an ample supply in her otherworldly reticule.)* and barked at a knock on the door. "I'm sure I know who this is. Come in gentlemen. The door is unlocked."

Holmes and Watson entered. The Doctor enthused. "Splendid performance, Baroness. Top drawer. You and Pookie had the audience mesmerized. The synchronized canine back flip and quick change was a masterpiece."

"Thank you, Doctor. It's a routine the dog and I have worked out for the Saintly Spectaculars. Of course, in Heaven, everyone knows how you're doing it but it's fun anyway. What say you, Holmes? How many of these do we have to do? Sebastian is befuddled but delighted. The slimy George Capstone is beside himself with glee. I don't have to be kidnapped again, do I?"

Holmes reached down and ruffled the dog's ears. "Congratulations Milady. The two of you were indeed spectacular. Sebastian held up his end, too. Well done. No. I've no need for you to be kidnapped. This time I want you to be seduced...by the Brighton Lothario, George Capstone."

"Are you serious? What a disgusting prospect. No thank you, Mr. Holmes. We ghostly actresses have our limits and standards and that certainly exceeds mine."

"Fear not! Your heavenly virtue will be preserved. Watson, Inspector Evans, Fordyce and I will arrive in time to prevent any untoward consequences but our overly friendly impresario must be caught trying to have his will with you. You'll be disheveled but in no danger."

"He'll be the one in in danger. If he goes too far, I'll flatten him and let Pookie chew on his leg."

Watson guffawed. "That would be another amazing performance, Baroness. Sorry, Madame LaTour."

"Indeed, doctor. Well, Madame LaTour was just getting ready to accept an invitation to a late night supper with Mr. Lechery, so I have anticipated you. You three better get ready to break in with the policeman to prevent an uninvited assault on an unconsenting lady. I shall practice my screams. But what has this to do the missing Carlotta?"

Holmes replied. "Leila Vance has finally been cooperative. She claims Charley has disappeared to avoid her theatrical predator. She refuses to return to the Gaiety or any other property Capstone owns or manages. I think I know where she is. Under threat of arrest for assaulting you, we need to get Capstone to agree to release them from their contract."

A Private Room at The Grand Brighton Hotel

"Thank you for this delightful champagne supper, Mr. Capstone. Pookie and I are enjoying it immensely."

72

"It's my pleasure, Madame LaTour. Please call me George. May I call you Rose?"

"Why, yes…George. I regret my stay in Brighton will be so short. I believe Sebastian and I have developed a very entertaining routine."

"It is more than entertaining. It is amazing. Almost miraculous."

She giggled. *(Little did he know.)*

"Are you sure I cannot persuade you to change your plans and stay on here in Brighton. I could make it most profitable for you. In several ways. You are a most charming woman, er, Rose. Is it true what they say about Frenchwomen?"

Rose LaTour aka Juliet Armstrong was no more French than the Tower of London.

She smiled, "Thank you, kind sir. I'm not sure. What do they say?"

"That you are always open for new adventures, especially of the amorous kind. Come here!"

He leaned over, grabbed her hair and attempted to plant a kiss on her lips. She squealed and backed away. The dog growled. Capstone kicked out at Pookie and lunged at the woman. Pawing at her dress, he tried another kiss.

She shouted in French. "M'sieur, Arrête! Immediament!" She screamed! "Au Secours!"

The door swept open and Anatole, the head waiter, Holmes, Watson, Fordyce and Inspector Evans rushed into the room. Fordyce, in true theatrical fashion, shouted, "Unhand her, you swine!" and threw Capstone to the floor. The dog bit his ear. The headwaiter took up a chair as a weapon.

73

Juliet backed away, straightening her gown and patting down her hair. Watson came to her aid.

Inspector Evans seized the impresario's wrists and shouted, "George Capstone, you are under arrest for attempted assault on this woman. I have several witnesses to that struggle. Are you willing to press charges, Madame?"

"On this monster, oui, oui, certainment."

Holmes winked at the policeman. "Let us consider this, Madame. If you press charges, you will have to stay on in Brighton as the case makes its way through the courts. You will miss several very lucrative engagements on the continent. On the other hand, there may be a solution at hand that punishes our theatrical producer appropriately and frees you to pursue your career. Mr. Fordyce, I understand you are bound by a contract that ties you to the Gaiety for ten more months. Now, if, in exchange for Madame dropping all charges, Mr. Capstone was to rescind that obligation, freeing you to take up an engagement in America, would you accept that as justice being done?

"It's up to Madame, of course, but I would welcome the opportunity to leave Brighton posthaste. I only wish I could find Charley."

"Another issue for another day. What say you, Madame? Would you be satisfied?"

"Mais oui. I wish to return to France and be rid of Brighton, the Gaiety and this disgusting fool tout de suite. Losing the quick change act will not be good for his business."

Capstone snarled, "Damned right it won't. I'd lose a packet."

Holmes laughed. "Being convicted of assault against a famous female performer will hardly help your profits. You may even lose the Gaiety."

(Pookie was concerned for the fate of Captain Billy's pooches.)

Capstone paused, "All right. I'll have my lawyer draw up the papers in the morning."

Inspector Evans said, "Meanwhile, I will hold you at the station until you do. A night in the nick might cool your smoldering ardor. Let's go!"

Holmes looked at the headwaiter. "Thank you Anatole. Sorry for the mess. I'll pay for the dinner and champagne."

"Nonsense, Mr. Holmes. The Grand cannot tolerate such behavior. It's on the house."

Watson grinned and murmured, "As is this whole adventure. May I assist you Madame Rose?"

"Merci, Docteur! Come Pookie, a Heavenly Chewy awaits."

The Metropolitan Police Station – Brighton, England

Next morning. George Capstone's solicitor has just completed the paperwork canceling the remainder of Sebastian and Carlotta's work obligation to the impresario. Holmes, Watson, Inspector Evans, Madame Rose and Pookie were witnesses. Sebastian Fordyce and George Capstone signed.

Suddenly, Capstone broke out laughing. "Here! This isn't legal. Charley O'Hara was also a signatory to the original contract. She's not here to sign off on this. This cancellation is null and void. I know my rights."

Holmes returned his laugh. "On the contrary, Mr. Capstone. This document will be perfectly legal in just a moment." He turned to the policeman and said, "Will you bring her in, please, Inspector?"

"Certainly, Mr. Holmes. Miss, please join us."

An incredibly attractive, tall brunette with a willowy figure and gorgeous blue eyes dressed in a simple street dress and shyly smiling, entered the room.

Holmes bowed and said, "Lady, gentlemen and dog. In response to the often asked question, 'Where's Charley?' may I present Miss Charlotte O'Hara aka Carlotta back from her recent hiatus."

Capstone's and Fordyce's jaws dropped simultaneously but for different reasons. One in frustration, the other in delight.

She hugged Sebastian and went with Holmes to the desk where the solicitor extended a pen and pointed to a series of pages requiring her signature.

While she carried out that task, Holmes explained: "After an exhaustive search, Watson and I uncovered a Brighton cab driver who is a fan of the music halls He remembered the highly attractive Carlotta and her remarkable act. He recalled taking her alone to the train station on the 13th but had no knowledge of her destination. That fact suggested that she had left voluntarily and had not been spirited away or was being held for ransom. However, that still left us with a number of questions as to her current status."

"I had a strong suspicion that her former roommate, Miss Leila Vance, was withholding information. When pressed, she admitted that she was aware of her roommate's plan to "vanish" and had promised not to reveal her activities of the past fourteen days to anyone. We then determined that Miss O'Hara was safe, sound and staying with her sister, Mrs. Maybelle Grimes, in their flat in Chiswick. I found and interviewed her and persuaded her to return and join us this morning. She is sorry she has caused consternation, but she has no intention of returning to the Gaiety Theatre. She no longer has to. America awaits. Inspector Evans has closed the books on her disappearance and Capstones' predation."

He turned to the pair. "I regret never having had the opportunity of seeing Carlotta and Sebastian in performance. Doctor Watson assures me your act is quite remarkable, especially the disappearances." They all laughed.

Epilogue

Outside The Metropolitan Police Station

"Well, Holmes and Doctor, it's time to retire Madame Rose LaTour and return Lady Juliet Armstrong and her faithful hound to Heaven's embrace. I never did get that Brighton donkey ride but the ice cream was sublime. Pookie and I plan to include our quick change act in the next Saintly Spectacular. A shame you won't see it. C'est la vie! Our best to Mrs. Hudson. I hope we'll meet again."

They flitted!

The Adventures of Sherlock Holmes and the Glamorous Ghost

Where's Charley?

The End

The Adventures of Sherlock Holmes and the Glamorous Ghost

Hymns, Hums, Handel and Holmes

Earth Time: Spring 1903 - Paradise Time: Infinity (as usual)

"Al-lay-lou-ya!" The powerful and exquisite voices of the joint Angelic and Saintly Choirs echoed harmoniously throughout the vaulted chambers of the infinite Cosmic Cathderal. Praises for the Almighty offered by the heavenly denizens under the leadership of St. Cecilia, patroness of musicians. The program concluded and Baroness Juliet Crestwell, nee Armstrong, gathered up her sheets of music. Patting the head of her dog Pookie who was lying at her feet, she prepared to flit back to her celestial mansion. A melodious voice sang out. "Milady Juliet. A moment, please!"

Juliet looked up at the eternally smiling face of St. Cecilia who was gesturing to her. "Oh, oh, Pookie!" she whispered, "What have I done wrong this time. Was my solo that bad?" Juliet has a superb contralto voice that delights everyone who hears it. Hymns, hums, arias, and songs. Her theatrical history made every perfomance a thrill.

"Lady Directress, is there a problem?"

"Yes and no, my dear. No, no! Your solo was absolutely splendid. The problem is not with you but you may be able to assist with the solution."

"Always willing to help, aren't we Pookie?' The dog waggd her tail enthusiastically.

They had exited the magnificent portal of the Cosmic Cathedral and were flitting along a golden pathway towards the mansions of the blessed.

"Actually, the issue is back on Earth."

78

Juliet frowned, "Oh dear, I've been temporarily restricted from going back down there. Pookie and I have been energetically bouncing between the transcendental and temporal. Perhaps too energetically! The Committee thinks I've been overdoing my earthly visits and besides, I have an obligation to your concerts and to the producer of the Saintly Spectaculars. I'm busier performing here than I ever was in London. I'm also helping Mr. Sherman at the Meadows. My dog and I are teaching some of the birds to fly in formation like the True Angels Aerobatic team. We are champion stunt fliers. "

"You certainly are an active spirit. I should very much enjoy seeing you and your wonderful dog in flight."

"I'll invite you to our next performance. Sorry, I cannot be available in London town, much to my regret. But needs must."

"A shame! But actually, this is a problem for your mortal colleague, Sherlock Holmes. His fame is well known here in Heaven. His sleuthing skills are needed. Are you familiar with George Frideric Handel's cantata *Ode for St. Cecilia's Day?* The premiere was on 22 November 1739 at the Theatre in Lincoln's Inn Fields, London. A little vanity on my part as the patron saint of musicians."

Juliet said "Yes I know the cantata. I'm a contralto but I sang the soprano's part once:

> Orpheus could lead the savage race,
> And trees uprooted left their place
> Sequacious of the lyre:
> But bright Cecilia raised the wonder higher:
> When to her Organ vocal breath was given
> An Angel heard, and straight appeared –
> Mistaking Earth for Heaven."

The saint laughed. "Wonderful! A lovely choice for such a lovely voice. I am flattered and so very pleased. Well, here's the issue. George Frideric Handel lived at 25 Brook Street in London for 36 years. During that time he created, published, signed and sold the scores to many of his works, including the cantata *Ode for St. Cecilia's Day.*"

He bequeathed many original manuscripts of his works to his amanuensis, Johann Christian Schmidt whose son John Christopher Smith, Jr,, Handel's pupil, presented them to King George III. Originally called the King's Library at Buckingham Palace, it is now the Royal Library. The collection comprises thirty-two volumes of operas, twenty-one of oratorios, seven of odes and serenatas, twelve of sacred music, eleven of cantatas and sketches and five volumes of instrumental music. A signed original copy of the Ode cantata has been preserved at the Palace. That is, until a week ago when it disappeared."

"Disappeared? Were the police alerted?"

"I don't know. I have heard all of this from George Frideric himself. He knows of your detecting adventures and would like to meet you. Are you willing?"

"Willing to meet the genius who is widely acknowledged as one of the greatest composers of all time? Of course!"

"Wonderful! A few more facts before I call to him. He was born in Halle Germany in 1685 and died in London in April, 1759. His earthly remains were buried in The Poet's Corner of Westminster Abbey. He never married. He spent time in Germany, Italy and England. He finally settled in London in 1711 at age 26. He became a naturalized British citizen in 1727. There his operas and oratorios gained wide acceptance and Handel became an established part of English music and society circles."

"In England he responded to different opinions and tastes and appealed to a wider public than on the Continent. More than anyone else, he helped to popularize music in Britain. His oratorios, cantatas, songs, and his wonderful instrumental works have both social significance as well as their purely musical importance. His music became an indispensable part of England's national culture. On the Continent, interest in his compositions grew in the late 18th century and reestablished him as a first rank Germanic composer."

"Of course the entire world is familiar with his masterful Messiah, Water Music suites and the Music for the Royal Fireworks but his immense musical output was truly prodigious and he is acknowledged as a unique genius of all time. A warning! When you meet him, he can simultaneously be charming, funny, blunt, tactless, and sarcastic but do not be put off."

Juliet smiled, "So can I. But I'm on notice. I am in awe but not overwhelmed."

"Let me call him!" She raised her eyes and silently murmured. No sound or motion for a few moments and then a shining cloud appeared in the distance moving steadily in their direction, accompanied by organ music.

"That's him. He likes to make an entrance."

The Baroness laughed, "So do I. Don't I, Pookie?"

The Bichon barked and did one of her famous back flips.

The cloud came closer and closer, the organ music reverberating louder and louder and finally settled in front of Juliet's opulent villa. A portly bewigged gentleman in his 70's dressed in a sparkling white robe emerged. The music came to a crescendo and ceased.

"Greetings Mein Herr Handel. Welcome to my humble abode."

"Oh no, Madame. Not Mein Herr! I am a naturalized English citizen. Just George will do nicely. Ah, three such lovely ladies. Cecilia, my dear! Wonderful to see you again. And you of course are the Baroness Juliet Armstrong with your splendid lady pup. Pookie, is she called? Two magnificent voices or is it three? Does the dog also sing? If she does, I will write her a Canine Cantata." He chortled.

"She growls, howls and barks but she is an accomplished dancer. Show him, Pookie."

The Bichon stood up on her hind legs, swiveled from side to side, twirled and finished with another of her signature back flips."

Handel laughed in glee. "It shall be called Dance Music for a Delightful Dog."

St. Cecilia smiled. "I have told Lady Juliet of the missing signed original score of your cantata, Ode for My Day. I am surprised that Buckingham Palace with all of its security would allow such a thing to happen."

"I regret to inform you, dear Cecilia, that yours is not the only dedicated document of mine that is missing. The Royal Library Curators, Palace Guards, and Scotland Yard have determined that at least twelve other tablatures and transcripts of my works have disappeared. Needless to say, I am sore distressed. This has raised major concerns with the authorities for the other works housed in the Royal Library and the rest of the Palace. A thorough review is under way. Some concern for the safety of the Royal Family has also been expressed but they come to Buckingham Palace so infrequently. They spend their time at Sandringham. Forgive my conceit but I believe an overly enthusiastic Handel collector is responsible. But who is it and how to get the items back? Some have been designated irreplaceable masterpieces. I should blush but I won't."

Juliet frowned and said, "Let us hope it is an acquisitive admirer and not someone set on destruction of your works. What can I do to assist?"

Her remark caused a worried pause. Then Handel replied, "If someone is intent on expunging my works, they have an immense task ahead of them. The copies number in the thousands throughout England and the Continent. Even in America where I'm not sure they know what music is. As to what you can do. I would like you to involve your esteemed detective colleague. I don't believe the Palace, Scotland Yard and the Home Office are up to finding the culprit and recovering the originals. The talents of Sherlock Holmes are required. I am sorry to hear you cannot personally be involved. Besides your musical and theatrical gifts, you and your dog have developed quite a celestial reputation as exceptional sleuths."

*****

221B Baker Street. Mrs. Hudson had just brought breakfast and the morning's mail up to the rooms of Holmes and Watson. The Great Detective set about disposing of the bulk of the letters, flyers and solicitations by tossing them into the fire. He set aside one or two handwritten missives on expensive stationery. Possible commissions! He was about to open them when he spied a glowing white packet lying by the door. It hadn't been there a moment ago.

"I say, Watson. Did you drop that large envelope on the floor?"

"Not I, Holmes. Did Mrs. Hudson lose it?"

He picked it up. "I don't think so. It's most peculiar. High quality envelope. Very fine texture. Intense white color. Directed to you and me. There is no return address, postmark or stamps. Wait! On the back is a legend in gold. " VIA **angelic postal service**"

83

The two of them laughed and simultaneously exclaimed. "The Baroness!"

Watson looked at him impatiently and said. "Well, don't just look at it. Open it up and read it. What does our celestial partner have to say?"

He unfolded a voluminous letter "She and Pookie have heavenly obligations and are constrained from flitting to earth at the moment but there is a confidential situation she would like us to look into. It seems a number of original signed scores by George Frideric Handel have gone missing from the Royal Library at Buckingham Palace. Palace security, the Library curators, Scotland Yard and the Home Office are involved but they are keeping a tight lid on their actitivies. The famous composer himself and no less a musical celebrity than St. Cecilia, the patroness of musicians, are requesting our intervention. The Baroness has promised them she would solicit our help. Included in the packet are several Angelic Postal Service return envelopes that we are to use in corresponding with her."

"I assume you intend to get involved."

"Of course, let's start with Lestrade."

*****

Once more down the seventeen steps, into the third cab in the queue and off to the Victoria Embankment and New Scotland Yard. Lestrade was in his stuffy office, a bit unusual for him. He spent most of his time out and on the prowl, so to speak. "Sherlock Holmes, Doctor Watson! Have you come to see how the professionals handle crimes?" He laughed. "Of course not. You have come to upset my digestion and ruin my sleep cycle. What can the Met do for you?"

Holmes smiled, "And good day to you too, Inspector. It may be we can do something for you. In fact, we have come to inquire after an event that has not yet gone public and may never do so if you authorities have your way."

"Come now, Mister Holmes. That remark borders on the slanderous. Only in very rare and perilous circumstances do we withhold information from the public."

Watson guffawed. "Does that include doings at Buckingham Palace?"

"Well now! We do keep a rather close eye on Buck House what with the new King and the Royal Family occasionally in residence or dropping by and all."

"We are here about the original Handel musical scores missing from the Royal Library."

The Inspector' eyebrows rose quizzically. "How do you know about that?"

"Let's just say I have my sources. Are you involved in the search or should I be seeking out one of your esteemed colleagues? Gregson or heaven help us, Athelney Jones?"

"Lestrade's eyebrows descended and his rodent shaped face took on a mournful stare. "No, for my sins, I, my sergeant and several constables have inherited that problem along with the King's Guard, Palace Library Curators and a couple of know-it-alls from the Home Office. Although the Guard and HO cares little about documents. They are actually most concerned with protecting the Royal Family if and when they arrive. Nothing seems to be amiss in that department, thank goodness. No connection. No matter where they reside, we have ample security surrounding them although they spend much of their time trying to ignore or subvert our protective measures. Save me from Royals."

"I have been strongly made to understand by the Royal Librarian that the missing musical scores are priceless and impossible to replace and therefore I'd better get my act together, fetch them back and slap the culprits into durance vile. The Commissioner has received strong representations from the King's Lord Chamberlain. Queen-Empress Alexandra, herself a musician, is greatly distressed by the loss. Now, just what is your interest in all this?"

Holmes smiled. "I have been commissioned by several unnamed parties to look into the vanished documents. There is a special interest in the works of George Frideric Handel which I understand make up the majority of the missing scores. I should like to interview the Royal Librarian or whomever of his curators are most knowledgeable about the number and nature of the absent manuscripts and tablatures. Is that possible?"

"It is indeed. I'll set it up."

Watson looked at the Great Detective. "I say, Holmes. Is this something we should discuss with your brother, Mycroft? Any embarrassment of the government tends to cross his desk. Security at Buckingham Palace and all the Royal residences is probably quite high on his attention index."

"A worthy thought, Doctor. Between our good policeman friend here and Mycroft's intervention, we should be able to make some progress with the Palace bureaucracy. Inspector, please let us know when we will have access to the Librarian and his minions. Meanwhile, I shall tweak a fraternal nose and avoid the Home Office at all costs."

*****

Back at Baker Stret next morning, Holmes forwarded a note to the baroness, using the Angelic Postal Service return mail facility.

"Your Ladyship, in response to your request and that of St. Cecilia and George Frideric Handel, Doctor Watson and I have initiated inquiries into the circumstances surrounding the disappearance of the maestro's personally inscribed sheet music. I will keep you informed of our progress and hope you will pass on notes of our progress to the saint and the composer. Our very best wishes to you and them and of course, your gifted canine. S.H."

He placed the missive in one of the angelic return envelopes, wrote Juliet's name on the front and placed it without postage or any further address on a silver tray we normally used for the post. A barely audible "whoosh" and the packet disappeared. Months earlier, Watson would have been shocked or at least surprised. Now, he merely chuckled and said, "The Royal Mail could take a few lessons from their celestial cousins."

Holmes agreed. "Let us seek out my brother. I doubt Mycroft would have this incident on his priority list were it not for the concern of the Royals and the involvement of the Home Office. I didn't mention Mycroft in my note to the Baroness. She is not very fond of the Senior Holmes sibling."

Watson laughed. "She's not very tolerant of Scotland Yard, either. She cannot abide Gregson and actively detests Athelney Jones. Not a very saintly attitude but then Lady Juliet seems to make her own rules. The divine authorities seem to accept her for her talents, energy and personality. I believe they welcome her rebeliousness. I think they are very fond of Pookie as well."

Sherlock Holmes grinned. "Face it, Watson, so are we. I am amazed that in spite of my lifelong protestations, we are partnered with a pair of female ghosts. Oh. well. Off to see Mycroft."

*****

Watson's note: The Diogenes Club, intent on matching the dour unsociable personalities of its members, stands unwelcoming in Pall Mall. It is unidentified to the outside world, allowing no one except members to enter its doors. I have noted in several of my previous literary efforts the peculiar rules that govern its atmosphere. No socializing or recognition of fellow members, no conversation at all except in the so-called Stranger's Room, an infrequently used apartment on the second floor, near the office of Mycroft Holmes, a co-founder of the establishment.

Sherlock Holmes and Watson were grudgingly and silently recognized by the Major-domo and Desk Clerk and waved up the stairs to the chamber where men may speak if they are of a mind. They awaited the elder Holmes. The Doctor laughed. "It's a shame our ghostly associate and her dog are not with us. She revels in cocking an invisible snook at the guardians of the Diogenes Desk and making faces at the members hiding behind their newspapers. She claims she is checking to see if they are still alive so she can inform the keepers of the Pearly Gates of their silent passing. Incorrigible!"

A door opened and Mycroft hefted his significant girth into the room and lowered himself behind a desk where a stack of Turkish Delights awaited. There was a coffee service on a sideboard filling the room with its tempting aroma. He waved them in its direction.

"Good morning, Sherlock, Doctor. Coffee? I assume you are here because of one of the conundrums you always seem to be wrestling with. Oh, I ended a sentence with a preposition. My command of our mother tongue is disintegrating."

"Holmes smiled. "You are forgiven, dear brother. Watson and I will not betray your weakness. The subject at hand is the disappearance of George Frideric Handel's signed masterpieces from the Royal Library at Buckingham Palace."

"Ah, so you've heard about that. What is your interest?"

"Why to recover them, of course and place the miscreants responsible in the tender loving care of Scotland Yard."

88

"There are a number of individuals and agencies who have already taken up that assignment."

Yes, but none of them is Sherlock Holmes. Palace guards, librarians, the Home Office. The Royal Household. Only Scotland Yard and I have any true detecting credibility. My client was quite specific in asking for my assistance. My anonymous client. Now, what are your thoughts on the subject?"

"The same as yours. No doubt an inside job."

"But with what motivation? Why Handel? Why musical scores at all? Money? They are virtually unsalable unless to a specialized collector. Perhaps, a musician with a warped set of values. I am on my way to meet with the Royal Librarian. I understand you know him."

"Yes, a puffed-up pedant with an oversized sense of his own importance. Quite unpleasant. Fortunately for him, he has a staff of curators who are competent and motivated. Fortunately for the Library, he leaves them to manage the establishment. He will no doubt turn you over to one of them if he condescends to deal with you at all."

"Well, perhaps we will glean some useful information in the process."

"Need I remind you that there is upset in the Royal Household over this affair, starting with the Queen-Empress. No doubt at her insistence, the King and Chamberlain have made their dissatisfaction known. The Librarian is much distressed but arrogant nonetheless."

"How do we keep the minions of the Home Office out of this investigation?"

89

Mycroft replied, "That will be my contribution. Let me repeat. This must be handled with some delicacy. I suspect the Royal Librarian is in danger of losing his job."

Watson chuckled, "In days gone by, he might be in danger of losing his head."

He laughed. "I shall call him and arrange an appointment. I doubt he'll refuse my request. I will explain that you have been called into action by powers on high. "

Little did he know. Or maybe he did.

*****

Buckingham Palace: Where is the Office of the Royal Librarian? They discovered the Palace has 775 rooms. These include 19 State rooms, 52 Royal and guest bedrooms, 188 staff bedrooms, 92 offices and 78 bathrooms. Needless to say, the Great Detective and Watson, his Stalwart Pathfinder, got hopelessly lost. Holmes, like most men, was reluctant to ask directions but they finally succumbed, their pride slightly damaged.

The Doctor chuckled, "I say, Holmes. What a wonderful place to hide. A miscreant could disappear in this labyrinth and never be found again."

"Unless he was pursued by Sherlock Holmes! Ah, here we are. The Royal Librarian. Let us hope Mycroft's good offices have had an effect."

A pale and undernourished young man in Royal livery was seated at a pale and undernourished desk in front of the Librarian's office. He brushed his drooping black hair out of his eyes covered by spectacles and asked, "May I help you, gentlemen?"

"Sherlock Holmes and Doctor John Watson to see the Librarian."

"Ah. Yes! The Librarian says he is far too busy to see you. His next open appointment is in three weeks, However, he has asked me to tend to your needs. I am Cuthbert Jameson, a Royal Library curator. How may I help?"

Holmes smiled enigmatically and murmured, "Probably just as well. We may get some intelligent, informed and useful answers." Aloud he said, "We are here on behalf of three highly placed and concerned individuals who wish to remain anonymous. *(Four, if you count Pookie.)* They have asked us to inquire into the circumstances surrounding the disappearance of the signed transcripts of George Frideric Handel's master works and hopefully recover them."

"You are in good company. Such esteemed personages as Queen Alexandra and the Chancellor of His Majesty King Edward have indicated their dismay about the vanishing scores. The Queen is especially upset. Handel is a great favorite of hers. She is a musician herself and often plays his works, transcribed for the harpsichord."

"Who is in charge of the Handel portfolio?"

"I am. I have given all the information I have to members of Scotland Yard, the Home Office, the Palace Guard and members of the Royal Household. There isn't very much to tell. For the past month, we have had a special exhibition of Handel's signed works on display in the King's Salon open to professional musicians, students and those members of society who have evinced an interest in the Master."

"All told, we have thirty-two volumes of his operas, twenty-one of oratorios, seven of odes and serenatas, twelve of sacred music, eleven of cantatas and sketches and five volumes of Handel's instrumental music. Only a dozen documents were on show. Among the signed scores now missing are fragments of *The*

Messiah, the cantata *Ode for St. Cecilia's Day, Music for the Royal Fireworks, The Arrival of the Queen of Sheba from Solomon, Judas Maccabaeus and the Water Music Suite. "*

Watson asked, "You have a guard on duty while the exhibit is open?"

"Oh yes. He patrols the rooms. The doors to the Salon are locked before and after hours."

"Who has the keys."

"I have a set. So do the guards. I believe the Librarian does but I'm not sure."

"May we go the Salon?"

"Certainly. Please follow me."

Up and down stairs, along corridors, in and out of anterooms and several large state rooms and they finally arrived at the King's Salon. The Salon is actually several large adjoining apartments separated by stately doors or tapestries. Stacks of books and documents on all sides and on free standing shelves reaching to the high ceiling. A number of glass covered tables and display cases. One large case was ominously empty."

Holmes looked at the curator. "Is that where the manuscripts were?"

"Yes!"

"The case is not locked."

"We leave it unsecured to allow access for other curators and professionals. All with strictly enforced restrictions and under the guard's or my supervision."

Holmes looked around. "All of these shelves, niches and closets would provide ideal hiding places for secreting the documents once they were removed from the case. There do not seem to be any places for a full-grown individual to conceal him or herself. "

"These rooms, indeed this entire Palace was not built with security in mind, Mr. Holmes. You are correct and Scotland Yard has pored over this entire space. Not a clue."

Watson asked, "Do you have any opinion on who our thief may be?"

"Whoever they are, they have an attachment to Handel. It could be a musician, composer, singer, collector of exotica. They only took the signed documents. I'm not sure how much of a market there would be for such things. You may wish to consult professional auctioneers."

"You have received no ransom demands or threats?"

"No. I would have thought we would. The Librarian is certain that we will."

The Doctor looked at him. "There is another possibility. A crazed individual who sought to annihilate memories of Handel by attacking and destroying his personalized transcripts."

Holmes interjected. "If that were the case, I believe we would be seeing tattered and disfigured remnants left behind as signs of his or her vengeance. No Watson, I believe the autographed scores are intact, hidden away from all of us who are seeking them. Thank you, Mr. Jameson. Is the King's Salon closed for the duration."

"Yes, indeed. The Royal Librarian has issued strict orders to that effect."

Holmes mumbled once again to himself, "Well, at least he's good for something." Aloud, "Please ensure it stays closed. A request. I realize I have no formal authority in this regard although we are working in cooperation with Scotland Yard. Please let us know immediately if you receive any communication at all."

Back to Lestrade.

*****

"So, Mr. Holmes, you and the Doctor are at much the same standstill as we members of law enforcement. We searched every nook and cranny of the King's Salon as well as the neighboring rooms and corridors. If those manuscripts still exist, they have been spirited away, probably out of the Palace altogether. In spite of their claims, the Library and the Palace in general are not the sharpest when it comes to security."

"Were any members of the Royal family in residence at Buckingham Palace at the time of the theft?"

"Do you suspect the Imperials? That's a bit extreme, even for you, Holmes. But oddly enough, while they normally live in Sandringham and York, Duchess Mary was at Buck House on that day with her children attending a commissioned concert of sacred music by the singers of St Martin-in-the-Fields. They were in one of the State Rooms, not too far from the King's Salon. What are you suggesting?"

"Just gathering data, Inspector. Who else was at the concert?"

"Only the Duchess' retinue, some members of the Palace staff and of course, the singers. It was a closed event."

"Have you interviewed all of the attendees, especially the singers?"

"Do you realize how many members there are of that choir? No, we did not and neither has the Palace Guard, the Home Office or the almighty Librarian. What are you suggesting?"

"Singers, Lestrade, musicians – possible purloiners!"

He looked to the ceiling. "Oh, all right. I'll have the choir called together at the church and interview each member but I think it's a fool's errand."

"It may well be." He silently thought, "Don't send Athelney Jones. He's a real fool."

Meanwhile, Watson and I will retreat to Baker Street and go over the terrain."

*****

Next morning, they discovered another gleaming white envelope bearing the legend in gold. " VIA **angelic postal service.**"

Inside was a single sheet of exquisite quality paper inscribed with a large question mark.

Watson chuckled, "Being a celestial has not not calmed the Baroness' impatience. Or perhaps Pookie is upset. Maybe St. Cecilia or the great Handel are becoming unstrung." He laughed at his feeble pun.

Holmes took the sheet and scrawled on it. "More suspects but the net is tightening. SH" He stuffed it into one of the return envelopes left by the Angelic Service, placed it on the mail tray and watched it disappear. Watson thought he heard the flutter of wings. After all, wasn't being messengers one of the primary duties of angels?

No sooner had this communications wonder taken place when Mrs. Hudson knocked and entered. "Excuse me, gentlemen but there is a member of the Royal Retinue here to see you."

A tall, dark haired, clean shaven, handsome young man in Palace livery stepped into the room. "Good Morning, Mr. Holmes and Doctor Watson. I am Sims, a footman in the service of Her Majesty, Queen Alexandra. I have here a writ summoning you immediately to her presence in Sandringham. I can provide no further details but I believe it is of some importance. A Royal limousine awaits to take you there. Since the Queen's Residence is over 100 miles away, may I suggest we leave immediately."

They both shrugged and hurried to pack a small bag for the trip. "I say, Holmes. Do you suppose Her Majesty wants to berate us personally for not recovering the Handel manuscripts. Damn unfair, if you ask me."

He replied, "And quite untypical of the Queen. She is known for her gentle and polite nature. No, I believe there is more to this than a simple royal rant."

They rolled along in luxurious silence for most of the voyage. Holmes stared off in an impenetrable trance. Watson pulled out a book and began to read about the Regal Abodes. It seems Buckingham Palace had been all but abandoned as a Royal Residence. It now stands as the administrative center for their Majesties. Queen Victoria upon the death of Prince Albert, retreated to Windsor Castle where she remained until her demise. The Duke and Duchess of York occupy York Cottage on the grounds of the Sandringham estate while Queen Alexanda's prinicipal home is Sandringham, itself. It was there that the limousine, the King's favorite, was headed.

Stopping once to refuel, stretch legs, pursue calls of nature and take on small refreshments, the vehicle moved on until in the early afternoon, they arrived at the estate. They were greeted by the Queen's Senior Lady in Waiting, the Mistress of the Robes, Louisa Jane Montagu Douglas Scott, Duchess of Buccleuch and Queensberry. Holmes recognized her since she had served Queen Victoria in the same capacity. They greeted each other familiarly. Watson simply bowed politely.

She said, "Gentlemen, thank you for coming. *(as if they had a choice.)* Her Majesty, Queen Alexandra, is eager to see you. She will be available shortly. You will be accomodated here at Sandringham overnight and taken back to London in the morning. You are invited to dine with Her Majesty this evening. Do not be concerned about dress. We realize you did not bring appropriate dinner regalia. Now, I must run a short errand on her behalf prior to your meeting. In the meantime, you will be conducted to your rooms."

She waved at a pair of footmen who took their small bags and led them up a series of stairs and down several corridors where they were admitted to two sumptuous adjoining apartments. Watson remarked, "Well, Holmes, if we are to be chastised, they are doing it in a most hospitable fashion."

"There is more here than we suppose, Watson. A royal audience and dinner! Hardly an expression of regal anger."

As they unpacked their meager belongings, there was a knock on their door. A footman stood at the entrance. "Gentlemen, I am here to lead you to Her Majesty's presence. Please follow me."

Once again down corridors and up stairs until they reached a large oaken door emblazoned with the Imperial Coat of arms. The lion looked especially fierce. The unicorn was maintaining his handsome profile and the two French mottoes "Honi soit qui mal y pense" and "Dieu et mon droit ' pretty much summed up the Royal Family and its history.

The Mistress of the Robes stood before the door and dismissed the footman. "Gentlemen, this is the Queen's personal drawing room. She is going to ask a particular favor of you which I am sure you will be capable of fulfilling and most willing to carry out." She raised an eyebrow in Holmes' direction.

"Milady, we will make every effort to accommodate Her Majesty as always. However, it is impossible for us to promise results until we are made aware of her request."

The Duchess smiled. "As I expected. The Queen awaits."

She knocked on the door and without waiting for a response pulled on the ornate handles to allow access to the surprisingly simple but well-lit apartment. The mandatory regal tapestries covered one wall. Pictures of royals including of course, Victoria filled the others. There were several large vases filled with a mixture of wild and cultivated flowers. A harpsichord sat in a corner of the room. The Queen sat on a comfortable but not ostentatious sofa, next to which was a table covered in what looked like manuscripts. However, most surprisingly, there were two small children, a boy and a girl, sitting next to her.

The Senior Lady in Waiting curtsied and said, "Your Majesty, as you requested, here are Mr. Sherlock Holmes and his associate, Doctor John Watson."

The two men bowed in appropriate fashion accompanied by barely suffused giggles by the little girl. They waited for the Queen to open the conversation.

"Gentlemen, thank you for coming all this distance to Sandringham. It is the preferred domicile of the King and myself. Being astute individuals, you have probably concluded what the topic of our conversation will be but for the benefit of these two scamps, I will state it clearly. I want you to surreptitiously restore these signed scores and tablatures of George Frideric Handel's works to their place in the Library in Buckingham Palace. They are to be found tucked away securely in a remote and sheltered spot with no indication of how they got there or by whom they were removed. Famous as you are for your stealth and cleverness, I am assuming that is within your capabilities. Am I correct?"

Holmes smiled, "Your Majesty's wish is our command. But please share with us how these documents came to be in your possession."

"I'll do better than that. I will let the perpetrators tell you themselves. Let me introduce two of my grandchildren. This young man is His Highness Albert Frederick Arthur George Saxe-Coburg-Gotha of York."

The solemn blond child scrunched up his noble nose and said, "Aww, Grandmama. Everyone calls me Bertie." He looked at the detectives. "I live over in York cottage with my parents, the Duke and Duchess of York and my brothers and sisters. I'm nine years old. This is my sister, Princess Mary. She's six."

The female sprite retorted, "I'll be seven in a month. And you just turned nine."

Watson chuckled. "The importance of accurate aging. Suppose one of you tell us how these documents ended up here in the possession of the Queen."

Bertie shoved his sister. "I'll tell. It was my idea."

Mary threw a royal pout.

The Prince said. "Mama took all of us to Buckingham Palace for a few days. While we were there we had to attend a concert of hymn singing."

Mary looked around at them all. "It was so boring."

The Queen restrained her laughter. "Mary!"

"Well it was, Grandmama! You wouldn't have made us go. Bertie thought so too. That's why we escaped."

"Go on!"

The Prince stood and shuffled his feet, ready for a recitation. "There was a pause in the singing and I thought, 'Here's our chance.' Mary and I were in the back of the room. I grabbed her hand. The rest of the kids were up front sitting next to Mama. No way they could get loose. The two of us crawled out of the room on our hands and knees. Nobody noticed. I put on the knapsack I always kept with me in case I needed it."

Holmes held back a chortle. These two sounded like slightly more literate members of his Irregulars. "What were you going to do?"

"Disappear and return when the singing was over. Mary decided she wanted to play Hide-and-Seek. There were plenty of rooms and corners to sneak around."

The girl shouted, "I was IT. Silly Bertie would never find me. I found this room with lots of books. I hid under a big desk. There was a guard but he didn't see us. He just walked right past and out the door. It was great place to hide."

The Prince ignored her. "That's when I saw them. There was this big glass case with a sign reading George Freddie Handles and a bunch of old music sheets with signatures on them. Mary can't read but I can."

"I can too."

"Anyway, I knew Grandmama was a musician and these would be things she would like to play on her harpsichord. I reached into the display case, took the pages and stuffed them in my knapsack to bring to her as a gift. After all, she is the Queen so anything in the Palace is hers anyway. I just thought she'd like to have them at Sandringham instead of London. When we got back to the room, the singing concert was over. Mama never missed us and I walked out with my stuffed knapsack. When we got back to York, Mary and I went over to see Grandmama and gave her the papers. She was upset. I'm still not sure why."

The Queen reached over and hugged both of them. "You are both dears but those pages of music belong in the King's Library. A lot of people are worried and unhappy about them being missing."

Watson thought "Including the composer!"

Holmes said, "Do not concern yourself, Your Majesty. The errant sheets of music will be unexpectedly discovered and returned to their rightful place. How they disappeared and who was responsible will be a secret held among the people in this room."

The Queen stared at Bertie and Mary. "Do you understand. You are not to tell this story to anyone, not anyone! That includes your parents. Your Mama would be quite angry."

She turned to the Mistress of the Robes and said, "I think it's time these two had their dinners. Thank you for fetching them from York Cottage."

The Duchess snapped her fingers and led the Prince and Princess out of the room. Mary skipped out shouting, "Bye. Mr. Holmes and Doctor. Have you ever played Hide and Seek?"

"Yes, milady, many times."

The Queen and the detectives broke into gales of laughter.

"I spoil them terribly but that's what a grandmother is for. I believe it will shortly be time for our dinners. We'll be served here in the drawing room. Perhaps a libation to start things off." She rang a bell for a footman. "One of these days you will have to tell me how you sneaked the documents back into the Library."

"It will be our secret, Majesty."

Watson wrote to Lady Juliet, *"Dinner was quite pleasant and as expected, elegantly sumptuous. The Queen and Duchess were both facile conversationalists but they managed to get Holmes and me into story telling mode. The Duchess was an avid reader of my published tales and the Queen admitted she had whiled away a few hours with a book or two of mine."*

"Her Majesty rose from the table and we assumed we were to be dismissed. Instead, she picked up the musical scores and went

101

over to her harpsichord. 'I do adore Handel and I must admit I was strongly tempted to keep Bertie's and Mary's gift. But that would hardly fit noblesse oblige. Before you leave with these treasures, let me play a few fragments of the Master's works.' We spent the next hour listening to the Queen of England entertaining us at her keyboard. A moment not to be repeated or forgotten."

"The evening ended with the Duchess providing us with a handsome leather portfolio in which to carry the priceless documents. The Queen presented each of us with a solid gold medallion commemorating the coronation of the King and herself. "A small token of thanks for services rendered."

"We retired to our rooms."

*****

Next morning in the limousine on our way back to London, Watson asked Holmes. "How do you intend to resurrect the missing musical scores without raising suspicions?"

"I do not. Mr. Cuthbert Jameson, our helpful Royal Library curator will make the discovery on my insistence that a second search of the King's Salon be mounted. This, of course, will be after, unseen by the guard, we deposit the documents in a hidden and unsearched corner of the library's vast expanse. Lestrade will be there to verify the finding. The Royal Librarian, absent as usual, will be relieved that his position is no longer in jeopardy although it should be."

As the Queen requested, they carried out the charade without the slightest indication of the young prince or princess' involvement. Cuthbert Jameson was lauded for his acute and persistent quest and Lestrade, the Home Office and Palace Guard were delighted to call off the search but only after the Royal Librarian was chastised for leaving the document case carelessly without a lock. He tried to pass the blame on to Jameson but his

102

excuses fell on deaf ears. A large glass breakfront with a substantial latch was immediately substituted and Handel's inscribed works were once again on display to the relief of all involved. The King's Chancellor and the Queen's Mistress of the Robes were accordingly informed of the discovery, restitution and re-presentation of the priceless works. The contribution of Holmes and Watson constituted a footnote in the official report of the incident.

*****

In the forecourt of Lady Juliet's celestial mansion a small group had gathered to hear the latest of George Frideric Handel's works being played by the master on an ethereal harpsichord. *Dance Music for a Delightful Dog.* Written for and dedicated to Pookie who alone of her canine associates had a keen sense of rhythm and even a recognition of melody. She frolicked to the composition, jumping, twisting, turning on hind legs and then standing on her forepaws and finished in time with the music in a series of her famous backflips.

The audience wildly applauded both the composer and the canine danseuse. Earlier, a transmission from Sherlock Holmes had arrived courtesy of the Angelic Postal Service, relating the tale of the purloined and recovered musical scores and Queen Alexandra's somewhat hesitant involvement in their return.

St. Cecilia, the Baroness, Pookie, Handel and several of his heavenly enthusiasts had all heard and rejoiced at the story. Lady Juliet looked at Handel and said, "George, you have been here in heaven for quite a few earth years although we are all living in eternity. Tell me! What does a musical genius do when he becomes even more immortal than he was."

He laughed, "Why, Baroness. You can answer your own question. He or she continues to perform their works and use their talents in an atmosphere of perfection. You perform beautifully at the Saintly Spectaculars, Cecilia has her magnificent Choirs and I continue to write my music, all in honor of the Almighty with the heavenly hosts as our audiences."

"Would you consider creating another work for an earthly individual if I could get it delivered?"

The Master looked at her, smiled and then laughed, "Why, of course. What a lovely suggestion."

*****

In the Queen's drawing room at Sandringham a familiar leather portfolio sat on the keyboard of her harpsichord. She summoned her Mistress of Robes and asked the Duchess, "Louisa, where did that portfolio come from?"

"Why, your Majesty, I don't know. Wait! It's the same leather portfolio we gave Sherlock Holmes to use in returning Handel's musical scores to the Royal Library. I recognize it. It was once my husband's. Has Holmes been here?"

"No, He has not."

"Have you opened it?"

"No, I thought it might be for you since it's your envelope."

"I think not. Let's see if it contains anything."

The Queen took up the portfolio and brought out several sheets of foolscap covered with musical notation. "Louisa, this is impossible. These pages are signed by George Frideric Handel. There is no date. And look, the title is *Incidental Music for Queen Alexandra*."

She ran the keyboard and played a few bars. "It's certainly his style. Could it truly be from him? Oh, I don't care where it came from. It's an exquisite gift."

Throughout the day, the Queen's drawing room was vibrant with heavenly music.

The Adventures of Sherlock Holmes and the Glamorous Ghost

The End - Hymns, Hums, Handel and Holmes

The Adventures of Sherlock Holmes and the Glamorous Ghost

A Family Reunion

Lady Juliet Armstrong and her canine companion, Pookie, were flitting back to her mansion over the golden heavenly pathways after a rehearsal with the Saintly and Angelic Choirs. St. Cecilia, choir director and patron saint of musicians, was elated at the performance and overjoyed at the reappearance of the missing Handel manuscripts at Buckingham Palace. She continued to thank the Baroness and her London colleagues, Sherlock Holmes and Doctor John Watson. The composer had written *Incidental Music for Queen Alexandra* as a gift to Her Majesty for her assistance in recovering the documents. The true story of the disappearance was carefully hidden away.

As she and the dog approached her stately home, she spied a tall, male figure in a white robe standing by the doors. Pookie barked momentarily more from surprise than hostility. The man seemed familiar. Was he?

He was. Her brother Arthur! Ever since his death in 1881 in the first Boer War, she had wondered about him and prayed for his soul. He was a teenager and she had been a child. Now here he was standing handsomely at her doorstep. She flitted up and embraced him. "Arthur, Arthur! *(Never Art or Artie)* It's really you and you're here in Heaven. I had been so worried about you. You weren't listed on the Celestial Registry."

"Nope. Spending a little purgatory time before being allowed to enter. I was a bit of a rake during my Army days and had some penance to perform. Nothing unbearable. It wasn't Hell. No fire. Just this state of exclusion that you want so hard to overcome."

"I've seen Hell and Satan. Horrible" *(See Volume One.)*

"Yep. Not somewhere I'd want to be. But now my long purification is over and I have a nice villa on the other side of the Elysian Fields. A few of my mates are here and I'm settling in."

"Was the delay really very long?"

"Well, it certainly seems that way while you're there. It's more a state of being than a place. A stay in Purgatory is helped along and shortened by people's prayers. Like yours, Mum's and Dad's. They finally let me out. "

"Mum and Dad! I hope they are still doing well. I'm ashamed of myself. You may not know this but Pookie and I make occasional trips back to Earth to work with the consulting detective Sherlock Holmes. During those sojourns, I've never gone to see them. I'm afraid I'd scare them half to death. Their ghost daughter returns."

"I'm sure after they got over the first shock, they'd be delighted. I notice you're still the rebel – wearing scarlet instead of white. But tell me about these jaunts with the Great Detective."

"Come inside. I'm so glad to see you. A little nectar and ambrosia and we can swap stories."

And so they did.

*****

221B Baker Street, London - Residence of Sherlock Holmes, Doctor John Watson and Mrs. Martha Hudson.

"Well, Holmes. A further thank you note from the Queen's Mistress of the Robes, Louisa Jane Montagu Douglas Scott, Duchess of Buccleuch and Queensberry. It seems Queen Alexandra got a splendid gift from George Frideric Handel. A dedicated piece. *Incidental Music for Queen Alexandra.* She is both delighted and astounded. Handel died in 1759. And now 145 years later, this

107

signed musical score appears. Did he write it as a ghost? How did it get into the Queen's hands?"

"I'm well aware, Watson. I sent it to her after I got it from Handel and the Baroness through the Angelic Postal Service. I used the same leather portfolio they gave me to return the documents purloined by the young prince and princess. The Queen and Duchess must know I was a party to the celestial gift. Let's say nothing more about it."

Mrs. Hudson knocked and hurried into the room waving a newspaper. "Oh, Mr. Holmes and Doctor. A terrible explosion and crash on the Brighton line near Croydon. A number of people killed and injured. The Police believe it was a deliberate attack. The London, Brighton and South Coast Railway (LB&SCR) are offering a large reward for information leading to the arrest and prosecution of the villains. Scotland Yard is involved."

She handed them the tabloid and as they read the report, Holmes was getting to his feet and grabbing his hat and cane. "Watson, first stop Scotland Yard, then on to Croydon!"

*****

Senior Director Raymond had instructed the Angelic Transport Command to send chariots to recover the souls of the dead passengers at the Croydon disaster. They numbered over twenty. Of course, not all would be allowed to pass through the Pearly Gates and the screening took place rapidly under St. Peter's supervision. An elderly couple caught Raymond's attention. Alvin and Lucinda Armstrong. Could they be? As they walked through the portal, clinging to each other, Raymond approached them. "Sir and Madame, allow me to introduce myself. My name is Raymond and I am Senior Director of Paradise. Welcome to your heavenly reward. I regret the tragic and violent nature of your demise but I can assure you all will be well henceforth. In fact, I believe I have some welcome news for you. Do you have a daughter, Juliet, and a son, Arthur, both deceased?"

The solicitor, for such he was, replied. "Yes we do. Why do you ask? Are they here?"

His wife looked at Raymond and her husband expectantly. "I do hope so. Can it be that we will be joined once again?"

"Yes, you will. I must stay here at the gates and help with the incoming souls but I will have an angel take you to them." He signaled a winged spirit over and issued instructions.

The angel approached and said, "Hello, Mr. and Mrs. Armstrong. I am called Mariel. Your daughter is quite famous here in Heaven and your son just arrived recently. Please come with me. I will take you to them."

He loaded them on a small self-propelled chariot. It took them a moment to realize they were dressed in sparkling white robes and had haloes atop their heads. Lucinda squeaked in delight. "I can't wait to see Arthur and Juliet again."

They whisked over the short distance to Lady Juliet's domain. Pookie jumped up from her place in the orangery and ran to the front door, barking at the chariot and its passengers. Juliet looked up from her conversation with Arthur and said, "I wonder what has that silly dog all upset. I better go look."

She flitted through the mansion and stopped at the opalescent portals in shock. *(She was never shocked. Shocking, yes, but never shocked.)* This time she was truly shocked. She looked at the angel and the smiling couple still standing in the celestial vehicle and let out a most unladylike whoop. "Mum? Dad? Is it really you? This is too much."

Arthur had followed her. He swept past Juliet and grabbed his mother's arm while holding out a hand to his father. The

Baroness embraced her Dad and started to weep tears of joy. "Come in, come in. What happened? Why are you here? I'm delighted you are but it means you're both dead. I'm both sorry and overjoyed. Arthur just arrived. Oh, my cup overflows."

Mariel did the angelic equivalent of clearing his/her throat and said, "Mr. and Mrs. Armstrong. I will leave you with your children to get reacquainted. Heavenly Real Estate has assigned you a lovely villa nearby so you can easily visit the Baroness. Mr. Arthur has a residence on the opposite side of the Elysian Fields near his wartime friends. That can be rearranged if you wish. Think about it. I will leave you now. Lady Juliet knows how to call me back. Welcome to Heaven!"

Pookie was watching all of this intently. She vaguely remembered the Armstrongs from when she was a puppy. She liked them. She did a series of backflips in welcome.

Lady Juliet, who seldom lost control, stood with tears running down her exquisite cheeks. She needed to talk with Raymond. "So tell us how you come to be here. Arthur has just emerged from Purgatory. I see you two didn't need to make the stop. Oddly enough, neither did I. I've often wondered about that but enough about me. What happened?"

Her father, Alvin said, "Train Wreck. Lucy and I were among a group of holiday makers heading for Brighton when there was an explosion on the tracks near Croydon. I think it was a bomb but I'm not sure. Went off right under the car we were in. Killed us outright along with a crowd of others. A group of soldiers on leave were victims."

He mother sniffled and said. "I feel so sorry for the people who were wounded. We're dead. Nothing to be done for us but they have to live with their injuries. Who would do such a thing? What do you think, Juliet?"

110

Juliet frowned, "I don't know but I can think of someone who will. It's déjà vu. Arthur's killed in the war. I'm shot. You two are blown up. It seems the Armstrongs are not fated to die in bed of natural causes. Why don't you three get settled in. I have to get together with Raymond. Have you met him?"

Lucinda replied, "Oh yes, lovely man. Is he in charge?"

The Baroness replied, "In a manner of speaking. Of course, the Trinity rule heaven but they have their executives. Raymond is one of them. A Senior Director. And he's not a man. He's an angel in every sense of the word. He and I have a long standing relationship and I need to see him about this train wreck."

*****

Inspector G. Lestrade's office in Scotland Yard. "Mr. Holmes and Doctor Watson. I am not surprised to see you. The explosion on the Brighton line, isn't it? Join the crowd. The Railway Inspectorate, the Home Office, the Army, the LB&SC Railway and local police and our unworthy selves are all involved in the investigation. The Brighton Line and their insurers are at the ready with reward money"

"I was about to leave for Victoria Station to board a special train to the scene of the disaster. Feel free to accompany me. The more the merrier. I don't mean to be flip but an event like this invites participants from all over. No doubt there will be a Parliamentary inquiry matched by several ministries. The press is running wild. And who knows how many private organizations will take a hand."

"Thank you, Lestrade. What evidence do we have of how, why and by whom the attack was made?"

"Not much evidence. Too many opinions. Anarchists, Fenians, trade unionists. There's a strike going on at Taff Vale Railway in Wales by the Amalgamated Society of Railway Servants (ASRS) that could lead to more activity. Some journalists have even blamed the Suffragists. I could see Emmeline Pankhurst breaking a window or two but bombing a train of holiday makers? Not likely! I know you don't speculate or give opinions but you're welcome to join our investigation."

They took a cab to the station and boarded the one car special. It took a mere 20 minutes to reach Croydon and the site of the wreckage. The destroyed train had been scheduled to make the one hour trip from Victoria to Brighton and was packed with Londoners on weekend outings. Its five car wreckage lay overturned on torn up tracks. The locomotive was derailed and the one car under which the bomb exploded was in splinters. The last of the ambulances and hearses had just vacated the site. Twenty two people killed outright, forty more injured, some near death. Teams of navvies, horses and machinery were struggling to clear the tracks, resettle the locomotive and right the unexploded carriages.

The crowd of curiosity seekers had begun to disperse. A group of seven well-dressed individuals had gathered down the tracks near a switch point and were engaged in vigorous discussion. Holmes, Watson and Lestrade walked around the worksite and approached the men. The wind was blowing steadily and the noise of the crews, horses and equipment made it necessary to shout.

A vaguely familiar, tall, burly, dark-haired individual in a bowler and topcoat yelled, "Ah, Inspector Lestrade. We've been waiting for you. Is this Mr. Sherlock Holmes and his associate?"

"Yes, I invited them to join me. Holmes, Doctor, you may remember Inspector James Fairwell of the Croydon police. Fairwell, would you present us to the rest of your party?"

"Of course!" His loud voice caused the others to stop their conversation and look at the newcomers. "Gentlemen, here is Inspector Lestrade of Scotland Yard and Mr. Sherlock Holmes, the famous detective. This gentleman is his colleague, Doctor John Watson. Let me introduce our group: Mr. Ernest Cartwright, Vice Director of the London Brighton & South Coast Railway; Chief Inspector George Humphreys of the National Railway Police; Colonel Michael Edwards of the Army's Criminal Investigation Division; Mr. Ronald Fisher, Vice Minister of the Home Office; Mr. Clive Ellington of the National Railway Inspectorate. Mr. Alec Gideon represents the Railway Passengers Assurance Company, the line's insurance firm."

Handshakes all around. Gideon spoke up. "On behalf of the Assurance Company, Mr. Holmes, I'm delighted you have joined us. I would like to commission you and Doctor Watson to join in this investigation. I'm sure Mr. Cartwright of the Brighton Line will agree with me."

Cartwright nodded and smiled.

Holmes smiled, "Thank you, Mr. Gideon. But first, in order for me to probe this event and the vicious criminals behind it, I'll need the agreement of the representatives of law enforcement here." He looked at the policemen and authorities in expectation. Fairwell and Lestrade were more than willing to let Holmes do his diligence as were the other policemen. The Home Office minister and the Colonel were hesitant but they were urged along by Mr. Ellington of the Railway Inspectorate.

The Vice Minister finally agreed but added in typical bureaucratic manner, "Gentlemen, we need to form an executive committee to pursue this matter. Our law enforcement colleagues will of course, participate. I will be happy to act as chairman and you, Mr. Holmes shall act on our behalf, being paid for your services by the railroad and insurance company. I will inform the press."

Oblivious to the cynical smiles of his colleagues, the politician left with Gideon and Ellington tagging behind. He was, no doubt, in search of the Fleet Street contingent and another headline, leaving Lestrade, Fairwell, Colonel Edwards, Mr. Cartwright and Inspector Humphreys of the Railway Police to fill Holmes in on what they knew.

The Consulting Detective turned toward the scene of the carnage and shook his head "A shame so much evidence has been destroyed or disturbed but the railway must be put back in service as soon as possible. Let us go to the site and see what knowledge we can glean."

*****

Leaving her family in the care of the angel Mariel, Juliet and Pookie flitted to the Pearly Gates where Mr. Raymond still stood directing the last of the victims through processing. Most were shuttled off to Purgatory. One hardened criminal was committed to Hell under his extreme protest and a few, such as Juliet's parents and several children, were granted immediate admission to the bowers of Paradise. In full sail, the Baroness approached the Director. Knowing quite well what was on her mind, he smiled and said, "No, Lady Juliet. I cannot permit you another trip to join your investigating comrades. The Committee says you are overdoing. The earth-bound police contingent has the investigation well in hand being led by none other than Sherlock Holmes."

"Oh, Raymond, let's not quibble. You know you're going to give in. My parents were killed in that wreck. Just like when I was shot. I want to join Holmes, find out who did it and see that they are punished on earth and in the hereafter."

"He doesn't need your help."

"I think he might. There are things ghosts can do, places we can go and persons we can track that even the great Sherlock

114

Holmes cannot. Besides, these are my mother and father. I'm not seeking vengeance. I'm seeking justice and preventing the villains causing more untimely deaths. We all come to the Pearly Gates eventually but the train wreck victims should have come in their due time. I feel the same about my brother in that terrible war. Who knows what good those people could have done on Earth before they entered the hereafter. So now, be your usual soft hearted self and say Pookie and I can go and join the Great Detective. You can smooth it over with the Committee."

The Directing Angel looked skyward in silent conference. He turned back to her. "One week and no transmuting into corporeal state. The dog may come with you. You may communicate only with Holmes, Watson and Mrs. Hudson. Let your parents know what you are doing. I will have Mariel checking in with them. For goodness sake, stay out of trouble. Both of you."

"You are a sweetheart, Raymond. We will be on our best behavior even if we encounter the swine who did this. You wouldn't know who they are, would you."

"No, Baroness, I would not. Have a good journey."

They flitted back to the mansion. Her parents and brother were still there getting caught up on their lives since they had last seen each other. Mariel was standing by.

Juliet announced she and Pookie were going earthside to confer with Sherlock Holmes and track down the railroad bombers. Her mother was upset. "You'll be in danger!"

"Mum, you'll have to adjust to being immortal. Pookie and I can be frustrated but we can't be harmed. I once met with Satan. Not a pleasant experience but I survived untouched. Don't you worry. We may be able to help the Great Consulting Detective. I want those fiends to face justice. On earth and in the afterlife. See you in five earth days. Feel free to use my mansion if you want to

115

keep meeting. Mariel will show you how to summon up some nectar and ambrosia. C'mon Pookie. We're off to see Holmes. For goodness sake, straighten your halo."

*****

Holmes, Watson, Lestrade and the remaining contingent had spent the last two hours walking around the scene of the disaster. The train was short - a locomotive and tender, one first class carriage, one second class carriage, two third class cars and a luggage van. Before the restoration teams had cleared away all the evidence, he had gleaned a few items that might provide a clue or two. A partially destroyed casing revealed the bomb was of military origin. Powerful enough to destroy one railroad carriage, distort the tracks and derail the other cars. They pointed that out to the Colonel who would set about initiating an inquiry about missing armaments in the London area.

What wasn't clear was whether the explosive was affixed to the rail car or attached to a switch point at Croydon. In the first case, a timer would be necessary and needed to be fastened at the railyard or Victoria Station. The second class car and its passengers would be deliberate targets. In the latter case, the bomb would have been planted earlier in the morning and the pressure from the cars passing overhead may have been enough to set it off. The target would have been random – part of the first train to come through those particular switch points.

"We need to find a timing mechanism of some sort. That may lead us to the culprits. Inspectors Fairwell and Humphreys, can you have your constables conduct a search for the remnants of some type of trigger device that might have survived the blast. I don't hold out much hope but it's worth the effort. Also, Mr. Cartwright, do we have a list of the passengers in that fatal car? This may have been an intentional individual murder with major collateral damage."

"My God, Holmes, what a callous way to kill someone off. Taking out a load of innocent passengers along with your target."

"No more callous, Lestrade, than arsonists wiping out entire households or a poisoned water supply."

The Inspector shook his head. "I can't wait to get my hands on these murderers. There were soldiers and children in that group. Looking forward to a holiday at the shore. Now gone!"

"We'll find them. Meanwhile let's get this search started and the victims identified."

The policemen set about organizing the search for the trigger in the debris that had been dragged off. Cartwright headed back to Victoria Station to get the passenger list which would be incomplete but helpful nonetheless. Holmes, Watson and Lestrade stayed on briefly but then took a police wagon back to London. The game was indeed afoot.

*****

Two shimmering wraiths flitted up the seventeen stairs of 221B Baker Street to enter Holmes' and Watson's shared rooms – empty at the moment. Juliet descended to the floor below and appeared to Mrs. Hudson. Pookie scampered in behind her. Momentarily taken aback, the landlady smiled at the Baroness and attempted to pet the ephemeral canine. When her hand went through the dog's back, she laughed. "Hello ladies. Welcome! I see you're not corporeal this trip.

'Good afternoon, Martha. Yes, we're back again. Heaven insists we stay amorphous and visible only to you, Holmes and the good doctor. Nothing solid this time."

"Well, it's good to see you anyhow, Lady Juliet and my little pal Pookie. What brings you back to London?"

"The Croydon train wreck. I have a strong personal connection to it. My parents were among the twenty-some victims who were killed. Scores were injured."

"Oh, my goodness! How terrible for you!

"Actually, they are in heaven right now. They were directly admitted. They deserve it. They are such lovely folks. They're getting settled. Oddly enough, my brother who was killed back in the first Boer War just emerged from Purgatory at the same time. We're having a family reunion in Paradise. But I want to find the blighters who did this. I assume Holmes has taken a hand in the investigation."

"Well, he and Doctor Watson left this morning to join Inspector Lestrade. I assume that's where they went. I don't know when they'll be back. Oh wait! I think I hear them."

Holmes and Watson came through the front door, engaged in conversation, and headed up the stairs. "Mr. Holmes, Doctor. Wait! Guess who's here!"

Pookie barked.

The Detective smiled and shrugged. "I should have known. Baroness, even in Heaven, you would have heard about the Croydon bombing."

"Hello Holmes, Doctor! I more than heard. Both of my parents were among the fatalities. Needless to say, I have a strong interest. Thank God, *(literally)* they are safe in Heaven. I left them getting adjusted to celestial existence. My brother, Arthur, just joined us as well. He died in the first Boer War in 1881. Recently released from Purgatory."

Watson shook his head. "I don't know whether to sympathize or rejoice with you, Lady Juliet."

118

"Both, Doctor! I'm happy for them but I'm outraged at such a heinous crime. I know! I know! Death happens every moment. I see them waiting at the Pearly Gates. Murders, accidents, sickness, old age. There's another war on with the Boers. Kill and be killed. But this one is also personal. Like my own experience of being shot. I want to find the killers who are so cavalier about taking innocent lives and maiming poor victims. I assume you're both deeply involved."

"Yes! In fact Holmes has been given the unwelcome commission by the railroad to find the culprits and determine the reasons behind the disaster."

The Detective shrugged. "Unwelcome, perhaps but appropriate, Watson. Who is better able to take on this task than I."

Juliet laughed, "Modest as ever, Holmes but I agree and I want to partner with you two once again. Pookie does too."

Holmes frowned. "Knowing you, Baroness, I realize it's fruitless to protest. Besides, it may be helpful to have pair of ghosts on our team. I assume Mr. Raymond has given you his blessing."

"We have a week among you mortals. We are restricted to appearing to only you three and we cannot become corporeal. Restrictive but those were the Committee's conditions."

"We can live with them. Come, we have some strategizing to do. Join us if you wish, Mrs. Hudson."

'Oh, I will indeed, Mr. Holmes. How about some tea to help the process along? Sorry, Lady Juliet. I can't serve you or your dog."

"I brought along a supply of Heavenly Chewies for my ravenous companion and I'm fine without food in my spiritual state. By all means, have your tea."

Before they could retire to Holmes' and Watson's apartment, a messenger arrived from Mr. Cartwright of the railroad. The passenger list had several noteworthy items. The train was fully occupied and then some. There was a contingent of 12 soldiers back from the Boer War and on leave in the second and third class compartments. Their commanding officer, a major, was in the second class car with them along with a second lieutenant.

In first class, there was a countess. Her retainers were in a third class coach. The rest of the first class occupants were the rich and landed, great and good of London. Two MPs and a minor minister or two with their families. They all escaped with minor injuries. At either extreme, the locomotive and tender and the baggage car were knocked off the rails but did not overturn.

Holmes and the Doctor "reviewed the bidding" for the Baroness and she in turn told of the incoming traffic at the Pearly Gates. The Detective looked at her and said. 'How would you like to return to Heaven and interview the victims who were admitted, including your parents. Perhaps they can shed additional light on means and motive. More about who was in that second class car with them. For that matter, did they know anyone else on the train? You can gather information from them. We can't."

The Baroness chuckled, "As I said to Raymond, 'There are things ghosts can do, places we can go and persons we can track that even the great Sherlock Holmes cannot. Besides, my mother and father were involved.' All right, but we'll be back, won't we Pookie?"

The dog barked, finished up her Heavenly Chewy and bounded through the closed door.

*****

The Armstrongs had retired to their respective villas under the guidance of Mariel. Lucinda was charmed by the grand size

120

combined with the homey atmosphere but somewhat dismayed by the absence of kitchen facilities. "However shall I make tea or dinner, Alvin?"

Her husband laughed. "Luci, you won't need to make tea or dinner. We're spirits. We don't eat earthly food anymore. The ambrosia and nectar are for us and we've an unlimited supply."

"Oh. dear. I think I shall miss having a cuppa."

The angel Mariel smiled and said, "Many of our new arrivals feel the same way, Mrs. Armstrong, but they soon adjust. I'm sure you'll love nectar. It comes in flavors."

"Oh well, God's will! Mariel, how is Arthur?"

"He is well and happy. He is living in more comfort than he has enjoyed in life or Purgatory. Several of his mates have nearby villas. They meet often. No longer sinful or raucous, of course. This is Paradise, after all but jolly times, nonetheless. They've been going to the shows and contests. They're playing celestial rugby. In fact, Arthur is fly-half for his team, the Heavenly Heavers."

"I'm so glad! He loved to play as a boy."

Alvin looked up and spotted his daughter and her dog coming through their large foyer. "Juliet, good to see you. Come join us. Your Mum was just getting acclimated to our new house and ambrosia and nectar instead of an afternoon tea."

"It takes a little doing, Mum but I think you'll love it. Are you all settled in? I assume Mariel has been taking good care of you."

The angel fluttered his wings and said, "I'll be off in just a few minutes. Several more new arrivals to assist."

"Before you leave, Mariel. How many victims from that train wreck are here in Heaven."

"Only eight. Twenty two died. The rest are in Purgatory except for one irredeemable soul. Satan has him."

"Did anyone come out of the second class carriage alive?

"No! Several people also died in the third class car. Caught when it overturned."

"What a shame! Can you direct me to the heavenly survivors? I'd like to ask them a few questions."

"Certainly. You can start with your own parents. Two of the other new arrivals are children - three and six years old. Their governess is with them. There are two soldiers – young lads. Their companions are off for brief stays in Purgatory. The other one is a pastry chef who was on his way to a job in a Brighton hotel. I guess we can gain access to the Purgatory group, if necessary. I wouldn't advise trying to reach the denizen of Hell."

The Baroness agreed and thought to herself. "I assume Holmes, Watson and Lestrade will be interviewing the wounded."

"OK, Mariel. Thank you. I'll be calling on you to talk to the other six spirits. Mum, Dad. Have a cup of nectar and come join me. I have a few questions I want to ask you."

"Of course, dear. Don't tell me you have turned detective. Who is this Sherlock Holmes I heard you mention?"

Her father laughed, "Luci doesn't keep up with the tabloid press or the activities of criminals. Do you, dear? Sherlock Holmes is the famous consulting detective whose adventures have been written up and published by his associate Doctor Watson. You know him, Juliet?"

"Pookie and I are his partners, Dad. We jointly discovered who murdered me and since then we have been active in a number of his activities. I'm sorry to tell you, I've been back on earth a number of times."

Lucinda frowned. "And you never looked us up. That's not like you, Juliet. Even when you became a baroness, you kept in touch with us. I can't say I liked your husband or his snobbish family."

"Mum, what would have been your reaction if Pookie and I appeared as ghosts? You would have been terrified."

"Well, you're both here now and I'm not terrified."

"That's because you, Dad and Arthur are also ghosts. Oh, we have so much catching up to do. But right now, what can you tell me about the rail car you were in?"

Alvin sat back. He was developing a liking for nectar and was intent on giving ambrosia a thorough trial. "Well, it was crowded. As far as I could tell the train had been overbooked. Even one or two of the first class gentry had ended up in second class. The weather seemed ideal for a relaxing weekend at the seashore. Everyone wanted an early start out of Victoria Station."

"A small Army group, home from the Boer War took up much of the space in our carriage. Young lads just out of their teens. A rowdy bunch except for two officers and sergeant who were with them. I spoke to the second lieutenant who said he and his men were exhausted but glad to back in Old Blighty once again. They didn't know whether they would be sent back. There were rumors that the war would soon be ending. We all hoped so."

"The major was stand offish and the sergeant was busy calming his charges down. A governess with two children was getting the full treatment from the soldiers and he was reining them in. I guess they had not seen English girls in a long time. The little boy who proudly announced he was six was fascinated by the soldiers. The three year old girl was upset by the crowding and set about crying. We and a pastry chef were the only other civilians in the car."

123

Juliet pressed on. "I suppose all your baggage was in the luggage van."

"Not at all. It seems the first class occupants had taken up all the storage room in the baggage car with their many trunks and bags and a shipment of mail was also in the van. We ended up sitting crowded with our luggage in the second class car. I haven't the slightest idea what it was like in third class but it couldn't have been comfortable. Thank goodness, the trip was to be short. Until, of course, the explosion."

Lucinda piped up. 'Yes, the explosion. It was terrible. Very powerful! I just remember the floor of the car opening up with a frightful roar and then I went black. I guess I died."

"Did the blast come from inside or outside the car?"

Alvin thought it came from outside but Lucinda was insistent that it came from one of the pieces of luggage on the floor. Juliet would have to check with the others to get a consensus. Holmes would need to know.

"Thanks. Mum and Dad."

"Did that help, dear? Oh, it's time for us to go see Arthur and his rugby team. Contact sports in Heaven. Who would have thought?"

The Baroness chuckled and called the angel. "Can I talk with the two Army men who are here? Then the pastry chef and finally the governess and her two little charges."

Mariel suggested they flit to the comfortable places set aside by Heavenly Real Estate for the soldiers. Pookie ran on ahead and settled down next to the two young corporals. Heddy and O'Reilly.

Heddy blurted. "Blimey, never met a Baroness before. A detective? You were on the stage, too? Is this your dog?"

"Yes, You're going to meet all sorts of different people here in Paradise. Some are even interesting."

They laughed.

"I'm investigating the explosion. I only have a few questions for you. Are all of your companions accounted for?"

"Yeah! Most of them are in Purgatory including the major and the lieutenant."

"What about the sergeant?"

"I think he's there too although some of us have often told him he could go to Hell."

They laughed again. Then O'Reilly paused. "Wait. What about Bowman? Where's he? Strange cove. Very moody. Not very sociable, if you get my meaning. I suppose he's in Purgatory with the rest of the lads."

Heddy nodded. "I guess so. Never saw much of him."

She replied, "Well, we'll check. One last question. Where did the explosion come from. Outside or inside?"

O'Reilly said, "I don't know. I was looking out the window at the Croydon switch points. The blast came from behind me. What about you, Heddy?"

"I'm not rightly sure. Probably outside but I won't swear to it."

"Thanks, chaps, enjoy Heaven. I'm appearing in the latest Saintly Spectacular show. Like everything else in Paradise, it's free. Come see me."

"Oh, you bet, Baroness! So long, doggie."

Well, this was proving more difficult than she expected. If the explosion came from outside the car, the culprit could be anybody. Inside, it was one of the occupants or perhaps a piece of luggage planted before the carriage filled up. Maybe Holmes and his friends can tell from the shattered wreckage which way the blast went off. Bother! Let's see what the chef has to say.

"Ah, the Baroness. Mariel told me to expect you. I was on my way to a new job at the Brighton Grand Hotel. Opportunity of a lifetime! Blasted away! Not much pastry work to do here in Heaven. Although, I could take up making ambrosia, I suppose. Well anyway, what can I tell you? I understand your parents were in the car with me. Are they here?"

"Yes, they are. So is my brother. We're having a reunion of sorts. Not how we wanted it to happen, however. Anyway, just one question. Do you recall the explosion before you expired."

"Do I? It made quite a boom. My ears were ringing before everything went blank."

"Did it come from inside or outside the car?"

"Inside definitely. From luggage on the floor. It was like being inside a drum."

"Thank you, Mr. Edwards. Please send me some of your ambrosia. I'm sure we'll be delighted. By the way, all the animals in the Meadows eat solid food. I'll put in a word to the keeper, Mr. Sherman. I bet he could use your help."

"From feeding duchesses to doggies. Quite a change but I bet the animals will be more appreciative. Yes, please do, Thank you, Baroness."

The angel Mariel was standing by. "I'm back. I assume you want to speak to the governess."

"Yes and the children too. It's amazing what sometimes little kids can tell you."

126

"Well she's with the children for the moment but her job will soon be taken over by their guardian angels. Their poor parents on earth are beside themselves in grief. The kids are in a special youngsters' dell designed for the little ones. Are you ready?"

"Back to my childhood. My parents think I never left it. Let's go!"

*****

Mrs. Hudson asked, "Have you any more clues, Mr. Holmes?"

"Too many, Mrs. Hudson, and they all add up to confusion."

"Oh dear! Have you heard from the Baroness?'

"No but I'm expecting to hear from her shortly."

We don't know how she does it but Lady Juliet and her dog once again chose that moment to put in a supernatural appearance. "Hello, Holmes! Hello Martha! Where is Watson?"

"Attending a press conference being held by Mr. Ronald Fisher, Vice Minister of the Home Office. I will no doubt be upbraided by the doctor for asking him to participate in such a useless pretentious exercise. I owe him one. Have you anything useful for us?"

"Yes, I believe so. That bomb was set off inside the second class car. Not all the victims agree but I'm quite confident. Now I know why you use the Irregulars so much. Children see and understand things that adults never recognize."

"Explain!"

She proceeded to rattle off all the evidence that she got from her parents, the Army men, the pastry chef and the governess who wasn't sure but thought it was set off in the interior of the passenger car. Suggestive but not yet definitive. But then, the little boy, six

127

years old, clinched it. He and his three year old sister were rolling a ball back and forth on the floor of the carriage. One of the soldiers shooed them away from a big black bag. The little girl failed to stop the rolling ball and started to cry. Her brother climbed over the bags and retrieved the ball but set off a whirring noise in the big bag. The soldier cried out and that's the last the boy heard. The bag, luggage, and car exploded blowing him, his sister and their governess to pieces. The little girl's ghost kept saying, "Bobby broke the train."

Bobby started crying. "I didn't mean to do it. I just wanted to get the ball back."

"It took a great deal of comforting by me, Pookie and the governess to calm them down. But the young spirit remembered what happened very clearly. Now, how do we use this supernatural evidence to solve the problem and who was the distressed soldier? One of his mates thinks a soldier named Bowman wasn't among the group shuttled off to Purgatory and he is definitely not in Heaven. We need to follow up on him. He's a Sapper and is trained in demolition. He was wounded in the Boer War."

Mrs. Hudson stared open-mouthed. Holmes said, "I must call Colonel Edwards."

The Baroness said, "I need to speak with Raymond."

*****

"Yes. Lady Juliet. Corporal Bowman is quite dead."

"Well, he's not here in Heaven. Is he in Purgatory?"

"No, I'm afraid we had to consign him to Hell. He was responsible for the explosion at Croydon killing over twenty people and wounding many others. He is unrepentant."

"I've spoken to the victims here in heaven. The little boy claims he accidentally set off the mine that was in the soldier's baggage."

"True, but Bowman intended to use the device to wipe out a large party of his fellow soldiers once they all arrived on several trains and were assembled in Brighton. The little boy caused it to go off prematurely in Croydon. Bowman was secretly married to a young South African girl who died in a British concentration camp. *(Another horror of a terrible war. Kitchener and the Royal Army has much to answer for! So do the Boers.)* He wanted revenge and was going to take it out on the vacationing war returnees. His only remorse is that fewer military men died than he intended. He had no interest in the civilians who perished. Fortunes of War! Satan has him."

"I wish you had told me earlier. Holmes is responsible for determining what happened. There's a major investigation going on – the government, press and public are in an uproar. The railroad is in disarray and the insurance will run in the millions."

"I'm sorry but I was taken up with processing the victims. I would have told you eventually. Now, what is Mr. Holmes going to say to all of his inquisitors."

"I don't know. Something clever no doubt. I'm going back."

*****

After the Baroness passed her information on to the Great Detective, and Bowman's history and circumstances were confirmed by Colonel Edwards, the foursome – Holmes, Watson, Juliet and Martha Hudson *(don't forget Pookie!)* sat in silence, pondering.

Watson spoke, "It was clearly an accident but how do we prove that to the public's and law enforcement's satisfaction? How do we tie the explosion to Bowman? What was he doing with a high powered mine in his baggage? On his way to Brighton, for goodness sake."

129

"I have convinced the military to agree with a story I have concocted. The various police are on board and as usual, the Home Office is clueless. The railroad and insurance company's liabilities are unchanged although they may sue the Army."

"Here's the account: The Royal Engineers while pretending to be on a weekend leave, planned to use a closed off section of Brighton Beach to test and demonstrate a new explosive land mine. Never mind that they have extensive test facilities elsewhere to accomplish that. Bowman was the Sapper in charge of the demonstration. He somewhat foolishly. was carrying the mine in a standard piece of luggage to disguise it. Because of overcrowding. he was forced to keep the bag in the second class passenger compartment instead of the luggage van. What no one appreciated was the effect the train's vibrations and bumps would have as they passed over the switch points. The mine was too sensitive."

"Oh, Holmes. Honestly, do you expect the press and public to buy that?"

"No, Baroness but that's the explanation they're going to get. There will be calls for courts martial and demotions but they will be lost over time in the military's bureaucracy. No mention of the children will ever be made. Officially, none of your heaven-derived evidence was ever available. Although he is imprisoned in the depths of Hell, Bowman's intents and motivation will never be mentioned. A whitewash I regret being a party to but all the alternatives are worse or less believable."

"What a terrible event! So much needless death and suffering. At least the new denizens of Paradise are happy and the recent occupants of Purgatory have their faith, hope and love to rely on. Especially hope and love. Come, Pookie. We're not needed here any longer. Let's go back to Heaven. I promised Mum, Dad and Arthur they can see us performing at the new Saintly Spectacular. Have you practiced your dance?"

The dog barked, stood on her hind legs, swayed and backflipped. She was ready.

The End

The Adventures of Sherlock Holmes and the Glamorous Ghost

A Family Reunion

The Adventures of Sherlock Holmes and the Glamorous Ghost

On the Dis-Orient-ed Express

Earth Time: 1903 - Paradise Time: Forever

The **ANGELIC POSTAL SERVICE** made its first delivery of the heavenly day at the mansion of Lady Juliet Armstrong, Baroness Crestwell (deceased). Actually, daylight was continuous in Heaven, time was eternal and sleep was unnecessary so a system of arbitrary days was created for the earth-born saints to be comfortable. The angels who had never lived with day and night, weren't affected.

Lady Juliet's brother and parents had recently arrived in Paradise. He had completed a stay in Purgatory and they had been killed in a tragic train wreck on a holiday excursion to Brighton. They were housed in sparkling villas not far from the Baroness' mansion and were adapting to heavenly life. Her mother, a librarian, had joined several book clubs and her father, a solicitor, had enrolled in a series of lectures on celestial law being taught by the most famous jurists of all time. Her brother, Arthur, late of the Army, had taken up his boyhood ambition and joined a professional level rugby team. Juliet herself was active with her dog Pookie in the theatre, celestial choirs and aerobatic competition. She also participated in sojourns back to Earth where she partnered with Sherlock Holmes.

The post included several invitations to social events; announcement of the new production of The Theatre Guild's Saintly Spectaculars 'Cosmic Carnival' starring (who else) Lady Juliet and Pookie, her Dancing Dog. The current issue of the Heavenly Herald newssheet was filled with items of interest to the Elysian denizens.

Pookie was a real canine talent but like all of her species was unable to read. So Lady Juliet set about announcing the news and information of interest to her dog. There was a notice of the upcoming aerobatic competition. The Baroness' Bichon Frisé was the Top Gun Champion in aerial dogfighting and wagged her tail furiously at the prospect of another midair contest. From the Meadows outside the Pearly Gates came the latest box scores of animal sport including doggy multi-dimensional fetch. The Bichon's team was leading the league.

"But, what's this, Pookie? A missive from Earth. One of those return envelopes we left with Holmes and Watson to use when we were searching for George Frideric Handel's missing manuscripts. Let's see what Mr. Consulting Detective has to say for himself."

She opened the sparkling white envelope and took out the message scrawled on a torn piece of note paper. Typical Holmes!

"Baroness and Dog! Your unique talents required. Come immediately if convenient. If inconvenient, come anyway. SH"

"Ooh, that man is intolerable. I don't know how Watson or Mrs. Hudson put up with him. He knows the Committee has insisted we cut back on our visits to Earth. I'll have to speak with Raymond. He and Holmes are compadres. Maybe they can swing something. Our unique talents are required. I wonder what cockeyed scheme he's involved in that requires the intervention of phantoms. Well, he knows how to stir up my curiosity. If we go, we'll have to rearrange our schedules a bit. Fortunately the Saintly Spectacular show and the flying competition aren't due to reopen for a while. OK, let's go find Raymond."

The search was short-lived. The angelic Senior Director was standing in the splendid foyer of the Baroness' home, floating as usual, a few inches off the floor. "I believe you wish to see me, milady."

"Indeed, I do, Raymond. You know, your foresight is actually scary sometimes."

"It comes with the job, Baroness. I believe I know what you want, as usual, and the answer is going to be 'NO'"

She waved the note from Holmes in his face and said, "It's a request from your earthly friend and my partner. He wants my services, No explanation."

"Well, this time, he's going to have to explain. This is Heaven and personalities are always pleasant but some of the Committee members are approaching cranky when it comes to your frequent earthward excursions. Tell Mr. Holmes to contact me directly."

"Who is the Committee?"

"Two Old Testament prophets, an archangel, an Apostle and for diversity's sake, three holy women. No names, please.'

"Oh, big guns! And when they're not deciding on my fate, what do they do?"

"Until your arrival, they had very little to do. Most celestial behavior is presentable and predictable but as you and your dog well know, you are not."

"Oh come on, Raymond. I actually believe the Committee enjoys dealing with me. I think you do, too."

The Senior Director smiled. "Perhaps, but have Holmes contact me by **Angelic Postal Service.** I'll see what I can do."

*****

"Have we heard from Lady Juliet?'

"No, Watson, and I owe Mycroft a response."

Mycroft Holmes, Sherlock's older brother, held a vaguely described position in the British government. The detective claimed he sometimes was the government. Acutely intelligent but lacking in vitality and initiative, Mycroft was in many ways the polar opposite of his hyper energetic brother. Physically bulky and slow of movement, he matched, even overmatched Sherlock's brainpower and acumen. He was also one of the founding members of the Diogenes Club, refuge of highly unsociable but well-to-do male members of London's aloof society.

Mycroft was aware of Lady Juliet, Baroness Crestwell. While the two of them cared little for each other, he was not above occasionally invoking her ghostly abilities and those of her otherworldly dog, Pookie, on behalf of his governmental duties. She, in turn, found him useful in supporting some of her adventures. A strange but ultimately, mutually useful relationship. Right now, he had a diplomatic assignment which would involve the terrestial talents of Sherlock Holmes and Doctor Watson coupled with the celestial gifts of the lady and her canine. He impatiently awaited news of their acceptance.

An angelic envelope arrived at 221B Baker Street. An equally terse note to Holmes was enclosed. *"Resistance from the Committee. Contact Raymond. JA."*

Muttering to himself, Holmes invoked the ghostly channel that he and Raymond had established during previous undertakings. He waited for the deep, ethereal voice to resound in his head. "Mr. Holmes, God love you. I've been expecting your call. The Baroness tells me you have asked for her services but have offered no explanation. I can't go to the Committee empty handed. Why is she and her dog required?"

Holmes responded, "There is an adventuress about to travel on the continent who is very likely to set off an international war if she is not stopped. All of our information is circumstantial and she will not allow anyone, male or female, to get close enough to establish actual proof of her intentions. An invisible spirit is required to track her and produce actionable confirmation of her activities. A spirit such as the Baroness."

"An international war?"

"The Countess is a courier. According to my brother, Mycroft Holmes, who is highly placed in the British government, she will be carrying documents that will trigger plans by the German Empire to annex Romania. She is supposed to be representing her business interests in Jerez, Spain and is going to a benign commercial conference in Constantinople on the Orient Express. We think her true destination is Bucharest and the Golescu Mansion, Romania's Royal Palace."

"Let me further explain. Due to Romania's disadvantageous location between the Russian Empire and Kingdom of Bulgaria as well as King Carol I of Romania's German heritage, the country has had a secret treaty of alliance with Germany and Austro-Hungary since 1883. The impulsive Kaiser wants to formalize that alliance into full annexation, making Romania a member of the German Empire. The documents contain his demands."

"He is using the Countess as his representative in order to mislead observers who would be suspicious of a formal delegation from Berlin."

"We don't know what the reaction of the King or the Romanian government will be. The Kaiser doesn't seem to care. The revelation may well trigger hostilities. Needless to say, Russia and Bulgaria will oppose such a move and may use military force against Romania, Germany and Austro-Hungary to ensure it doesn't happen. It's not clear how the Ottomans will react."

"So what do you want our Baroness to do."

"Determine what the Countess' mission really is. Are we correct? Who is directing her? If the documents exist and are indeed in her possession, we want to relieve her of them and cut off the coup d'état."

"A saint must not steal, Mr. Holmes."

"No, Mr. Raymond, but I can. Watson and I will also be on board the Orient Express with Lady Juliet and Pookie traveling from Paris to Constantinople. We'll be disguised as commercial travelers."

"Is this woman the famous or infamous Irene Adler?"

"The Woman? No, she is not. She is the Countess Maria Altanova or at least that is what she is calling herself. She leaves Spain for Paris with her maid and secretary tomorrow. She will then take the luxurious sleeper eastward across Europe to Constantinople. Watson and I will be in the same carriage. We very much want Baroness Juliet to join us to observe and report. She and Pookie can flit directly to the Gare de l'Est from Paradise."

"I will see what I can do. We don't need another war."

*****

"Well, Raymond. What has the Committee decided?"

"Somewhat to my surprise, Baroness, they've agreed that you can once again join Sherlock Holmes. They have a strong aversion to wars. Ten days maximum this time. You and Pookie must remain incorporeal most of the time and visible only to Holmes and Watson. You may turn physical only if absolutely necessary. I'd say, 'Stay out of trouble' but I know otherwise."

137

"You must be at the Gare de l'Est tomorrow for a departure at 18:25 Paris time. Holmes and Watson will meet the two of you there. According to Heavenly Travel Management, you will board the train and proceed over the next three or more days to Constantinople by way of Strasbourg, Munich, Vienna, Budapest and Bucharest. You are supposed to arrive at your final destination at 16:00 but there may be a few delays. An empty sleeper cabin has been set aside for the two of you but I imagine you will not make much use of it. Holmes will brief you on your mission."

"Oh, good! Pookie and I can spend another lovely day in Paris before getting on the Orient Express. We can catch a show or two and maybe an opera. I'll check the fashions for Madame Clarice. We'll be by ourselves but after our last trip, I feel like an old experienced Parisienne. Flitting down the Avenue Des Champs-Elysées. A shame we won't be able to eat or drink. At least, I won't. I'll have to pack a large supply of Heavenly Chewies for little Miss. Oh, Raymond! Where is the Gare de l'Est?"

"In the 10th arrondissement on the right bank. I'll have an angel direct you there. Holmes will know his way around the other cities where the Orient Express stops although you will have very little time for being celestial tourists. The train keeps a tight schedule. Take care, Baroness. You and Pookie behave."

*****

Déjà vu chez Paree. They're back! First stop-the fashion houses. What's new?

"Oh. Pookie, those creations were delightful but Madame Clarice and Miraculous Modes are still far ahead. Oh well, since no one can see us except Holmes and Watson, flaunting new styles would be a waste of time. Watson has some eye for feminine beauty. Holmes is a loss. Anyway, they'll be here tomorrow. All right, on to the shows. But first another ride on the Seine. Tomorrow we'll be off across Europe. "

*****

Next day 18:00 Paris time. "Thank you, Meriel. I'm not sure we would have found the station by ourselves although Pookie has a marvelous sense of direction. Give my best to Raymond. Here's the train, Miss Dog. Compagnie Internationale des Wagons-Lits. That sounds so much more distinguished than the Sleeper Car Company. The famous Orient Express. Oooh, it does look luxurious. Pookie, look at those women in their haute couture traveling outfits. Can you imagine what they have stored away in the baggage vans. I wonder which one of them is our assignment. Speaking of assignments, where is our detective duo? It's getting close to departure time. Now, where are they?"

A pair of well-dressed commercial travelers appeared through the steam surrounding the locomotive and adjacent cars. Lady Juliet suppressed a giggle. Holmes wore a light brown wig and a short mutton chop beard and sideburns. Gold rim glasses rounded out his appearance. He seemed a bit shorter and was without his famous pipe. That must have been bothersome. His clothes were well cut but just a bit flashy. A homburg finished off the image. Wonder of wonders, Watson was clean shaven. No moustache. He wore a business man's bowler and a modified chesterfield coat. He sported a limp and used a cane.

They successfully merged into the group of travelers boarding the luxury cars. Holmes nodded in the Baroness' direction as they mounted the steps behind the porter with their in-cabin luggage. He signaled the two of them to follow. Pookie bounded up ahead of the porter and turned about looking for the compartment the ghosts were to occupy.

139

"Voici, Messieurs Charles and Washburn. Welcome aboard. All the way to Constantinople. I hope you will greatly enjoy your voyage. Merci, Monsieur Washburn. Most generous. Here is your attendant, Antoine."

A short, somewhat rotund official in blue Wagons-Lits livery approached, smiling under his well-tended mustache. "Gentlemen, welcome. 4A is your double compartment. Let me assist you."

He stepped in ahead of them. Turning down the two beds, plumping pillows and running the water in the sink. "I suggest we keep your windows closed as long as we are inside the terminal. Once we are beyond the station and tunnel, you will be able to enjoy some fresh air if you desire. Les bains and toilettes are at the far end of the car. May I assist you in unpacking your luggage?"

Charles *(Holmes)* said, "That will not be necessary. Thank you, Antoine. I am somewhat surprised that our neighbors have not yet boarded."

"A rather unusual situation, gentlemen. The only other occupants of this carriage is the Countess Maria Altanova and her maid. They are already in suite 1A. Her secretary, Monsieur Lucas has a single room in 2A. 3A is empty but will be occupied in Munich. The other two compartments in this wagon are yours, 4A. 5A has been paid for but will be unoccupied during this trip. I suspect it is the Countess' doing. She insists on maximum privacy."

(Antoine was only partially correct. The Countess had indeed taken the large compartment in the front of the car and had ensured the adjacent cabin was reserved for her secretary. Mycroft Holmes had arranged for the empty compartment on the opposite end next to the detectives to accommodate the Baroness and her dog, although strictly speaking, they required no room in their ghostly state.)

Washburn *(Watson)* chuckled. "The Countess need not worry about us. We have no intention of invading her privacy." Silently, Juliet laughed and Pookie whined. *"But we do!"*

"Gentlemen, as soon as we are underway, we will be serving dinner in the restaurant car. It is right down from this one. I believe you will find our cuisine is of the very finest in all of Europe. Prepared in small, mobile kitchens but by genius chefs. In the meantime, we are offering complementary drinks and aperitifs. As soon as you are settled in, you may wish to go there and meet some of your fellow travelers."

Charles *(Holmes)* replied. "Thank you, Antoine. We will. Perhaps we will meet the Countess after all."

"I doubt it, Monsieur. She will be taking all her meals in her compartment. So will her maid. You may run into her secretary, however. I believe, he will use the restaurant facilities. Is there anything else I can do for you? It seems I will not be very busy on this trip. Although I expect the Countess' maid will be making demands. She seems a bit pushy for a domestic. But who can tell." He shrugged and left the room.

Juliet looked at the two 'commercial travelers' and grinned. *"May I suggest we communicate telepathically. Our attendant may start eavesdropping out of sheer boredom. Pookie and I will accompany you to the restaurant car. I want to familiarize myself with our traveling companions. We are probably not the only ones aware of the Countess' mission. And Doctor, perhaps you can find a tidbit or two to feed my ravenous canine companion. Even as a ghost, she eats. I keep meaning to ask Mr. Sherman about that."*

"Good thinking, Baroness. I believe Mr. Raymond passed on my briefing to you."

"Yes, Holmes. I thought I was rid of trains after that Brighton disaster but I guess Pookie and I are doomed to exist on

141

rolling stock. Very posh rolling stock, I might add. My mother will be quite impressed. I suppose my job is to spy on the very secretive Countess and find out what these documents are that your brother seems to think will set off another war."

"That summarizes it quite nicely, Lady Juliet. Then Watson and I will go into action to purloin what you have discovered."

Watson interjected, *"Tell me, Holmes. Do you think we will have competition on this train."*

"Absolutely, Doctor! Mycroft is highly skilled but so are our potential adversaries. Their agents may not yet be on board. Remember we have stops in Strasbourg, Munich, Vienna, Budapest and Bucharest before she reaches the conference in Constantinople, if that is really where she is going. We may also have to take steps to keep the lady alive."

The Baroness winced. *"Oh dear! More possible mayhem. I thought this would just involve some well-executed stealth."*

"If Mycroft is right, violence is not out of the realm of the possible."

Watson asked, *"Just who is this Countess Altanova?"*

"Good question, Doctor. We don't know much. She suddenly appeared on the international scene. There is an Altanova estate in Jerez in the Andalusian region of Spain but it is not clear whether the lady has any affiliation with it. Count Altanova is dead. Mycroft is convinced that she is traveling under an assumed name and title funded by an as yet unknown entity. Probably Germany. That is something we wish you to uncover, Baroness."

"Maybe Pookie and I should just move in with her and her maid for the next three days."

"Not a bad idea but we may want you to track her secretary as well. Monsieur Lucas. To say nothing of any other of our fellow passengers who strike us as suspicious."

"We'll be busy little bees, won't we. Good thing, we don't sleep. The Crestwell Detective Bureau is on the march. On to the restaurant car."

Just then, the conductor's whistle sounded, a chuffing sound echoed though the car and the train began to move. On to Strasbourg - 250 miles and 8 hours away arriving well after midnight with several administrative and operational stops enroute.

Travelers from the other carriages had already descended on the dining car. Holmes and Watson were escorted by the maitre d' to a table for four. "Gentlemen. Will you mind sharing a table with other passengers?"

"Not at all." *(The Baroness and Pookie perched on two of the plush chairs, anticipating they would have to move eventually.)* "Perhaps two dry sherries while we peruse the menu."

"Immediatement! Bon Appetit!"

Juliet looked around at the other diners. *"Recognize anyone, Holmes?"*

"Not yet, Baroness. Let us hope we are not recognized."

"Oh, oh! You are about to be joined."

The maitre d' was returning with two glasses of sherry and a tall Germanic individual in tow. He was dressed in an impeccable evening suit with a small decoration in his lapel. A slight bulge near his left shoulder was no doubt caused by a carefully holstered small pistol. Clean shaven with his hair cut short but flawlessly combed, he wore steel rimmed spectacles. "Messieurs Charles and Washburn, may I present Monsieur Lucas Koch. His compartment is 2A in the same carriage as yours. May he join you?"

143

Watson extended his hand. "Of course! You must be traveling with the Countess Altanova. Charles and I are in 4A."

The secretary, for such he claimed to be, bowed stiffly, shook Watson's hand and looked carefully at both of them. "I am pleased to meet you."

Holmes greeted him and said, "Good evening. Forgive my curiosity. We were given to understand that the Countess was Spanish. I doubt that is your ethnic origin."

"No, I am Swiss. My family has served the Countess and her forebears in Jerez for three generations. I see you are enjoying one of our fine wines." He turned to the maitre d' and ordered a dry Sherry for himself.

Lady Juliet who had taken Pookie on her lap, looked the newcomer up and down. *"He's a fake, Holmes. He has a gun. I smell German or Austrian government. The Countess' Secretary? Codswallop! I bet he's her bodyguard and he's trying to suss you two out."*

"I agree, Milady. Well, two can play at that game. Let's see what develops."

"This would seem to be a perfect opportunity to examine his compartment. Watson, can you manage to steer a little food in Pookie's direction while I'm gone or should I bring her with me. No, forget that. I want her to do some sniffing around. She hasn't got Toby's or Celeste's phenomenal skill but she's no slouch. C'mon little one. Let's go spy. Maybe I'll look in on the Countess while I'm there in the sleeper car. Speaking of sleep, let me know when you two will be heading off to dreamland. I'll be awake and prowling around till we get to Strasbourg. Ta, ta!"

Holmes had been holding this ethereal conversation while looking over the menu and sipping his sherry. He looked up and caught Lucas Koch staring at him. The 'secretary' asked, "Tell me,

144

Mr. Charles. What causes you and Mr. Washburn to make this long but hopefully, pleasant journey. I assume you are going all the way to Constantinople."

"We are. I don't think I would be violating company policy to tell you we represent a rapidly growing manufacturer of motor cars and we are finalizing contracts with the Ottoman government. Sultan Abdul Hamid II has a great enthusiasm for automobiles and wants his government offices and military fully equipped. What of you? Is the Countess on a similar mission of commerce or is her trip to Constantinople of a philosophical, cultural or social nature?"

"A bit of each. The Countess is a woman of wide ranging interests. Her father and her husband were major acquaintances of the Sultan's until their deaths. This is not her first journey to Constantinople. She is seeking to enhance Spain's historic relationship with the Empire. Charm and diplomacy! Between us, one of her objectives is to try and loosen the Sultan's prohibition of wine for the followers of Islam. Christians and Jews are permitted such indulgence. She is hoping to persuade the Sultan to extend the privilege to Muslims. It would be quite lucrative for the Jerez and Spanish economies. She has other objectives, of course."

Watson interjected. "I understand the Countess is very protective of her privacy."

"Indeed! When I tell you her father was murdered, perhaps you will understand."

"Are you her bodyguard?"

He laughed. "Gentlemen. I am hardly physically or mentally fit nor trained for such a role. Besides, Lady Altanova will not countenance such an imposition on her seclusion. She chooses her companions and associations carefully and shuns most social interaction."

"Yet she embarks on, forgive me, a mission of salesmanship."

"True. As I said, she can be most charming and diplomatic when the occasion demands. She is something of an enigma."

"So we are unlikely to meet her."

"Only by accident."

The waiter approached the table and all conversation ceased while they placed their orders. The fourth seat remained empty. They agreed on a bottle of 1900 Bordeaux.

A light rain built up into a steady downpour as they rolled out of the Paris suburbs and across the French countryside. Sociable small talk took up the spaces between servings. The maitre d' was correct. The food and wine were exceptional. Herr Lucas Koch slowly relaxed in the company of these two amiable Englishmen unaware that at that moment two temporarily corporeal wraiths were examining his single cabin, opening and closing drawers and personal baggage, and making ready to move on to the Grand Suite deluxe accommodations of the Countess and her maid.

*****

"Pookie, if this Mr. Koch is a secretary, he is lacking the necessary equipment to do his job. I would have expected at least a portable desk and a supply of ink, writing implements and stationery. Not many secretaries travel around with boxes of ammunition. Clothes, a locked document case that we can't open, toiletries and not much else. He travels in Spartan fashion. I wonder what and whom we'll find next door. We'll have to change into our intangible mode. Can't reveal ourselves to our persons of interest. What's the matter?"

146

The dog was pawing at the turned down bed. She whined and flipped back a sheet with her nose. She sneezed. A bottle tumbled out from under a pillow.

"Ah, ha, you clever pooch. What have you found? Let's see."

She picked up the unlabeled bottle and gently twisted the cap. A collection of small white pills appeared. She shook two of them into her hand. *"Oh dear! I want to give these to Holmes to identify but I'll have to stay physical in order to get them to him. No, I have a better idea. Pookie, you stay physical. I'll tie these in your red bow and you go wait for Holmes and Watson in the space between our compartments. I'll change to evanescent and tell Holmes to return to his compartment and you. This spying is getting complicated. All right. Off you go. Be careful."*

The dog tilted her head, gave a silent bark and waited for Juliet to open the door of Lucas' compartment. She ran off down the aisle to compartment 4A and hid out of the sight of the attendant. Juliet flitted out of the sleeper car and into the diner where Holmes, Watson and Lucas were polishing off cognacs and conversing.

"Thank you, Mr. Charles and Washburn. This has been very entertaining. I look forward to having the use of an automobile myself. I doubt I can afford one but perhaps the Countess will. Who knows. I might add 'chauffeur' to my list of duties." He took out a gold pocket watch and said "I must check on her ladyship and see if she has any assignments for me before she goes to bed. Good evening to both of you. Perhaps we will meet yet again on this trip."

"Good night, Herr Koch. It has been very pleasant dining and talking with you. Please give our best regards to the Countess."

The secretary headed to the exit of the restaurant car as Juliet wafted in in her ethereal state. *"Well, we timed our exit from his room correctly. I'm going to follow him back but I wanted to tell you that his room is quite sparse and minus all the accoutrements you would expect a secretary to have. Pookie found a bottle containing pills under the pillows of his bed. I tied two of the tablets in her bow. She's in her physical state and waiting for you to come back and retrieve the pills. I wonder what they are. Then she and I will 'disintegrate' and enter the Countess' Grand Suite and eavesdrop. Busy, busy, busy!"* She flitted away.

"What say you, Watson? Shall we see what our little canine spy has tied up in her ribbon. They could merely be digestive pills but why hide them in the bed? No, there is something to this. Let's find Pookie."

Paying for their drinks, they left the lounge, smiling at the other travelers who were still digesting their splendid meals. Through the connecting passageway, past the dozing attendant and on to their twin cabin door where they found a white furball wagging her tail. Watson leaned down, petted her and untied her bow, spilling the two pills into his hand. *"Good girl, Pookie. Here, let me tie your ribbon again and you can flit off and join your mistress."*

She fussed impatiently while he fixed her bow and then turned back into the ghost she was and headed to the other end of the car where Juliet waited. *"In the words of Mr. Carrol's young maiden, 'curiouser and curiouser,' Pookie. We'll let Holmes puzzle about those pills. Let's see what's going on in the Countess' suite. I wonder what she looks like."*

They landed in the suite as the maid, Carlotta, was clearing the dishes from the evening meal she had shared with the Countess. Koch had just entered after a brief stop in his own compartment. The noble lady was ensconced on a large double bed in a dressing gown with a damp towel over her eyes. From what they could observe, she was diminutive, pale of complexion with dark hair splayed over a pair of pillows. The towel covered most of her face.

Koch looked at the maid. "How is she, Carlotta?"

"No change, Doctor! She picked at her dinner and I believe she is ready for her next dosage."

The Countess groaned and trembled but the towel stayed fixed across her brow.

Juliet reacted sharply. *"Doctor!? Ah, ha. Pookie. That's a surprise. As I suspected, he's no secretary. The plot thickens. No wonder they insist on privacy and isolation. Her ladyship is being treated for some condition tied to this mission of theirs. It may explain the tablets Doctor Koch had hidden away in his bed. As Holmes would say, 'Let us both see and observe.' Is this Carlotta really her maid? Is the Countess really a Countess? Is anybody who they say they are? Holmes and Watson as automobile salesmen! You and I are using our real identities but no one knows we are here. When we get back to Heaven, let's see about turning this into a mystery farce for the Theatre Guild. My mother will love it."*

A knock on the door. The steward, Antoine and a rolling tea caddy to collect the remains of the dinners. Carlotta blocked his view of the bed and the recumbent Countess. "Was everything satisfactory, Miss? Do you require anything else before going to bed? We are still a few hours outside of Strasbourg."

"No, no! All was fine! Please see to it that we are not disturbed when we arrive in Strasbourg. Tomorrow morning, you may bring two continental breakfasts at 09:00. Brioches! European coffee, no tea! We should be well on our way to Munich by then. Thank you. Good evening!

She almost dumped the dishes on him and summarily closed the suite door. She turned to Koch and whispered. "I hope we can keep this up until it's time for me to take on her identity. You're sure King Carol is not familiar with her."

He chuckled and whispered back, "Don't worry. This Chloral Hydrate will keep her subdued. The King doesn't know her. He thinks she's coming on a visit to promote one of her charities." Aloud he said. "Countess, it's time for your motion sickness medicine again. You have been afflicted all the way from Jerez. It will help you survive this journey. These carriages run smoothly but the tracks in some places are quite old and primitive. Here, I have mixed it with a fine sherry for you. Another excellent product of Jerez."

The Countess groaned, "All right, Doctor. Carlotta, help me sit up. I feel so dizzy. I think the cure is worse than the sickness."

Koch grinned, "You are adjusting quite nicely. A few more doses and you won't notice the symptoms at all."

The maid assisted her and she slowly sipped the wine laced with the sedative/hypnotic drug. "There you are, Countess. You'll be better in no time."

The lady fell back on her pillows and into a deep sleep.

The maid turned to the doctor. "How did you induce the motion sickness symptoms in the first place."

"She is highly suggestible. I simply warned her of the possibilities and she did the rest. The medication is most effective. She will be out for the duration of this trip and will remember nothing."

"How long before we reach Munich? "

"It's 250 miles from Strasbourg. About 6 hours but we haven't reached Strasbourg yet. We'll arrive at the München Centralbahnhof mid-morning. After that, Vienna, Budapest and then Bucharest. "

"Who is this Generalfeldmarschall Koenig who'll be coming on board."

"He's Chief of the Kaiser's General Staff. He'll be in disguise. Herr Karmann, a rich industrialist and his aide. He will be the force behind our little expedition. You will take your orders from him. Remember, you are just the courier who is to gain access to King Carol without raising suspicions. Once you have made your delivery, Koenig will take over and we will disappear. We'll bring the Countess to Constantinople on the next Orient Express. She'll never know what happened."

"This all seems to be too much cloak and dagger. Unnecessarily complicated."

"I agree but Koenig has an overgrown sense of the dramatic and he is paying us."

The Baroness had been taking all of this in and getting increasingly aggravated. *"All right, Pookie. Time to get together with Holmes and Watson. If the outcome wasn't so serious, this would be an operetta bouffe. Let's flit."*

Holmes and Watson were just thanking Antoine for bringing them two cognacs. "Gentlemen, I think the Countess is ill. She was in her bed when I came to retrieve their dinnerware. That arrogant maid shooed me away before I could determine anything."

Watson almost gave away his true self by remarking, "It's been my experience that lengthy travel can have a debilitating effect on some people. Not all that unusual."

Holmes gave him a cautionary look. "We constant travelers see that wherever we go especially on rails or water. Perhaps one day, we'll all be flying, Antoine."

"Let us hope not, Monsieur Charles. That would be the end of my job." He laughed and withdrew.

151

The two specters took up their place in the center of the compartment. *"Well, gentlemen. We have a lot to report. The Saga of the Countess on the Orient Express."*

While Pookie demolished several Heavenly Chewies, Juliet proceeded to play out the conversations and revelations they had uncovered complete with dramatic asides. Ever the actress! Holmes had his suspicions confirmed that the 'doctor' was dosing the Countess with chloral hydrate to keep her docile, submissive and semi-conscious. At least they knew she was a real Countess. But who was the maid? She was to be the courier pretending to be the noblewoman. This was Mycroft's target. But now a new player was about to enter stage right. Generalfeldmarschall Koenig, Chief of the Kaiser's General Staff, probably the architect or composer of this international, political but hopefully not bellicose exercise. They must wait for the train to reach Munich.

Watson was concerned about the Countess' welfare but at the moment had no way of checking on her without giving away their identity and mission. He hoped Koch was a real doctor and a conscientious one at that.

*****

On to Munich. Breakfast in the compartment. Juliet and Pookie went exploring in the other cars. Few of the passengers were up or had their doors open and the Baroness did not want to invade their privacy. She only did that when a possible criminal activity was in progress. Pookie had no such concerns and wandered in and out of the closed cabins, observing in true Holmesian fashion. Doggy privilege! A few things to attract her attention but nothing that looked dire. Nothing she could eat.

Now that they knew the documents with the German demands on Romania had not yet reached the train, Holmes and Watson settled down to work out overall strategy. They must capture the letters signed by the Kaiser before they could be presented to King Carol. Koenig could bluster away but minus any tangible proof he was representing the real Kaiser Bill, he would be subject to both suspicion and possible arrest. All would eventually blow over but hopefully, faced with a fiasco, the irresponsible Emperor would change his plans. Or at least they and Mycroft hoped so.

The München Centralbahnhof was undergoing significant upgrades and modifications that promised to last for several years. When completed as the Hauptbahnhof, it would handle most of the long distance traffic for the growing and prosperous city.

Generalfeldmarschall Koenig had traveled the 365 miles from Berlin to Munich by auto and was not in a pleasant mood when they arrived at the station. To make matters worse, the Orient Express had not yet arrived. It had been delayed at the French-German border and had not been able to make up all the lost time. While he waited fuming in the staff car, taking his temper out on his hapless aide, he conjured up images of the German, Austrian and Hungarian rail system under the control of the Empire's Army. Of course, those fools, the French would continue to be a problem until such time as they fell to the single eagle of Berlin. It was coming.

So was the train. It pulled into the station and a swarm of attendants rushed to take up their respective duties – helping a small number of passengers debark, loading and unloading baggage, taking on coal, water, food, drink and other supplies for the next leg of the long trek and helping the new passengers come onboard and settle in.

Koenig, in somber but well-tailored civilian clothes, left his similarly garbed aide to see to their luggage and followed the liveried steward, Antoine, up the boarding staircase, down the first class aisle and into Double Compartment 3A. He was annoyed that the Countess had the luxury suite. His aide would be the recipient of his chagrin but Prussian discipline took over. All the compartments in the carriage were now occupied or in the case of the baroness, at least spoken for.

Antoine did his greeting. "Herr Karmann, welcome to the Compagnie Internationale des Wagons-Lits Orient Express. This is your compartment for the remainder of our journey to Constantinople. *(The Germans were booked to the end of the run but would be getting off in Bucharest.)* While I arrange your hand luggage and freshen your beds, may I suggest you and Herr Osmond go to our restaurant car and enjoy a complimentary welcome aboard cocktail, wine or aperitif."

Generalfeldmarschall Koenig, who hated the French on general principles, controlled himself, nodded his head, snatched his briefcase and stomped off in the direction indicated by the steward. His aide, Colonel Schwartz *(Herr Osmond)*, could catch up with him when he had seen that their luggage had been safely secured in the baggage van.

Koenig entered the diner car and spotted Doctor Koch who was waiting for him. None too subtly, he took a seat next to the physician and greeted him in High German. Koch replied in Switzerdeutsch as expected. They exchanged banal remarks about the weather and the journey that contained coded identification phrases. Satisfied that he was talking to his confederate, Koenig ordered a glass of schnapps, apple brandy, and toasted his good health. Osmond entered the car, sat down next to the German and was introduced to the Swiss doctor. He, too, ordered a brandy. After all the drinks were free.

All this was taking place under the scrutiny of Charles *(Holmes)* and Washburn *(Watson)* who were sitting in the next row of banquettes. Lady Juliet and Pookie were invisibly watching and waiting. Holmes spoke telepathically. *"Baroness. Our*

154

representative of the Kaiser has arrived. Please follow him and his associate and report back as soon as you can."

The conductor's whistle sounded, the steam from the released brakes hissed and with a gentle rocking motion the Orient Express was once more on its way – this time, 280 miles to Vienna and 133 miles thereafter to Budapest. 12 hours in all including border crossings and replenishment. They would be in Budapest's Keleti station very early in the morning.

Koenig finished his brandy, signaled his assistant and left the restaurant car, supposedly to take a nap. In the sleeper car, they eluded the attendant and entered compartment 3A. They were unaware that two specters had also joined them. Several minutes later, a light tap on the door and Doctor Koch, careful to evade Antoine, entered the room and saluted the Chief of Staff. Lady Juliet and Pookie settled in to "see and observe."

"Herr Doctor. I understand that you are a major in the reserves of the Empire's Army. How did a Swiss reservist earn the opportunity to serve the Kaiser in such an important role?"

(Juliet wondered, too.)

"Herr Marschall, I am a member of the Kaiser's personal covert intelligence unit. I am a licensed doctor and have successfully carried out several important missions for the All Highest in European as well as Eastern countries. I am not surprised that you are not familiar with me or our organization. We work very hard to keep our existence and operations secret. It would seem we have been successful."

(This did not sit very well with the Kaiser's Chief of Staff who believed he was entitled to total access to the Emperor's military, political and international activities. On the other hand, he knew how volatile and unpredictable Wilhelm II could be. He remembered the conflicts between the Kaiser and the Iron

155

Chancellor, Otto von Bismarck. After this brief episode was successfully completed, he would investigate this clandestine group and have it dismantled, if necessary.)

"So it would seem, Doctor! Now, let us update each other."

The Baroness chuckled. *"Yes and let's update me. Is the King in for a surprise?"*

Juliet noticed the Generalfeldmarschall did not further acknowledge the Doctor's military rank or affiliation with the Emperor. *"We have some discontent here, Pookie. Sparks may fly. I'll need to tell Holmes and Watson."* The dog cocked her head and scratched her ear.

Colonel Schwartz, *(Osmond)* began, "So, Herr Marschall, Herr Doctor. Countess Antonova is on her way to Constantinople to participate in a commercial conference and to visit the Sultan. She hopes to persuade him to allow his Islamic subjects to enjoy the wines of Spain as do his Jewish and Christian citizens. On her way, she has been granted an audience with King Carol I in Budapest. She has a similar mission to promote the wines of Spain. But thanks to you Doctor, the Countess will not be conscious or able to meet the King.

Now, here is the complex part of the scheme which I haves worked out. As you know, King Carol has Germanic forebears but has little or no respect for the Kaiser and refuses to speak to him or his representatives. So, we will practice subterfuge. Her maid, Carlotta, will go in the Countess' stead. Imagine the King's surprise when she presents the Ultimatum from the Kaiser demanding the annexation of Romania into the German Empire. Imagine his further surprise when you, Herr Marschall appear to enforce the demand and prevent the King's staff from arresting Carlotta. I have the signed ultimatum and will hold onto it for safekeeping unless you want it now.

"Yes, Schwartz. Give it to me. I will decide whether to give it to this maid or hold onto it myself when the time comes." The Colonel opened his briefcase and passed the documents to the Generalfeldmarschall who locked them in his holdall.

He continued, "Since she is known by the Sultan and members of his court, the real Countess must be revived in time to finish the journey and be a party to the conference in Constantinople. You must attend to that, Doctor. The Countess must remember nothing of the past three days except you have been treating her for extreme motion sickness. She will be told Carlotta had been taken ill and removed from the train in Budapest. I will hire a substitute maid to join us in Budapest."

Doctor Koch looked at the ceiling. This plan was too clever by half and full of holes. "Suppose the King reject's the Ultimatum."

"Then the Generalfeldmarschall will point out in great detail, the military consequences of his obstreperousness. The King will be reminded that he already has a secret alliance with Germany and Austro-Hungary. The Romanian army is no match for the Armies of the Kaiserreich."

"There are other countries involved. Russia, Bulgaria, England, France, The Ottoman Empire."

Koenig responded, "The Kaiser is almost hopeful that they will seek to interfere. He does not believe in diplomacy. He prefers battle. Deutschland, Deutschland uber Alles! Now let us prepare. When the time comes, I must disguise myself as the assistant to the fake Countess. Did you prepare that, Colonel"

"Of course, Herr Marschall. Actually, your business attire is quite adequate but we shall have to alter your facial appearance and complexion a bit to give you an Iberian look.

Juliet, who had been taking all of this in somewhat calmly, blurted telepathically. *"Pookie this could be the beginning of a Pan-European conflict. We have to stop this."*

The dog growled silently. They flitted from the room in pursuit of Holmes and Watson. The Orient Express rolled on in pursuit of the Austro Hungarian Empire at Vienna and Budapest.

*****

Back in compartment 4A: *"Here's the plan, gentlemen. Generalfeldmarschall Koenig will accompany the bogus Countess as her personal assistant in her visit to the Royal Palace. Once before the King, he'll identify himself and present Germany's demands. They're hoping King Carol will refuse the ultimatum. The Kaiser wants war. The more countries the better. Oh. Holmes, we have to stop this. By the way, where are we?"*

Watson replied, *"We have just left Vienna, Lady Juliet, on our way to Budapest."*

"Oh, drat! I did so want to spend some time in the city of palaces. The music, opera and symphony, ballet and dance, the balls, the parks. Pookie wants to meet the Lipizzaner stallions. She has equine friends back in theMeadows. Some of them are graduates of the Spanish School. Oh, well! Nothing for it. Before we go back to Paradise, we're flitting back to Vienna. Meanwhile, back to business. You have to snatch those documents before Koenig can use them"

Holmes confirmed, *"Yes, Baroness, somewhere between Budapest and Bucharest, the Kaiser's ultimatum will disappear. If Koenig is embarrassed in the process, so much the better. You say the documents are in the Marschall's possession?"*

"Yes, his aide-de-camp, Colonel Schwartz or Osmond had them but turned them over to Generalfeldmarschall Koenig or Herr Karmann, as he calls himself. . (Lord, doesn't anyone on this train

158

use their right names! The Doctor and both of you are disguised. Only the Countess is still using her correct name and title but the maid is pretending to be her. At least Pookie and I are properly identified but nobody knows we're here besides the two of you. This is worse than one of the farces I used to play in back in London.)

"Fear not, Baroness! All will be resolved shortly."

"I hope so. On the one hand, this is ridiculous. On the other, it could be catastrophic. And Mycroft is sitting back in the Diogenes Club pulling some of the strings. I give up. Come on, Pookie. I'll get you some Heavenly Chewies. Watson, let me know when we reach Budapest. That's supposed to be a beautiful city."

Holmes laughed, "Cities."

"What?"

"Budapest is actually two separate municipalities spanning the Danube – Buda and Pest."

"Oh, no! More misidentification. The Hungarians play fast and loose with their city names. Are we going to Buda or Pest?'

Watson said. "Pest!"

Pookie growled.

"No, I didn't mean you, Pookie. That's the name of the city."

The dog wasn't mollified.

*****

The Orient Express arrived at Budapest's Keleti station in the late evening. A beautiful and busy edifice. The Marschall and his adjutant had just finished off post prandial glasses of Hungarian Tokaji (Tokay) wine in the restaurant car. The meal itself had been excellent. Koenig (Karmann) rumbled. "I'm sorry I joined this train in Munich and missed the first night's dinner. In spite of all their faults, the French can produce splendid cuisine. I shall have to spend more time in Paris after we conquer them. Come, Colonel, let us retire to our room."

As they moved into the sleeper carriage, the Marschall turned to Schwartz and said, "Go up to the Countess' suite and check that 'alles ist in Ordnung.' I do not think Doctor Koch is that dependable. I do not like relying on him or that maid, Carlotta. The Countess must be kept in a semi-conscious state until after we confront the king in Bucharest. We will need another maid for Lady Altanova so she can move on to Constantinople. The railway can probably provide one. See to it."

"Jawohl, Herr Marschall. I shall speak to the carriage attendant after I ensure all is well with the Countess. I will tell him Carlotta has taken ill."

He left and proceeded to Suite 1A. Koenig entered 3A, the double cabin. No sooner had he stepped inside when he heard a knock on his door. "Monsieur Karmann, It is I, Antoine. May I enter and arrange your bed?"

*****

The Baroness had followed the Colonel to the Countess' suite where the lady lay in a drug-induced stupor. He spoke harshly and at length to the doctor and maid, going over their instructions repeatedly and stressing how the Kaiser dealt with incompetence. When he had convinced himself that they understood their roles fully, especially Carlotta, he decided to return to his compartment where the Marschall would be waiting for a full report.

He entered the cabin and to his surprise and that of the ghosts who were following him, found it empty. He thought Koenig had gone to the toilettes and he settled down to await his return. After half an hour, he decided to investigate. He shouted for Antoine who had no idea where Herr Karmann might be. He had last seen

160

him when he turned down the bedding. Perhaps he was bathing. Murmuring about the incompetent French, he told the attendant to accompany him. They systematically searched each one of the cabins including 4A, that of the Englishmen, Charles and Washburn. They allowed that while they would recognize the distinguished business man, they never actually made his acquaintance. "No idea where he is." Cabin 5A was as empty as it had been throughout the trip. *(Except for a couple of sassy phantoms.)*

*****

Next morning, the two detectives were seated in their cabin when a knock came on their door. Thinking it was Antoine with an early breakfast, Watson opened the portal to an individual in the uniform of the Hungarian Police. "Jó reggelt! Good morning, gentlemen. I am Inspector Béla Halász of the Rendőrség, Railway Division." He extended a warrant card. I am here to investigate a tragic accident that has taken place here in the Keleti Station. A gentleman who was occupying the compartment next to yours, 3A was struck and killed very early this morning by an inter-city commuter train. As best we can tell he was wandering on the tracks just outside the sheds. Can you cast any light on this man and why he was on the tracks.

"No, Inspector. I believe his name was Karmann but I can't be sure. We were never introduced, do you see. He joined the train in Munich but we had no dealings with him. Excuse me for being somewhat unfeeling but do you propose to delay the departure of this train as a result of this incident? We have important business to transact in Constantinople."

"We have just completed questioning the passenger sharing the compartment with him. He had no idea why the gentleman was wandering around the tracks. He did not know much about the victim. He says they were put together because there was no other available space in first class. Do you know who is occupying 5A? The attendant says it has been paid for but empty. That makes the victim's traveling companion's story most peculiar. We are detaining him for further questioning. No one else in this carriage including the sick noblewoman in 1A and her attendants could provide any more information. Strange! There will be a brief delay as we consolidate our findings but you will soon be on your way."

"Thank you, Inspector. I hope you can get to the bottom of it. Very unusual!"

The Baroness waited until the policeman left and turned to the detective. *"Holmes, did you..."*

"No, Lady Juliet. I am not a murderer but I have a few suspicions."

"You believe he was murdered, then."

"Very likely!"

"By one of his motley crew?"

"I doubt it."

"But then who?"

"Patience! I think we will know shortly."

They looked out the windows of the compartment in time to see the Police taking Colonel Schwartz *(Osmond)* into custody. He was not carrying a briefcase or portfolio. Where were the documents? Did the Marschall have them in his possession when he was killed?"

Watson shook his head, *"I say, Holmes. Do you think he did it?"*

"No, the German government will step in shortly and connect the mangled body with the Generalfeldmarschall and the Colonel's real identity will then be revealed. He'll be on his way

162

back to Berlin in 24 hours. I wonder what happened to the ultimatum documents which now will not be delivered."

Suddenly, the train began to move. On to Bucharest. The longest leg in the Orient Express journey. 16 hours covering a distance of about 520 miles from Budapest-Keleti to Bucuresti Nord Station with stops for border crossing and topping up.

"Well, it seems we have been cleared by the Hungarian authorities."

"Yes, Baroness but there still remain some complications to be worked out."

A knock on the compartment door. Antoine. "Excuse me, Doctor Watson and Mr. Holmes."

"I say, Antoine, you seem to have us confused with someone else."

Holmes intervened. "It's all right, Watson. He's well aware of who we are and I know who he is. May I introduce Capitaine Henri Duclos of the Deuxième Bureau-French Government Intelligence. He and his associates have been monitoring the so-called diplomatic activities on this journey. Although, they recently decided to take action. Is that not so, Capitaine?"

"Eh, Bien, Monsieur Holmes. I see your brother Mycroft briefed you fully about our interests in preventing this coup d'état in Romania. Indeed, we have acted. Herr Karmann was assisted in his wanderings on the Keleti tracks with a dose of chloroform. A bit of poetic justice considering their treatment of the Countess. Which is why I am here."

"Doctor, we need your assistance in restoring Countess Altanova to her normal self. Doctor Koch and the formidable maid, Carlotta, made their escape from the train just before it left the station. We have operatives searching for them but I don't hold out much hope. Meanwhile, the Countess requires medical attention to offset the effects of the Chloral Hydrate they were dosing her with."

Watson shook his head, "There is no known antidote but generally the effects wear off in a short period of time. Let us hope she does not have a heart condition. Chloral Hydrate overdose can be fatal to cardiac patients. I shall look in on her shortly. What do we do for a substitute maid?"

"We anticipated that requirement. The Railway provides female domestic support to those passengers requiring it. The Countess has a new maid, Mlle Chloe Martin. She is one of ours - a military nurse. We have cancelled the Countess' meeting with King Carol, pleading quite truthfully, medical issues. The King isn't bothered. One less silly audience. He knows nothing of the ultimatum or of Germany's plans for his country. He will be warned through diplomatic channels."

"The Countess must be ready to meet with the Sultan in Constantinople. Let us hope she will be recovered. She will be told Doctor Koch and her former maid were both taken ill and removed from the train in Budapest. The Compagnie Wagons-Lit will attend to their needs and those of the Countess. Needless to say, the Compagnie will actually be the Deuxième Bureau and we do not expect to find those two conspirators. It is not clear how the Hungarian Railway Police intend to handle the Marschall's unfortunate accident. What the Kaiser's reaction will be to his plans being scuttled is anyone's guess. He is erratic, to say the least."

Holmes asked, "What became of the documents? Were they on Koenig's body?"

"No!" he laughed, "They made their way into the firebox of this train's locomotive. They are probably helping to propel us toward Romania this very moment. What are your plans?"

"Depending on the Countess' recovery, we will leave the train in Bucharest and return to England. I'm sure my brother will be pleased with the outcome although longer range, the Kaiser is unpredictable."

" Indeed! Now, Doctor, would you please accompany me to Suite 1A."

The Baroness was beside herself with indignation. *"Holmes, this has been the most frustrating exercise I have ever embarked on."*

Pookie thought she heard the word 'bark" and proceeded to.

"Yes dear, You're annoyed, too. Nobody was or is who they said they were. The Germans, Swiss, Spanish, even the English. Everyone lies. Even the train company is being used by French Intelligence. They should call this the Dis-Orient-ed Express. Well, I know what Pookie and I are going to do. We still have some earthly time before the Committee, bless them, insists we return. We're flitting to Vienna. We'll attend the opera, symphonies, ballets, shows and Imperial Balls. Pookie will meet the Lipizzaner horses. They talk to animal spirits. And we shall ride up and down the Beautiful Blue Danube before heading back to Paradise and Mum, Dad and Arthur. Au Revoir, Holmes, or should I say Auf Wiedersehen. Have a safe journey. Give my best to Watson and say hello to Mycroft."

Off they went. A little dog dancing to a sparkling contralto singing the Blue Danube Waltz.

The End

The Adventures of Sherlock Holmes and the Glamorous Ghost

On the Dis-Orient-ed Express

The Adventures of Sherlock Holmes and the Glamorous Ghost

Tails from the Vienna Woods

Prologue

"Here we are, Pookie. Vienna! City of Music! City of Dreams! City of Imperial History! City of Glorious Architecture! Listen to me! I sound like a travel brochure."

The dog barked and executed a precise and enthusiastic backflip.

Baroness Juliet Armstrong and her steadfast Bichon Frisé companion, Pookie, were sitting in front of the huge Schönbrunn Palace awaiting an outdoor concert by the Vienna Philharmonic Orchestra and the Vienna State Opera Ballet. Pookie had taken Juliet to the famous (or infamous) Schönbrunn Zoo where she communed sympathetically with the inmates.

Earlier they had flitted around the Ringstrasse, taking in the State Opera, Museums, Parliament, City Hall and the Burgtheater where they witnessed an exceptional matinee performance by Hedwig Bleibtreu as Joan of Arc. The Baroness, an actress herself in light hearted comedy, was overwhelmed.

Much of Vienna's grandeur is due to its long serving Habsburg monarch Emperor Franz Joseph and his wife of 44 years, Empress Elizabeth, nicknamed Sisi. She was quite famous for her beauty and influence. Unfortunately, she was assassinated by an anarchist in 1898. It occurred to the Baroness to look up Empress Sisi when she returned to Heaven. She sounded like a women who would share Lady Juliet's sense and sensibilities.

The Emperor and his wife lived at one time or another in both Schönbrunn and Hofburg Palaces. Pookie and Juliet would soon be enjoying the concert by the 1,441-room Rococo Schönbrunn and tomorrow morning would go to the smaller but no less elaborate Hofburg, one wing of which houses the unique baroque Winter site of the Spanish Riding School, dedicated to the preservation of classical dressage and the training of Lipizzaner horses.

The first horses of the Riding School came from Spain. The Lipizzan horse is one of the oldest breeds in Europe. The breed got its start in 1580 when Archduke Charles of the Austro-Hungarian Empire established a stud farm at Lipizza near the Adriatic Sea.

It wasn't clear whether it was Juliet or Pookie who was more eager to see these phenomenal animals and their skilled riders in full performance. With her many trips to The Meadows, the dog had established solid friendships with a wide range of horses – wild, domestic, racers, draft, carriage, military, performers – including several Lipizzans who had passed on after their glory days.

Tomorrow's Morgenarbeit *(morning exercises)* would be the last before the summer break when the horses and riders return to Heldenberg in lower Austria about 30 miles north-west of Vienna, for rest and relaxation. The ghosts were delighted with their fortunate timing. They had caught the troupe before its departure. Pookie was looking forward to talking to these equine geniuses. Meanwhile, the sun was setting and the concert began. The Baroness began to hum with the orchestra. "Oh, Pookie, I love the Strausses, all of them." She waltzed around and finally collapsed next to the dog who was dancing on her hind legs. Viennese delight!

*****

09:30 in the Hofburg Spanish Riding School and the Lipizzans were getting their final brushing before their morning performance. Their coats were actually a cover of white hair over grey bodies. In the first six years of their lives, they transitioned from dark colors to neutral grey and then on to the cover of white. During their performances, their sparkling manes and voluminous snowy tails glowed in the lights of the Hofburg chandeliers.

Riders, grooms and stable workers were busy making sure their equine stars were at their very best. Even though this was a morning training exercise, a large crowd of spectators was anticipated. They would be there to see the magnificent show but also to bid farewell to the company for the summer months. Immediately after the performance, the horses would be rubbed down and taken on board a series of wagons to be transported to the summer stables at Heldenberg. They would not be ridden over the 30 mile trip for fear of doing damage to their splendid legs and powerful bodies.

As Lady Juliet wandered through the stables, being recognized as a ghost by some of the older horses, Pookie struck up an instant friendship with Pluto Altima, the senior stallion. All the stallions had two names – the first was one of eight lines of sires - Pluto. The second, the name of his dam-Altima. The company laughingly called him Der Alte. The Old Man! He was thirty eight and still going strong. Lipizzans lived to an old age.

Pookie was telling him of the wonders of Heaven and the horses, including former Lipizzans, who resided on both sides of the Rainbow Bridge – in the Meadows and Paradise. The stallion was captivated. Though he much enjoyed being a world renowned show horse, he also wished for something different. This dog was describing a life beyond life.

The bell rang and the riders and grooms walked their eight charges out of the stables and into the entrance to the Winter Riding Hall. All riders wore the traditional uniform: brown tailcoats, bicorne-style hats, white buckskin breeches, white suede gloves, and black top riding boots. The dressage was fabulous and unrivalled anywhere in the world and possibly even Heaven.

168

The phantom horses in Paradise gave occasional performances without riders to the delight of the saints and angels.

The show began with "All Steps and Movements of the Haute Ecole" followed by "Pas de Deux", (Two horses performing as mirror images.) "The Grand Solo" and "The School Quadrille." The proverbial show stopper was "Airs above the Ground" where the horse rears back on his hind legs and then leaps forward through the air with his forelegs tucked in and hind legs kicked out.

"Oh, Pookie, That was wonderful. I wonder if Holmes and Watson ever saw this. I hope the Celestial Lipizzans perform shortly so Mum, Dad and Arthur can see them. Where are you off to? Going back to congratulate your new found friends? Don't forget! A ride on the Danube awaits and then back to Paradise."

The curly white canine looked at the Baroness, barked, stood on her hind legs, jumped forward and kicked, leaving Juliet collapsed in a fit of laughter. "Oh my, a Spanish Riding School Bichon. Are you going to include that in your aerobatic routine? And you're all white too with a hyperactive tail. Such a show off!

I'll meet you down by the docks. I guess we could flit up and down the Danube but I'd rather ride a boat. Right now, I'm going to St. Stephen's Cathedral. Those wonderful mosaic tiles on the roof and the awesome interior. I'll see you later. Congratulate the horses for me. A shame you can't talk to the riders. Handsome bunch!"

The dog ran off in search of her new found friends. She flitted into a scene of controlled chaos as each stallion was rubbed down by his groom in preparation for his individual journey. The stable hands were maneuvering the 'circus' wagons into place and packing the horse's equipage along with the rider's and groom's baggage. The show horses numbered twelve in all. Eight performers and four support animals including the bay stallion whose dark color is seen as a mark of good luck. The younger stallions had been transferred yesterday and were already bounding around the South Austrian fields.

Pookie approached Der Alte who was taken up with being prepared for transit. She barked a greeting. The horse whinnied suggesting she flit along with his carriage and they would have a chin wag when the caravan reached Heldenberg. It would take only a moment to flit back to Vienna and she would certainly be back in time to join Juliet for the boat ride. Instead, she opted to fly on ahead to Heldenberg. As befitted his rank, Der Alte was loaded on first and his wagon moved out of the Hofburg, into the city streets and onto the country roads. Pookie arrived and decided to look around the Heldenberg complex while she waited for the wagon.

Little did she know, the horse would not be coming. A suspicious accident caused a damaged wheel on the second wagon and the entire train was stalled until repairs could be made. All except the first wagon carrying Der Alte which proceeded on its route unaware that no one was behind. As the carriage entered a wooded area, a group of masked marauders on horseback rode up and stopped the wagon, brandishing weapons at the groom and rider who were in the drivers' seats.

The villains grabbed the two Spanish School employees, gagged them, tied them up and left them on the roadside. They drove the circus wagon off in a new direction. Throughout this, they said not a word but showed by gestures that they were in earnest. The Lipizzan star had been stolen.

*****

Hours later after the broken wheel on wagon number two had been repaired and the caravan restarted, they came upon the two unlucky drivers lying by the roadside on the way to Heldenberg. One of the riders saw and recognized his distressed colleagues and

170

called a halt to the procession. When the story was told, the caravan continued on to its destination but one of the riders took the bay stallion and raced back to Vienna and the Hofburg. Shock permeated the Director's Office. The police were summoned and an investigation initiated. The Emperor was advised. He was infuriated and ordered the detectives to "Get the horse back quickly and unharmed."

Pookie had been waiting at Heldenberg for Der Alte's wagon to appear and when the others arrived in a panic and the noble horse was nowhere to be seen, she decided she must find the Baroness and quickly. A high speed flit to the Danube docks where Juliet was waiting, none too patiently, for her dog to appear. "There you are, finally!"

The dog barked vociferously, whined and tugged at her clothes. "What's the matter, girl? What do you want?"

The dog ran off, turned and came back several times - a sure sign she wanted Juliet to follow. "Don't you want to go for a boat ride?"

Pookie growled and once more pulled on Juliet's dress.

"All right! I'll come with you. Lead on!"

They flitted off, the dog in the lead and landed in the Hofburg offices of the Spanish Riding School Director, Herr Leitner. He was shouting at his subordinates and the detectives from the Gendarmerie. "The Emperor is distraught as am I. That horse is irreplaceable. Where is he?"

"Oh dear, Pookie. Der Alte has disappeared. We must act. I know who can find him. Where is he?"

****

Countess Maria von Kaufmann was 12 and spoiled rotten. Her parents could deny her nothing, including a glorious horse from

171

the Spanish Riding School. Her mother, the Grafin, a shrew of the first order, succeeded in all circumstances to make life miserable for her husband, the count *(or Graf)*. She was ably aided and abetted by the brat. Nothing would satisfy the young noblewoman other than she should have a Lipizzan in her stables.

The Graf suffered from several major shortcomings. First, he was incredibly stupid. Second, he was a bully except in the case of his wife, whom he sorely feared. Third, he had no respect for the possessions and relatives of others, including wives. He made up for his wretched home life by harassing the women of his household and estates. He knew nothing about horses except what his whining daughter told him in her demanding way. Finally, he was an unrepentant skinflint who would never spend money when he could steal or extort it or the things it could buy.

Not for him to bargain for an inexperienced Lipizzan colt. He commanded his men to capture a mature and fully trained performer. He left the details to Karl, his estate manager and his groom – who were stellar examples of depraved villainy. "Maria wants a Lipizzan. See to it!"

*****

"Where is he?" She didn't mean the horse. She meant Sherlock Holmes and of course, Watson. If her calculations were correct, the two investigators should have left Bucharest after ensuring the stability of Countess Altanova and gotten aboard a westbound Orient Express train heading back to Paris and then on to England. They would not have gone on to Constantinople unless something dire had happened. She estimated they should be at or leaving Budapest with Vienna their next stop. "Come, Pookie. We need some detecting skills. We need Holmes and Watson. Let's do some high speed flitting. We'll follow the railroad tracks." The dog barked approval.

She was right about the train. After a brief stop at Budapest, it was set to cover the 133 miles to Vienna in relatively short order. Now, are they on board? "Since Mycroft is paying for this trip, let's start in first class and see who we can find."

No luck. "Wait, of course. It's lunch time. They'll be in the restaurant car." The word 'restaurant' set Pookie's stomach to rumbling. A Heavenly Chewy was needed. As the Baroness reached into her reticule, she spotted the two of them, no longer in disguise although Watson was still clean shaven. Success."

"Messrs. Charles and Washburn, I assume." She chuckled telepathically. The dog snuffled.

Watson reacted first, almost speaking out loud. *"Oh, I say, Baroness! We thought you two would be back in Paradise by now."*

"We would have if it wasn't for an incident we ran into in Vienna. Actually, Pookie ran into it. A priceless Lipizzan horse whom she had befriended has gone missing. We suspect foul play. We could use your sharp eyes and keen intellect. Major upset at the Hofburg Palace. Emperor Franz Joseph is deeply disturbed. He's giving the Gendarmerie fits. The Spanish Riding School has been a favorite of Austrian royalty for hundreds of years"

"And you want me to just barge in and take over an investigation."

"Just like you always do. Come on, Are you so eager to get back to Mycroft's tender loving care?"

Watson winced. He had been feeding tidbits to the dog. He wondered how a ghost dog could eat earthly food but Pookie could and did.

"All right. We should be in Vienna in another two hours. Fill us in on this disappearance."

*****

In the Graf's stables, Der Alte wasn't taking kindly to captivity or his captors. The groom tried several times to set a bridle on his head and a bit in his mouth and was rewarded for his efforts with a sharp bite and kick. The groom took a whip to the animal, causing him to rear up and descend heavily on his oppressor, breaking his arm. He screamed and lashed out with the whip in his other arm. He looked at the estate manager. "Get him under control, Karl"

Karl knew only one way to get a large, heavy, threatening animal under control. He reached for a rifle against the wall and swung it at the horse's head. The weapon went off placing a bullet squarely between the stallion's eyes. He fell on the groom crushing him. Der Alte died but like the hero he was, took his enemy with him. Karl looked at the two bodies and ran from the stables as fast as he could.

*****

The Orient Express pulled into the Vienna Westbahnhof on time. Holmes and Watson had surprised the Wagons-Lits attendant by telling him they would be debarking and spending a few days in the City of Music before resuming their trip. They retrieved their sparse luggage from the baggage van and headed for a cab to take them to the Hofburg Imperial Palace and the Spanish Riding School. Juliet and Pookie were sitting next to them as they clattered through the streets. Telepathically, she asked. *"How do you propose to get yourself engaged in this matter, Holmes?"*

"Nothing simpler, Baroness. I have performed several services for His Imperial Majesty and I have a good relationship with the Commandant of the Directorate General for the Public Security"

She huffed, *"I might have known."*

174

They arrived at the Palace and after a brief round of reacquaintances, the Emperor's Chancellor was summoned. "Mr. Holmes, how unusual but timely to see you. I am sure the Emperor will welcome your visit. We have a bit of a problem at the moment that you may be able to help use solve."

"I am pleased to once again be of assistance to His Imperial Majesty. Is this about the missing horse?'

"Yes, how do you know about it?"

"As a consulting detective, I have my sources."

The Baroness chortled.

"Is Commandant Steiner of the Directorate General involved?"

"Yes, he is. You should know that the Spanish Riding School and its splendid horses hold a very special place in the Emperor's heart. It has been so with the Austrian royalty going back over 325 years. The loss of a primary stallion is of very great concern, especially this one, Der Alte, a very senior equine. Come! His Imperial Majesty will be pleased to see you again. Doctor Watson, I am happy to meet you once more. It has been a while. Forgive me but you look a bit different.

"An experiment, Lord Chancellor. I am clean shaven."

"Ah, yes, of course. I'm sure it's for a good cause."

They walked the halls of the Palace until they reached the Emperor's audience room. The Chancellor spoke to the guards and the doors were opened revealing Franz Joseph and Commandant Steiner engaged in active conversation.

The Chancellor cleared his throat and said, "Pardon, Your Imperial Majesty but I believe you will be pleased to see your visitors. Mr. Sherlock Holmes and Doctor John Watson.

The ghost added, *"And Lady Juliet Armstrong, Baroness Crestwell (deceased) and her dog Pookie, (also deceased.)*

The Emperor smiled; "Ah, Mr. Holmes, Doctor. What wonderful timing! Are you aware of our equine dilemma?"

"Yes, your Imperial Majesty. We are here to assist Commandant Steiner if he wishes to afford himself of our services. There will be no fee, of course."

Juliet laughed, *"Perhaps a gold medal, a bauble or a knighthood if you are so inclined."*

Franz Joseph frowned, "I cannot stress how important the return of that stallion is to me. Please, gentlemen, put all of your efforts into finding him."

"We shall, your Imperial Majesty."

Dismissed from the Emperor's presence, Holmes turned to the Commandant. "Can we go to the scene of the abduction. I trust no evidence has been disturbed."

"That is next on my agenda. My officers have been given strict orders to preserve the site for detailed examination. I little realized you would be joining us but given our past history, you are most welcome."

The Baroness quipped, *"I didn't realize we would be participating in a crime scene lovefest."*

The Bichon growled. *"Oh, I'm sorry, Pookie, I momentarily forgot this is a special friend of yours. I am truly concerned."*

A police carriage took them to the roadside location where the Spanish Riding School groom and rider had been tied up and left. Holmes took out his magnifying glass and said, "Look here, Steiner, I think we may have a significant clue. The rider said the abductors were on horseback and they took the wagon containing Der Alte as is. They did not transfer him to another vehicle. Notice, one of the wheels has a fault. A crack in the round. Let's see where it leads." They climbed back on the police carriage and periodically stopped to see if the trail was still revealing itself. It was.

Commandant Steiner remarked. "This bunch were real amateurs. Using the School wagon without examining it for any telltale signs. Let's continue to follow the marks. Thank goodness it hasn't rained."

Eventually the trail led up to a medium sized schloss outside the city. The estate of Graf von Kaufmann. The marks disappeared as they entered a long gravel driveway. The mansion was significant in size and décor. There were stables in the rear. Holmes, Watson and Steiner looked about. They spotted the Spanish School wagon. Several bay horses were in their stalls but no sign of the stallion. Where could he be?"

They decided to ask the Graf to join them in a conference with the Emperor. Could he shed any light on the missing equine? He reluctantly agreed. Who could defy Franz Joseph? The Grafin insisted on accompanying them and twelve year old Maria who had never met the Emperor decided she would come along. She was sure she would charm his Imperial Majesty.

Juliet remarked, *"I'd like to smack that willful brat, Pookie."*

The Grafin insisted on using their formal carriage pulled by two beautiful black Friesians. They would arrive at the Hofburg Palace in style. Little did she know how they would leave. Their daughter, in her finest dress, chattered away about how she would lord it over her acquaintances. *(she had no friends)* She had been to the Palace and met the Emperor. Holmes, Watson and the Commandant followed in the Police carriage.

The Chancellor was on hand to meet them. He looked at Holmes, Watson and Steiner, nodded knowingly and opened the door of the audience room. His Imperial Majesty was engrossed in a document and took a few moments to look up. The men in the party bowed as one. The Grafin made a flamboyant curtsey and Maria almost fell over as she performed her clumsy obeisance.

Without waiting for the Emperor to begin the conversation as court protocol called for, the twelve year old blurted out. "Your Imperial Majesty! I am Countess María von Kaufmann, daughter of the Graf and Grafin. I am pleased to meet you. I am here because I know all there is to know about horses."

The Chancellor grabbed her arm to silence her. The Count looked embarrassed but his arrogant wife looked at her child with admiration. The Emperor ignored them. He turned to the detectives. He beckoned them to approach his throne and quietly asked. "What have you learned?"

Out of the nobles' hearing, Commandant Steiner told him of finding the school's wagon but no horse. The estate manager and groom were missing as well. He intended to arrest them when they were found. He strongly suspected they were acting under the Graf's orders but the evidence was insufficient."

Oblivious to what was going on at the throne, the twelve year old turned to her parents, stamped her foot and shouted, "Mutti, Vati, the Lipizzan horse you promised me is dead. Karl said so. I can't ride a dead horse. You must get me a new Spanish stallion. Only another Lipizzan will do!"

The uproar in the room was deafening. The Graf tried to silence his daughter but she chattered on. "By the way, Karl says the groom is dead, too."

The Emperor shouted, "Silence! Count von Kaufmann, I have heard enough."

The Count pleaded, "Your Imperial Majesty. I know nothing."

"Your daughter says otherwise."

"All hearsay. She is only twelve."

Juliet laughed, *"Twelve going on thirty. The arrogant little twit is a complete copy of both her parents. Stupider than her father and selfish as her mother."* Pookie growled.

The Emperor frowned. "I believe her. My advisors tell me it will be difficult to convict you, Count. Nevertheless, I will act. As of this day, you, your family and household are banished from Vienna. Your estate will be sold and the proceeds given to the Spanish Riding School in reparation for their loss."

The Countess shrieked and fainted. Her daughter joined in the hysterics.

The Emperor, unmoved, continued. "You may go to your summer schloss in Transylvania or leave my empire altogether. If found back here in this city, you or they will be immediately arrested. I have so instructed Commandant Steiner. Now get out of my sight."

They aroused the sobbing Grafin. As they staggered from the room, the daughter was heard to ask, "But what about my new horse?"

Franz Joseph turned to Holmes, Watson and Steiner. "Thank you, gentlemen. I regret Der Alte's passing but each of you shall be rewarded for your detective skill. All three of the Kaufmann's are monsters. I wish I could punish them further.

The Baroness shook her head. *"I know someone who will. I feel sorry for the household staff."*

Holmes replied, *"Don't! I'm sure most of them will abandon the mansion rather than be exiled in Transylvania."*

179

They left the audience room. *"Pookie, it's time for us to return to Heaven, We don't want to upset the Committee. Goodbye Holmes, Doctor. Have a pleasant journey on the Orient Express."*

Watson smiled. *Au Revoir, Baroness, Pookie. We'll meet again. I'll have grown back my moustache."*

They all laughed. Telepathically, of course!

*****

Mr. Raymond stood at the Rainbow Bridge to welcome the earth travelers back. "You're on time. The Committee will be pleased. Before you return to your mansion, you may wish to stop at the Meadows - specifically the Equine Plains. A friend of Pookie's is waiting."

They flitted over and spotted Mr. Sherman. "Greetings, Lady Juliet. Greetings Pookie. Come and meet our latest entrant. Oh, but you already know each other."

Standing in a field of succulent grass was a tall, muscular and incredibly beautiful white stallion, gently waving his immaculate long Viennese tail. Behind him, off to the side, seven more stallions had gathered but were giving him room as befitted his status. Der Alte! The Old One. Lead stallion of the Spanish Riding School for close to forty years. He looked up, spotted Pookie and reared up on his hind legs in greeting. The dog bounded toward him, doing somersaults as she went.

The Baroness looked over at the manager of the Meadows and said. "Mr. Sherman. I have an idea. What would you say if I could get these stallions admitted to Heaven? I could have Heavenly Real Estate create a splendid stable for them next to my home. They would be free to flit back and forth from my stables to the Meadows and the other horses. In return, they would do an occasional show for the Theatre Guild as denizens of Paradise."

180

Sherman loved the idea as did Raymond. The Committee agreed. Pookie presented the proposal to Der Alte who was eager to experience what Paradise was really like. He persuaded the other Lipizzans to join him. They agreed, provided they could return to the Meadows when they wanted to. A magnificent stable sprang up behind the Baroness' complex and eight white stallions, all proudly wearing haloes, cantered in precise order into their new home.

Juliet's Mum, Dad and brother Arthur were delighted and came by frequently to see them. Flocks of angels arrived and discussed whether it might be possible to find a unicorn or two to join the group. The Baroness was pleased.

Epilogue

The Elysian Stadium was packed beyond capacity. *(Considering everyone, angel and saint, was pure spirit and took up no room, that meant no crowding at all.)* An organ pealed joyously. *(Handel had composed "Music for Tails from the Vienna Woods" for the occasion.)* A brilliant light burst forth from the far side of the arena and a riderless equine column slowly progressed out onto the field. Lady Juliet, in a scarlet tailcoat, white leggings, boots, and top hat crowned with a jaunty glowing halo led the procession of eight dazzling white horses to the center of the ring. Der Alte was in the lead position.

Her contralto voice rang out. "Virtuous and Angelic beings, welcome to the Heavenly Theatre Guild's Saintly Spectacular presentation of the Lipizzaner Equine Spirits. Wild but silent applause. *(The clapping hands of wraiths make no noise.)* A more boisterous contingent including Juliet's brother Arthur and his wartime mates shouted exuberantly. They indeed could be heard.

The audience included the seldom seen Queen Empress Victoria, Prince Albert and the Austro-Hungarian Empress Sisi.

181

Juliet had met her and introduced her to the horses she so much adored. They were now fast friends.

In front seats, the Baroness' parents watched, mesmerized as the tightly formed column moved to Handel's music in a routine of synchronized maneuvers. On the sidelines stood Mr. Sherman and his staff from the Meadows, glowing with pride. As Juliet moved out of the ring and left the horses to carry on their performance, Mr. Raymond murmured to her. "You can't see them but the Committee is here. The Almighty are looking on, as well. Horses are much favored creatures."

She replied, "I'm sorry Holmes and Watson can't be here to see this but they have witnessed the earthly version. On the one hand, it's a shame Der Alte died. On the other, I am delighted he and his fellow stallions can put on this show."

The horses moved at various speeds and directions, crisscrossing, peeling off, backwards, forward, side to side. All in meticulous lock step. Then seven of them moved to the sides of the Arena leaving Der Alte in the center. Glowing in the lights, his glorious tail waving, he reared back on his hind legs and held a momentary pose. The Levade! Next he executed the piece-de-resistance, The Courbette and "Airs above the Ground." Leaping forward and kicking out behind, he seemed to fly. As he landed, a tiny white dog raced out into the center space, jumped and landed on the horse's bare back. Pookie! Der Alte trotted in a wide circle as the dog did a pirouette, multiple backflips and stood erect on her hind legs swaying on his back. Finally, she jumped to the ground and the horse and dog in joint motion rose forty five degrees and soared in the air. The crowd went wild *(or as wild as heavenly beings are allowed to go.)*

Raymond had the last word. "We'll have to organize an ethical convocation to deal with this. Those two thieves stole the show."

182

The End

The Adventures of Sherlock Holmes and the Glamorous Ghost

Tails from the Vienna Woods

The Adventures of Sherlock Holmes and the Glamorous Ghost

Angels We Have Heard on High - A Novella

Prologue

Earth Time: 1903 - Paradise Time: Eternity, as usual

"Well, the sun is still out. Endless day! How about some nighttime! You know, Pookie, I sometimes wish for a little rain here in Heaven. Or alternate weather of some kind. Even a London fog. No hurricanes, storms or blizzards, thank you. The heavenly clouds are lovely and the breezes are gentle but they never produce any real weather. I suppose I'm just being picky about things being so ideal. I guess that's what happens when you have an occasional opportunity to venture to Earth. You never quite adjust to perfection when you return. I wonder how Mum, Dad and Arthur are coping with being in Paradise."

The speaker, as you may have suspected, was Lady Juliet Armstrong, Baroness Crestwell, (deceased). She was addressing her canine companion of 15 earthly years and now, eternity, Pookie, a highly talented, intelligent and spirited Bichon Frisé. The dog cocked her head, scratched her ear and let out a gentle whine. Spoiled and bored. It was a while since she had participated in a vigorous round of multi-dimensional fetch with her companions at the Meadows on the other side of the Rainbow Bridge. Maybe she would flit over there and see what she could stir up. Or she could practice her aerobatics. Or she could visit her friends, the Lipizzaner stallions. The equine showboats.

It wasn't clear what the Baroness was going to do. Her celestial calendar was usually filled with events – singing with the Angelic and Heavenly hosts; flying with the True Angels aerobatic team; performing in another Saintly Spectacular variety show;

184

posing enigmatically for Leonardo da Vinci; visiting with other immortals including her parents and brother. But at the moment, there was a void. It had been a while since she had been permitted to once again join Sherlock Holmes, Doctor Watson and Martha Hudson in an Earthside adventure. The Committee, whoever they were, was concerned about her spending too much time outside the perimeter of Paradise, which was, paradoxically, infinite. Explain that, if you can.

She was about to content herself with trying on several of Madame Clarice's new creations from Miraculous Modes, all in scarlet, of course, when she noticed a pair of angels flitting along the golden walkway outside her mansion. Nothing unusual about that. This was Heaven and angels of all type and rank filled the atmosphere. Messengers, worshippers, transporters, defenders, personal guardians. Some of them got to spend a major part of their existence on or near Earth and other planets depending on their assignments. All of them beautiful and genderless. Created to serve and happy to do so. *(Or at least, most of them. There was/is Lucifer!)*

Hmm! These two were approaching the opalescent portals of her home. Perhaps something new was in the blissful wind after all. She glided to the doors accompanied by her dog and waited to greet them.

They were both dazzling, changing colors as they moved. Their wings were folded down their backs in the usual position of rest. One was slightly taller and bore him, her or itself with a bit more authority.

A dazzling voice said, "Greetings and God's blessings upon you, Baroness."

"And on yourselves, angelic beings. Welcome to my abode. May I know who you are?"

The taller one responded. "I am called Ezrafel and my companion is Armadel. We are Guardian Angels for beings on Earth. Although I did serve once on an exoplanet. Is this your dog? Is she the famous Pookie, holder of the Top Gun title in dog-fighting aerobatics?"

"She is indeed!"

The capricious canine rose on her hind legs and executed a formal bow producing an outpouring of angelic laughter.

Juliet continued. "I only recently met my own Guardian Angel. Orifiel. Are you acquainted? He preferred to use the male pronoun in conversation, by the way."

"As do we. Yes, we know Orifiel. In fact, that is how we have come to be here. At his advice."

"Well, you both have my attention. In what way do we have mutual interests."

Armadel, who had been silent until then, replied. "We are the Guardian Angels of Sherlock Holmes and John Watson."

The Baroness gaped. "Has something happened to them?"

"No, no, Lady Juliet. They are as well as they usually are. Right now, they are sleeping but we are capable of keeping watch over them while we are engaged elsewhere. Watson is my charge and Ezrafel sees to Holmes. Guardian Angels have no special gift for prediction but we are concerned for their future welfare. Our primary role is not to protect their human lives although we do act on their behalf. They will all die sometime. We are charged with protecting their souls enabling us when the time comes to lead them to Heaven."

"Holmes and Watson have lived for so long running from one hair raising exploit to another that we fear they have exhausted

186

their supply of good earthly fortune. Unlike cats, there are no numeric projections of how many lives human detectives have."

Ezrafel interjected, "Of course, you are familiar with Holmes' close call at Reichenbach Falls with Professor Moriarty. And Watson has been shot several times. There have been many near miss incidents."

Juliet shook her head. "Yes. They lead dangerous lives. It's a requirement of their chosen professions. But they do good. I'm not sure what you wish from me."

"It is not yet time for their physical demise. But it could happen. We want you to persuade them to retire. You can communicate with them directly. We can only do so implicitly. We realize retirement guarantees nothing. They may be struck by lightning or a runaway beer wagon but the odds on their continued survival improve if they abandon their constant flirtation with danger."

"Oh, gentle beings! You give me far too much credit for influencing those two. Peril is Holmes' lifestyle and Watson is dedicated to support him. I'd rather try to redirect the Thames River. Besides, at the moment the Committee has proscribed my returning to Earth. It seems they were concerned by Pookie's and my lengthy stay in Eastern Europe, even though we helped avert a war."

Armadel replied, "We were afraid that would be your reaction. The two of them are pushing the limits of their personal safety. We don't want them to die prematurely. Perhaps a little urging by you via Angelic Mail would help."

"All right. I'll send them a suggestion but I doubt it will do much good. By the way, while you're here, could you answer a few questions for me. I keep meaning to ask but I never do."

"Certainly, if we can."

"Well, my mother wanted to know, 'How many of you are there?'"

"God created us, so only He knows for sure but we believe our number is infinite. There is one of us Guardians for every planetary mortal and we are only a part of the vast Angelic community. As you know, there are many ranks and orders of Angelic Beings - Cherubim, Seraphim, Thrones, Dominions, Virtues, Powers, Principalities, Archangels, Angels and we're organized in many ways for different functions- legions, choirs, guardians, messengers and all."

"I'll tell Mum. My father is a bit of a smart Alec. He came up with that old question that philosophers used to chew on. 'How many angels can dance on the head of a pin?' Your answer?"

"Angels are pure energy and intelligence. No bodies, no genders. We, like you, can adopt corporeal bodies when necessary. But in our primary state, an infinite number of angels could dance on the head of a pin and still leave room. Never tried it myself. Seems like a useless activity. What about you, Armadel?'

"I enjoy dancing but not on pins."

"I doubt that will satisfy Dad but it'll have to do.. You know what lawyers are like."

Angelic laughter is charming. Pookie barked along with them. "All right, celestial beings. I'll contact Holmes and Watson. I'm not optimistic. Say hello to Orifiel for me."

Chapter One

Watson had remarried and was operating *(no pun)* out of his Queen Anne Street surgery and residence leaving the Baker Street premises entirely to Holmes and Mrs. Hudson. He made ample use of a 'locum' substitute so he could continue to accompany Holmes on his many adventures. His wife was amazingly tolerant of his absences and used the time to visit her many relatives throughout England. Their recent journey across Eastern Europe on the Orient Express had consumed a major part of their time and energy.

A year or two older than Sherlock and increasingly bothered by his Jezail bullet wound, the doctor had resolved to slow down his maddening pace. He despaired of Holmes ever adopting a similar strategy. Little did he know.

In his office, he was surprised to find a snow white envelope lying in his mail receptacle amid a pile of bills, circulars from drug companies, requests for contributions, medical periodicals, two social invitations and women's magazines for his wife. No notes or missives from Holmes. The front of the envelope bore his name in scarlet, lady-like script and nothing more. On the back, emblazoned in gold were the words Angelic Postal Service. From the Baroness!

He walked through his office door into the house he shared with his wife, poured himself a brandy and settled into a comfortable reclining Morris chair. Having delayed long enough, he used his letter opener and proceeded to withdraw and unfold a lengthy message from Lady Juliet.

Dear Doctor Watson

May God's blessings descend upon you in great abundance. Pookie and I have happily returned to Paradise with the added joy of being once again with my family. I am now the proud sponsor of the Heavenly Lipizzaner Troupe - eight wonderful snow-white horses plus one curly haired white dog. Der Alte and Pookie are the lead performers in their breathtaking show of precision dressage. I do so wish that you and Holmes could behold their splendid star turns in the Theatre Guild's Lipizzaner Saintly Spectacular. They are marvelous. Oh. Empress Sisi and I are now friends. She is a great enthusiast of the Lipis as she calls them.

Enough chit-chat. I am writing to you on behalf of your Guardian Angel Armadel. He has been with you all your perilous life and yet I'm sure you don't even know his name. He and his companion, Ezrafel, have been charged with keeping you and Sherlock Holmes safe in spirit if not in body in spite of your best efforts to perish. I believe they are nearing exhaustion if such a condition can befall beings of pure essence. Anyway, they are mightily concerned for the welfare of the two of you . They are hoping I can convince you both to retire or at least take up less dangerous activities. Although I am skeptical of persuading you, I have promised them to intercede. I am sending a similar letter to your (and my) delinquent partner.

Please have the courtesy and consideration to ponder my request and reply via Angelic Post. I share your Guardian Angels' worries. Since your entry through the Pearly Gates is not guaranteed, I would much prefer to see you both settle into peaceable relaxation on Earth. The criminals we will always have with us. Holmes and Watson, we will not.

Blessings and Great Affection for You, Holmes and Martha Hudson,

Lady Juliet Armstrong, Baroness Crestwood (and Pookie.)

Watson laughed but then paused, read and re-read the letter. He knew that while she only knew the half of his adventures, his wife would be overjoyed if he abandoned his life as the detective's active colleague. The missive was unsettling. He would speak with Holmes.

*****

"Yes, Watson. I received a similar message from the Baroness. Interesting that we do indeed have Guardian Angels. I occasionally suspected as much but until Lady Juliet a while back upset my unconditional commitment to the physical and terrestrial,

190

beings of pure spirit were not on my agenda. So they wish we would retire in order to preserve our existence? I appreciate their concern but my existence depends on the challenges inherent in my life style. I told her I would take her request under advisement. Meanwhile, I *(we, if you are so inclined)* have an urgent and confounding task to deal with."

The doctor nodded. "Once again, you have piqued my interest, Holmes. I thanked the Baroness and gave her and her angels a similar response."

"I think the angels are ours, not hers."

"You believe in them?"

"Do you believe in the otherworldly Baroness?"

"Of course! She and her dog are quite real."

"Then Guardian Angels should not be beyond your credence."

Watson grumbled, "I suppose not. But what is this task you mentioned? Goodness knows we've had a variety lately. Averting a war, solving a trainwreck, restoring missing music, finding missing artistes, French intrigue. What's left?"

"Personal threats! A note signed by S.M."

"Oh, I say."

"Not only to me. You and Lestrade as well. We are all promised a horrible death."

"Well, we have managed to establish a large collection of enemies in our years. Who is it this time?"

"I believe S.M. is none other than Sebastian Moran."

"Isn't he still in prison?"

"I don't know. It seems not. We'll know more of that shortly. Lestrade is on his way."

Chapter Two

The Baroness had just returned from a session in her stables with Mr. Sherman, Pookie and the Lipizzaners. Empress Sisi had been there giving the horses her full imperial attention. Der Alte had permitted her to place a saddle on his back and ride around the compound. She was ecstatic. The dog and several other horses were engaged in perfecting their acrobatic performances. The Theatre Guild had scheduled another series of equine shows and the troupe was building its repertoire. Heaven was being charmed by white horses *(and a sassy white dog.)*

As she flitted around the side of her mansion, she came face to face with two angels – Ezrafel and Armadel. "Baroness, God's blessings and greetings!"

"And the same to you, angelic beings. I suppose you have come to see if I have any news from your protégés."

"Yes, and we have some news as well."

"I did send letters to them via Angelic Post as you requested. I got the responses I expected. 'Thank you for your concern. We will take your suggestion of retirement under advisement.' They are stubborn although I'm not sure about Watson. I think he's getting tired. What is your news?"

"They have been threatened with a horrible, painful death along with Inspector Lestrade. A note signed by S.M. They believe it's Colonel Sebastian Moran."

"Oh, Holmes called him 'the second most dangerous man in London.' Professor Moriarty was the first. We are pretty certain the Professor is dead. Isn't Moran in prison?"

192

"Maybe not. We don't know. He rejected his guardian angel years ago and we have no definite proof."

"I didn't know you could reject an angel. I'm sorry, dear spirits. Faced with a threat like that, there is no way Holmes will retire. Neither will Watson. Even if they wanted to, I don't think they can. They'll need to fight back. I'll try again after they have settled this issue. Meanwhile, would you like to meet some marvelous horses?"

*****

As evening enveloped London, Inspector Lestrade tromped up the infamous seventeen steps to Holmes' rooms at 221B Baker Street without the aid or guidance of Mrs. Hudson. She too was beginning to show a bit of wear and tear but had some very enjoyable memories after first being introduced to Lady Juliet Armstrong. She dreamt of a return trip to Paris.

The policeman shrugged off his lightweight coat, removed his less than reputable hat and flopped into the basket chair facing Holmes and Watson. The doctor offered him a glass of brandy which he gratefully accepted. After a sip, he pronounced. "As of one hour ago, Colonel Sebastian Moran was transferred to an isolation cell in Wormwood Scrubs. With the closing and pending demolition of Newgate, prisoners are being moved to other venues. I have been assured that Moran is still a guest of His Majesty."

Holmes looked to the ceiling. "Well, there are several possibilities. 1) Moran plans but has not yet executed an escape. The note is an ironic warning of things to come. The Scrubs is not as well controlled as Newgate was. 2) The inmate at Wormwood Scrubs is not Moran but someone posing as him and Moran is once again at large. 3) The threat did not come from the Colonel. S.M. is someone else."

Watson blew out his cheeks. "That certainly gives us a lot to think about but little to act on. Whoever this S.M. is, they are being very elusive. Does the note offer any clues, Holmes?"

"Addressed to the three of us. Just six words. *'A horrible death awaits you three.'* Signed S.M. Commonly available envelope and paper. The traditional untraceable block letter printing, no postal markings, obviously dropped off by a messenger. No misspellings or other anomalies to reveal identity. No useful fingerprints or other indications. Except! Here, smell the envelope."

"A weak and delicate scent. Feminine. Possibly the paper was in a drawer with a sachet or undergarments. Hardly in Sebastian Moran's league. Is S.M. a she?"

"Perhaps or she is a confederate of Moran's."

Lestrade shrugged. "I'll have to take the note as evidence, Mr. Holmes. Threats call for a formal criminal investigation. Especially when one of the targets involves an officer of the law, namely me." He laughed. "It could be my wife. But the initials are wrong. She just left me again. Tired of my lengthy absences."

Watson frowned, "Sorry to hear that, Inspector. Hopefully, she'll calm down and return."

Lestrade shrugged, "Probably, she usually does. Anyway! I've asked the warden at the Scrubs to set up a rotating guard on Moran's cell. I don't want him getting chummy with any of his gaolers."

Watson looked at Holmes. "You don't think it's Moran, do you? Possibly, an imitator or someone who shares the same initials. In other words, it could be anyone. Male or female."

"Very astute, Doctor. We need to narrow it down. I believe that's our only option."

Lestrade chuckled. "Which is no option at all. I think it's time I had a chat with the Colonel."

Chapter Three

Pookie looked up from her nap in her cloud-surrounded bed and yipped. Those two angels were back again. Only this time there was a third. She watched as they floated into the entrance way to the mansion and looked around. Juliet was in the stables with the Lipizzaners. The dog flitted in their direction, barked and herded them toward the opulent outbuildings where the horses could spend their time if they so chose. The angels waved at the Baroness who was just finishing up brushing one of the stallions' sparkling coats. She waved back, patted the horse and floated over to greet the trio. "Armadel, Ezrafel, once again greetings and blessings. Back so soon? I don't think I know this angelic being."

"No, you don't, Lady Juliet. Let me introduce Caradel. Another Guardian Angel like ourselves."

"Welcome, Caradel. Whom do you protect?"

"Someone you know. A law officer."

"Who?"

"Inspector Lestrade."

"That's a relief. I half expected you to say Athelney Jones. I pity his angel."

They laughed that wonderful celestial chuckle. "So do we all."

"Let me guess. Holmes, Watson and now Lestrade are all tied up in a threatening situation."

"Got it in one, milady. All three of them may be targets for murder. Obviously, we are concerned."

"Should I contact them?"

"They are well aware of the threat. They do not know who is responsible. Neither do we. Perhaps Sebastian Moran, Perhaps not."

"I wish I could join them but the Committee will have none of it. Being incorporeal can be a major advantage in detecting."

"True, but one needs to be able to communicate directly with our mortals to have any real effect. We know you can but we have to rely on more subtle modes of influence. Angelic Hints."

"Those three can take care of themselves. They are quite skilled in tracking down 'wrong 'uns.' I've seen them in action many times."

The dog barked. "Yes, we know, Pookie. You're an active detective, too. Such an intelligent girl."

"Well, our charges will be waking up shortly. Back to our stations."

"Before you go, say 'hello' to the Lipis. They are quite clever as well. I'm trying to develop another career for them in crime fighting. Of course, they greatly enjoy being show horses but Mr. Sherman's staff tells me they are envious of some of the equines that helped the American sheriffs and cowboys. Some of the war horses are real heroes, too. The Lipis' discipline can be a real asset. They have wonderful memories and are marvelously strong. I plan to talk to Holmes and Mr. Raymond about establishing a corps of stallions and mares as heavenly law enforcers. Equine guardians. I don't know how the Committee will react to that."

The angels approached the Lipizzans, stroked and patted them and spoke to them in universal celestial language. The horses snorted and whinnied in reply.

196

The Baroness smiled. "Ah, they have a new set of friends. Bring your heavenly associates to meet them. The Lipis look like angels.

Armadel chuckled, "Or we look like white horses. Maybe Pegasus."

Chapter Four

Lestrade exited 221B and strode over to the police wagon that was waiting for him. First thing in the morning, he'd go to Wormwood Scrubs and face down Colonel Sebastian Moran. Meanwhile he had an appointment with a property agent. There is an Inn, *The Jaunty Brigadier*, in Sheffield, South Yorkshire that he was interested in. He was a few short months from retirement although he did not advertise the fact. He was tired of police work and he hoped his wife would react positively to the prospects of being an innkeeper. She was from the Yorkshire area.

The driver left him off and was dismissed by Lestrade. "I'll take a cab home, Jackson. Thanks for the lift."

A well-lit ground floor office with large bow windows. A brass plate on the paneled oak door announced" Jeffrey Harkness - Commercial and Residential Property Agent. Lestrade tapped the heavy knocker and waited. The door opened, revealing a short, middle aged individual, clean shaven, dark haired, steel rimmed spectacles in a dark red waistcoat, white shirt and grey cravat. His trousers were sharply creased and the luster of his boots spoke of someone who took special care of his appearance.

"Ah, Inspector Lestrade, Good Evening! You're prompt. As usual. No doubt a habit drawn from your police discipline."

"Mr. Harkness, greetings. I gather from your wire that you have some news for me."

"Indeed, I do, Inspector. I have received word from my colleague, Mr. Ferguson, in Sheffield that the property I told you about could become available in the not too far distant future,"

"The Jaunty Brigadier Inn?"

"The very place. Its owner is planning retirement and selling up in a few short months. A bit ironic, isn't it? Both of you are retiring but he is heading for his rosebushes and you are interested in his place of business. Of course, he is much older than you. We all of us lead such different lives.   Are you interested enough to travel the 160 miles north to Sheffield to examine the premises and the business which I'm told is quite healthy? Ten guest rooms and an owner's suite, all in first rate condition and a flourishing kitchen, dining room and highly popular pub. There are hotel and kitchen staff eager to stay on. I'm sure an astute individual such as yourself could make quite a profit of it."

"Do you know the price the owner is asking?"

"No, I do not. My Sheffield colleague is a canny Yorkshireman who keeps such information to himself. I suspect the price for a former Chief Inspector from Scotland Yard would be quite reasonable. But first things first. Can you take the time to travel up and inspect the property for yourself."

"I believe so. I'll be back to you shortly." *(He thought:. But first I'll have to convince the wife to come back, think it's a good idea and accompany me to Sheffield. I believe she'd be happy running a profitable inn and me not running off to another case. We'll see.)*

*****

Watson was in a quandary. The threatening note had rattled his nerves but the prospect of another adventure was too good to let pass. He had a backlog of completed stories tucked away in the tin dispatch box he kept in a vault at his bankers, Cox and Company.

198

He was overdue to bring some of them to his literary agent and publisher. The Strand and other publications couldn't get enough of his stories of Holmes' exploits. The Consulting Detective considered them overly sensational and annoying. Watson, in a moment of pique, had challenged his colleague to write one himself. He was greeted with silence.

"All right, Holmes. Let's search out this mysterious S.M. I resent being threatened. Who is he?"

Holmes took a sip of his brandy "He is a she, Watson! Lestrade will get nothing but abuse from his visit to Sebastian Moran tomorrow."

"A woman with the initials S.M.? A relative of Moran. He never married. As far as I know he has no wife, daughters, nieces or female cousins.'

"No. but Professor Moriarty did. He had two married brothers, oddly enough both named James, like himself. One was a colonel, the other a station master. Hardly professional associates of the Napoleon of crime. Both dead at this moment. Natural causes. Over the years, I have kept close watch over the Moriarty's. I believe the colonel had a daughter, the professor's niece. Selene Moriarty."

"And you believe she is the source of this threat? Why? Why now? Moriarty died at Reichenbach in May 1891. It's 1903. Twelve years. What in his history would prompt this Selene to seek vengeance on the three of us now?"

"Not his history, Watson. Hers! I am speculating. As you know I seldom do but I believe the lady just came of age. I believe she will acquire a very substantial inheritance from her deceased uncle, the Professor conditioned on her eliminating you, Lestrade and me. It is the sort of diabolical plan he would have created in case I managed to outlive him. – which I did."

"But why her? Surely Moran would have been a better choice."

"The Professor never trusted Moran in spite of his being his second in command and his brothers seemed to be upright citizens who would never have carried out the commission."

"But you believe this young woman would?"

"I suspect the riches promised are spectacular. Over time, the Professor amassed from his crimes, a huge hidden treasure trove which we were never able to locate. If some of his genes found their way into Selene's personality, her cupidity matched with blood lust and revenge should be sufficient motivation for her to act against us. Let us see if Lestrade uncovers anything with Moran. I doubt it will be of any use."

*****

His Majesty's Prison - Wormwood Scrubs: The Governor greeted the recently promoted Chief Inspector Lestrade. "Welcome to the Scrubs, Chief Inspector. What can I do for you?"

"Thank you, Governor. I want to interview Colonel Sebastian Moran. A matter the Yard is investigating."

"Ah, the infamous Colonel! A recent transfer from Newgate. Glad they're tearing that rat hole down. Well, he's certainly a surly customer. At the Yard's request, we have put him in isolation and increased the number of guards in his sector. What's the issue? I don't have that large a staff that I can double up on every blighter we allow in here."

"We suspect he's going to try an escape based on some threats we think he's issued."

"Who has he threatened?"

"Sorry, that's confidential. Let's just say some important people in his history."

200

"Well, he certainly has a history. Him and the infamous Professor Moriarty. Thank God, that fiend is dead. Er, He is dead isn't he?"

"Yes, for twelve years now. Gone for good. Or actually, gone for evil. He can't come back. Fortunately, there are no such things as ghosts to worry about. *(Little did he know.)*

"All right! I'll call a gaoler to take you down to solitary. Not a very pleasant place."

"He's not a very pleasant bloke!" They both laughed.

Down to the isolated confinement area and Sebastian Moran's cell. A guard was standing by, no doubt bored out of his mind. He saluted the gaoler and the chief inspector.

The gaoler rapped on the door and shouted. "Moran, you have a visitor."

A growl from within, a bang on the door and a returned shout. "Get stuffed, screw! I don't want a visitor unless it's the governor to let me out of here. Why am I in solitary? This is worse than Newgate."

"Stand back, Moran. I'm going to unlock the door. Don't try anything. There's three of us and we have weapons."

He took out a set of keys and advanced on the heavily secured entry. Several locks to open. Then, he slid a steel bar sideways and the door was unbolted.

Lestrade stood in the opening of a dark and confined space – a bed, a chair and slop bucket. The smell was overwhelming. Moran stood at the back wall and sneered.

"Lestrade! I might have known! Still botching things up at the Yard? What do you want?"

"Chief Inspector Lestrade to you, Moran."

"Colonel Moran, copper!"

"I doubt it. Not in here! I want to know how you've been able to issue notes threatening death?"

"You're off your chump, Lestrade. Look around you. Does this look like a high society drawing room? See any paper, pens or ink? Fancy desk? Messengers standing by? What threatening notes? To whom?"

"You know to whom, Moran. Make it easier on yourself. Own up!"

"Oh, that old wheeze! Are you going to get me out of here if I confess? No? I didn't think so. Own up to what?"

"Sending a death threat to Sherlock Holmes, Doctor Watson and me."

"Oh ho! So, someone's on your case, are they? Good for them! Well, it's not me."

"The note is signed S.M."

"And you immediately concluded it was me. Go back to detective school, CHIEF Inspector. There are thousands of S.M.'s in London. Samuel Melbourne, Sidney McPherson, Stephen, Simon, Scott, and Spencer; Mayhew, Morton, Magnuson, McDonald. There are women too. Sarah Mowbray, Susan McIntyre, Sophie Montgomery, Selene Moriarty."

"Wait a second! Selene Moriarty!? Why did you pick that name?"

"I don't know. It just came to me. I made it up."

"You didn't make up Moriarty. That name is burned in your soul. Who is Selene Moriarty?"

"Haven't the slightest idea."

202

From his expression and sound of his voice, it was clear he was lying. Lestrade gestured to the gaoler. "All right. I've heard enough. Lock him back up."

Moran shouted once again. "Let me out of here. I want my solicitor."

Lestrade sniffed. "He's long since dead, Moran. Your turn! Maybe you'll soon join your infamous boss, The Professor, in Hell. Thank you, gentlemen. Keep him here a while longer."

The door slammed shut, the bolt slipped back in place and the locks turned.

Chapter Five

Holmes was seated in his basket chair and Watson was on the chesterfield. Lestrade tracked a furious pace back and forth in the confined space.

"You're sure he said Selene Moriarty."

"Oh, yes. I even challenged him on it. Moriarty's an unusual but well-known name. So is Selene. Who is she? Does she really exist? Is she related to the Professor! Is she the source of our threats?"

"I believe so." The Great Detective shared his knowledge of Moriarty's niece and his theory about her coming into a major windfall if she succeeded in doing the trio in. "Her first mistake was writing and sending the note. Gratuitous bile. She may be dangerous but she is also emotional. She could have hired someone to do away with us silently and without warning but she couldn't resist a bit of drama beforehand. She's a vicious amateur. That works in our favor."

Watson coughed. "Fine, Holmes, but most successful murders are committed by amateurs. Killers for hire are rather rare."

"Let us hope she is too wary and greedy to use a professional. She wants revenge but I doubt she wants to pay someone or subject herself to possible blackmail. A corrupt lawyer or banker is probably managing the inheritance. If she succeeds, I wouldn't want to be in that individual's place. He or she would have to be eliminated. No, I believe she will work alone, reporting the results to her escrow administrator in order to take possession of her legacy but then cleaning up loose ends."

Lestrade humphed, "Well, in addition to finding her, we need to find this executor of Moriarty's will."

"Splendid idea, Chief Inspector. Watson, I think it is time to visit the repository of all London scandal and gossip, the St. James Street Club that accommodates Langdale Pike. If anyone knows the details of Moriarty's bequests it will be him."

"You know how I feel about that rumor monger, Holmes, but I suppose you are right. Do you know him, Lestrade?"

"The Yard has been known to use his services from time to time but I have never met the man."

Holmes chuckled, "A deficiency we shall have to repair forthwith. Let us go."

Watson raised an eyebrow. "What, no calls for games being afoot?"

Holmes laughed, "A cliché, Doctor, a cliché. Onward!"

They thundered down the seventeen steps and hailed the third cab that came into view.

'We must stop at a wine shop. A bottle of fine cognac in exchange for information."

Chapter Six

"Yes, yes! I agree! I think that Weimaraner was cheatin₋ really sinful thing to do in celestial multi-dimensional fetch. N wonder he hasn't been admitted to Heaven over the Rainbow Bridge. All right! I'll report him to Mr. Sherman and the Animal Conduct Board. We can't allow that sort of thing, can we? Anyway, your team won regardless. "

The Baroness was trying to assuage her irate Bichon's annoyance as they returned from a spirited sports session at the Meadows. Sweet though she was, Pookie was a fierce competitor. She had not won the Top Gun Award in aerobatics several times by being a canine wallflower. But she played strictly by the rules. Lady Juliet was never quite sure what the rules were in multi-dimensional fetch. But Pookie did.

"Let's stop by and see the Lipis. I'm sure Der Alte will be glad to see you. You two have certainly perfected your show routine. Your double backflip as he kicks out is pure genius. The whole troupe is marvelous. The representatives from the Theatre Guild were quite impressed. They have several shows in the planning process. *'The White Tailed Wonders'* I'm thinking of changing my ring mistress costume from scarlet to white satin for this one routine although white is hardly my favorite color. Oh. look! We have angelic company. Armadel, Ezrafel, Caradel! Blessings and greetings."

"And tó you, Baroness." The three guardian angels had been feeding the horses cosmic carrots and ruffling their manes. They got substantial equine kisses in return. The angelic community was in love en masse *(no pun)* with the Lipizzaners. "We come with an update on the situation with our three mortal charges."

They proceeded to tell Lady Juliet the latest news about Selene Moriarty and the detectives' attempts to find her and the executor of the Professor's will. They also mentioned Lestrade's retirement plans for the inn in Sheffield.

The Baroness looked upset. "This woman sounds fierce and if her legacy is as substantial as you say, greatly motivated to do our three friends in. I feel quite helpless. However, that's interesting news about Lestrade. Now, if we can only get Holmes and Watson to follow suit."

Ezrafel responded, "I think they are capable of dealing with her, milady, but we wish this encounter would provide sufficient motivation for Holmes and Watson to join the ranks of the leisure class at its conclusion. Holmes is beginning to show his age and Watson's wife, his agent and publisher are increasing the pressure for him to turn his attention full time to his medical practice and alternatively bring out more of his adventure stories and memoirs. That should keep him busy. We hope. Holmes is a tougher nut to crack."

"Holmes has an utter disregard for his physical limitations. Eating, drinking, sleep, danger mean nothing. A serious slip or near miss might convince him that he is no longer invincible but I have my doubts. He certainly gave my letter short shrift. The man is most irritating. Let me know if and how I can help. Meantime, these glorious horses, their canine companion and I are rehearsing for their next spectacular. Be sure all of your heavenly partners come to see them."

"Is it true Empress Sisi is sponsoring the Lipizzans?"

"Yes! They are officially known as Her Imperial Majesty's Equine and Canine Company. Pookie, the little egotist, has become unbearable. Who needs a Baroness when she can have an Empress. However, she still knows where to go for her Heavenly Chewies."

At the mention of food, the Bichon set up a whine, disturbing the horses. Der Alte pushed her with his nose. She licked his face.

The Baroness didn't see Mr. Raymond until he was floating right in front of her. The angels made a small bow in his direction. After all, he was pretty close to the pinnacle of the angelic hierarchy. Lady Juliet was summarily unimpressed. To her, he was just a sweetheart pushover to be manipulated and cajoled. Unfortunately, this time her charm wasn't working. She was being confined to Paradise. Hardly a punishment but she wanted to get back down to Earth and mix it up with Holmes, Watson and Lestrade. Selene Moriarty needed her wings clipped..

The Director smiled. "God's blessing on all of you. Aren't these equines wonderful? Mother Mary, St. Francis and St. Eligius have a special love for them. St. George, too. And before you ask, Baroness, the answer is still 'No!" The Committee is unmoved. Trying to get Empress Sisi to intercede on your behalf didn't work, either. Sorry!"

"Oh well, Raymond. It was worth a try. But, it's a vital situation. Holmes, Watson and Lestrade are in mortal danger."

"I know and so does the Committee but those three have been in tougher spots than this before and emerged triumphant. Not always unscathed but triumphant nonetheless. This time I don't think they require you and your dog as evanescent protectors. You Guardian Angels are using all your resources, are you not."

The cosmic beings shook their heads and wings in affirmation.

"Good. I'll make the following concession, milady. If it looks like things are getting out of hand and your presence could make a positive contribution, we'll allow you to go. But don't count on it. You neither, Pookie."

207

The dog whined again.

Raymond continued. "By the way. I have seen your parents and brother. They seem to be adjusting to Paradise very nicely."

"Yes, I am so delighted. Mum has her book clubs and she comes down here to see the horses every day. Dad is immersed in heavenly legalities and Arthur is a Rugby All-Star. All is well with the Armstrong family."

"Good! I look forward to your troupe's next performance. God's blessings on you all."

Chapter Seven

After a brief detour at the wine shop, Holmes, Watson and Lestrade resumed their journey to St. James Street.

Lestrade asked, "Why are we engaging with this Langdale Pike?"

"He is the wholesale purveyor and collector of London's gossip. If anyone has information on Selene Moriarty and her executor, Pike is our man. Our alternative would be a survey of our underworld connections, Lestrade. Pike is more reliable. He sits in the bow window of his club, apparently immobile and inert and yet he has his antennae sharply tuned for the latest disgraces, rumors, scandals, relationships, transactions, tittle-tattle, crimes and outrages. He filters these and passes them on to the press and chattering classes, all for a price of course. He and I have a reciprocal relationship. If Selene Moriarty is being served by an unscrupulous banker or lawyer, Langdale Pike will know who he is."

As Holmes, Watson and Lestrade descended from their cab at the St. James Club, Langdale Pike spied them from his bow window perch. His curiosity was immediately piqued. Holmes never approached the club unless he had some reason to deal with

Pike. He was also interested in the other two accompanying the detective. This was no social call.

As they entered, he waved an indolent hand in Holmes direction and drawled. "Mr. Sherlock Holmes. Always a pleasure. Are you buying or selling?"

"A bit of both, Langdale. Perhaps a swap may be in order."

"Ooh, interesting. Please have a seat. We can speak confidentially here. Perhaps a bit of liquid refreshment to facilitate the discussion?"

Holmes produced the bottle of VSOP cognac. "I am told the quality of the club's cellar has gone downhill. This may compensate. Feel free to imbibe. I and my companions will abstain."

Pike was familiar with Watson and knew he was not on the Doctor's Christmas greeting list. He languidly nodded in his direction. "A pleasure to see you again, Doctor Watson."

Watson grunted.

"And let me see. Ah yes. Chief Inspector G. Lestrade of Scotland Yard. I am honored, sir." He opened the bottle and poured himself a generous tot. He waved his glass at the three. "Are you sure you won't join me? No? Well, on to business. Now, in what way can I make my humble self of use to you gentlemen?"

Holmes responded. "We conjecture that Selene Moriarty, the niece of the late and unlamented Professor, has just come of age and stands to be granted a very substantial inheritance from his hoard of ill-gotten gains. The transfer of her legacy has one major condition. She must kill the three of us. Needless to say, that event has little appeal."

Watson coughed loudly. "I say, Holmes! Should you be telling this to a known gossip peddler. The story will be in the streets and possibly the press within the hour."

Pike smiled, "Fear not, Doctor. Mr. Holmes and I have conducted numerous highly confidential exchanges and I doubt he would be here if he did not believe in my trustworthiness. Some of our previous transactions would have gotten both of us killed if they were discovered by the wrong persons. Now, I have reason to believe your conjecture, Mr. Holmes but I doubt you are here just for confirmation by a "known gossip peddler."

"I need several things from you, Pike. Is Selene Moriarty indeed the niece of the Napoleon of Crime? Has she been offered this perverted bequest? Since we have received a threatening note signed S.M., I believe she is and has. And finally, who is the executor of this command for vengeance from beyond the grave?"

"I believe I can be of some assistance. But I think another bottle or two of fine brandy is in order, Mr. Holmes."

"Aha! A three bottle problem. Say on! You know I am good for it."

"Ironic that we should be discussing brandy since Selene Moriarty is already a liquid heiress of sorts. She owns a pub 'The French Bottle' passed on to her by her murdered husband. Albert Soames."

Lestrade looked up. "Killed in a bar fight with a customer. Both died in the fracas. Case rapidly closed."

Pike continued, "Correct! She is indeed Moriarty's only niece. She had married Soames in her teens but refused to change her name. Proud of her heritage. Correct me, Chief Inspector, but I believe her premises hosts a number of reprobates of interest to your organization."

Lestrade chuckled, "Of course, The French Bottle and Slippery Selene. I never made the connection. Thought her last name was Soames, not Moriarty. Damn stupid of me! I'm overdue for retirement. She's a real slick character herself. We're sure she's been involved in all kinds of felonies with her barfly clientele but we've never been able to hang anything on her. She is certainly capable of murder. I'll bet she's really looking forward to the opportunity to reap riches from vengeful mayhem. She's her uncle's girl."

Holmes responded, "If she is, then I misjudged her. She will not take it on herself to do us in. The Professor never got his hands dirty. She'll shop it out, let her lackey take the risk of killing us off, collect her bequest and take off to lead a life of new found luxury. Now, Pike, who is her executor?"

"You have multiple choices. The Professor had several lawyers and his original banker is dead. Management of his estate was passed on to the badly misnamed firm of Worthy and Sons. A more dishonest organization would be very difficult to find. Jonathan Worthy should be your first stop but there are other possibilities. Come back if you need to."

"Thank you. We shall beard the widow in her den of iniquity and then move on to the infamous banker. Several bottles of VSOP cognac will be in your possession by end of the day."

*****

Watson was flummoxed. As they hailed a cab, he sputtered. 'I say, Holmes. Do you trust his word? How does Langdale Pike do that? Does he really just sit there and sweep up, retain and trade tons of information? From all over London?"

"Oh, not just London, Watson. He has connections on the Continent. I am led to believe he deals with North America as well. Canada and the United States. And yes, I trust him and no, I do not know how he does it. He stumbles every now and then but on this subject, he is most believable. London's underbelly seems to be an area in which he is most knowledgeable although he is equally au courant with the toffs, nobility and royalty. He puts Fleet Street to shame although feeding the press is a major source of his earnings. He is quite unique."

Watson raised his eyebrows and turned to Lestrade. "Chief Inspector, where is this French Bottle? I assume that's where we are heading."

"On the outskirts of Covent Garden near but just outside Seven Dials. Not exactly fashionable, Doctor. The Yard and local police do a lot of business in that area."

The cab pulled to a halt. "Here we are, gents. Are you sure this is where you want to go? Not sure I'd want a pint of ale from this place!"

He was right. The French Bottle was hardly suggestive of fine dining or potable beverages.

Watson demurred, "Holmes, Lestrade. We are walking into a trap. If she wants us dead, this is her chance."

Holmes disagreed. "No, Watson. She'll set it up so nothing leads back to her. Too many witnesses in the pub."

Heads turned as they entered the tavern. Well-worn tables, a long bar that had seen better days. Straw on the floor and heavy smoke in the air. The clientele were all male of the rough and not terribly ready variety. Behind the bar, two figures – a tall, blocky bartender with a nose that had been displaced several time, dark, stringy hair, a dirty apron, piggy eyes and a cauliflower ear. A permanent frown rounded out his appearance.

At the other end, stood a dark-haired young woman of generous proportions clad in a green satin outfit that would have looked appropriate on a West End Stage. Her face was heavily made up from brow through cheek to chin. A smile revealed teeth that were not well cared for. Her deep set eyes were reminiscent of a certain Napoleon of Crime. No doubt about it. The Professor's niece. She along with the rest of the clustered group stared at the three newcomers.

Lestrade walked to the bar ahead of Watson and Holmes. He ignored the bartender and turned his attention to the woman. "Good afternoon, Widow Soames or should I say Miss Moriarty."

"Inspector Lestrade, isn't it? Who are the two toffs with you? Slummin', are you gents? Welcome to the French Bottle. What did you call me? Moriarty? Afraid I don't answer to that name. Selene Soames, that's me. Albert's widow. Now, what can Louie and I do for you. I don't imagine yer out for a pot of Seven Dials Porter."

"It's Chief Inspector. We came to congratulate you. We heard you're about to inherit a large pile of the readies now that you're of age."

"Ha! From your mouth to God's ears, copper. Don't I wish. I've been 'poor Selene' all me life and damned likely to stay so. Albert was a sweet man but left me nothin' but this rat infested dump. Who are these two?"

"Where are my manners? Let me introduce Mr. Sherlock Holmes and his associate Doctor John Watson."

"Ooh hoo! The famous detective." She turned to the group who were listening to the conversation. "Gentlemen, be on your best behavior. The law is upon us. I ask again. What can we do for you?"

Holmes, who had been silent up to now, responded. "It is what we can do for you. A word of warning. Think twice before making more threats and earning your inheritance. We have a similar message for Mr. Jonathan Worthy."

"What threats? Who the hell is Jonathan Worthy? You been hitting the cocaine again, Sherlock? Yes, I know about you. I'm tired of this. Unless you want to order a pint or two, I'll ask you to leave me premises."

Several of the toughs started to rise from their chairs. "Now, now, boys! Nothing to get upset over. These three were just going."

Lestrade turned and stalked out of the ill-smelling bar. Holmes and Watson took up the rear. It took several minutes to hail a cab. Not many were willing to cruise in the area.

"Well, that didn't get us anywhere," said Lestrade.

"On the contrary, Chief Inspector, she knows we are on to her. She can't waste time if she's going to carry out her mission. We need to deliver a similar message to her soon-to-be benefactor. Watson, do you know where Mr. Jonathan Worthy may be found?"

'Langdale Pike gave me his direction while you were ordering up the additional bottles of cognac. He has an office right near the Old Lady of Threadneedle Street but has no affiliation with the Bank of England."

"Capital! On to confront Professor Moriarty's executor!"

Chapter Eight

They were in a typical well-appointed office of a not so typical personal banker. If Mr. Worthy had any additional staff they were hidden on the other side of several doors that lined the wall behind the secretary/receptionist's desk. Wooden file cabinets, locked, lined an opposite wall. A few hunt prints were the total decorations.

"Do you gentlemen have an appointment?"

A blonde, comely woman of middle years, conservatively dressed with minimum makeup stared at them.

Lestrade flashed his warrant card and said, "No, We do not but this is important Police Business. I am Chief Inspector G. Lestrade of Scotland Yard and these two gentlemen are Mr. Sherlock Holmes and Doctor John Watson. You may be familiar with their names."

The raised eyebrows of the secretary spoke volumes. She indeed knew of this trio and was torn between somehow trying to deflect them from Jonathan Worthy's presence and chancing a conflict with law enforcement. Prudence outdid loyalty. "I'll see if Mr. Worthy is available."

She rose, knocked on a paneled walnut door and entered, closing it behind her.

After a few moments, the secretary emerged and said, "Mr. Worthy will be with you shortly. May I ask what this is about?"

Lestrade gave her a cold stare and said, "No, you may not. Our business with your employer is personal."

She retreated to her desk and trying to be nonchalant, riffled through a stack of papers. She was equipped with a telephone from the Westminster Exchange and what seemed to be a recent typewriter. The phone rang just as Worthy's door opened. Like most phone users she spoke in a very loud voice to the caller. Worthy frowned and motioned for the threesome to come into his office. He gestured toward three chairs somewhat hastily positioned in front of his large walnut desk and sat himself behind it.

A tall cadaverous man, somewhat reminiscent of Professor Moriarty with slumped shoulders, high forehead, thin hair and receding jaw, he did nothing to hide the hostility in his glare at the detectives. Lestrade began the introductions but was cut off.

"I know who you are but I have no idea of how I can be of service. Please enlighten me."

Holmes responded. "Since we are being direct, let me do just that. We have good reason to believe that you are the executor of the will of the long deceased Professor James Moriarty. We have further reason to believe that a provision in his testament calls for the delivery of a very substantial sum to his niece, Selene Moriarty known also as Selene Soames, on condition of her ensuring the deaths of the three of us."

The banker broke out in a sardonic laugh. "Thank you, gentlemen. I had reason to believe I was going to go through this day without any entertainment. Your comedy has remedied that problem. In fact, I have never heard anything so ridiculous in all my life. But I will briefly humor you with a response before I throw you out of my office. As you well know, bankers and lawyers are bound by strict rules of confidentiality when it comes to clients, living or dead. So I can neither confirm nor deny the relationships you ascribe to me."

"As to threats on your lives, Chief Inspector, any member of your esteemed force would laugh at you in total ridicule to think that I would have any involvement in such a preposterous endeavor. I have never seen a case of triple paranoia before. I must confess it piques my interest but not enough to tolerate your presence any longer. Please leave or I shall call building security to have you ejected."

He stood and opened the door. "Miss Warburn, these gentlemen are leaving. If any of them should attempt to return, they are to be denied entry."

They exited the building. Lestrade shook his head. "I'm going back to the Yard. He's lying but I don't know how to shake him."

Holmes smiled, 'I think I do. I shall be back to you shortly. Come Watson. Let us take a cab. The third one, if you please."

"What do you have in mind, Holmes? We got nothing useful from him. "

"To the contrary, Watson. We've set the cat among the pigeons. Now we must observe their behavior and protect ourselves in the process."

"Observe them, how? Are you planning one of your disguises?"

"No, I've already anticipated the need for surreptitious observers. I believe they will shortly be at our disposal."

Chapter Nine

Mr. Raymond stood in the large foyer of the Baroness' mansion. Lady Juliet and Pookie has just returned from the Meadows with the Lipizzaners. The horses had tossed off their discipline, ran free and capered over the limitless hills and fields. Now they were returning for a substantial feed of heavenly hay and water and a rest.

"The boys really enjoyed that, Raymond. There were a couple of mares in the party as well. What brings you to Crestwell Manor?"

"You got your wish. You are to go immediately to London and 221B Baker Street. It seems Sherlock Holmes, the Doctor and Chief Inspector are all under serious threat of possible murder. Their Guardian Angels have appealed to the Committee to respond to a request from Holmes for your and Pookie's services in tracking the suspects. A bit of clandestine observation is necessary. You'll stay evanescent. When the Committee heard that all three of them were in danger and Professor Moriarty was reaching out from Hell to have his revenge, they acquiesced to your return. Frankly, I am surprised. Don't waste earth time. I'll have the horses taken care of. I'm sure Empress Sisi would love to supervise."

The Baroness laughed. "Well, maybe I can personally persuade the three of them to retire. Pookie, we are needed earthside. Let's go, lazy."

The dog yawned and did one of her signature backflips.

*****

Holmes and Watson were about to enjoy another one of Mrs. Hudson's excellent dinners when the two wraiths appeared in the spartan dining room. Pookie barked her greeting and Juliet sang a verse of *Britannia Rule the Waves* in her marvelous contralto. They all fell to laughing.

"I wondered if Chief Inspector Lestrade would be here. He doesn't know we exist, does he?"

"No, milady and there's no point in trying to enlighten him. He doesn't believe in ghosts."

"Like someone else I once knew. So what is this assignment you have for us?"

Holmes and Watson alternately outlined the situation between bites of savory roast beef and Yorkshire pudding. Pookie was upset that she couldn't participate in the repast. The Baroness gave her a Heavenly Chewy but that didn't satisfy.

"So you want us to track this banker and this pub owner. You expect they will be getting together shortly to deal with the fact that you are on to them."

"Exactly! We suspect she will act rapidly before we can gather more evidence and arrange to frustrate their plans. I believe she has a paid assassin in that group of barflies that inhabit her den of iniquity. After we've been disposed of, she'll probably do him in. Once her inheritance is passed on, Jonathan Worthy will be next unless he has plans for her demise."

218

The Baroness laughed. *"They seem like a real group of pals. I get you before you get me. OK, where do we go?"*

Holmes paused. *"I think you should put Worthy under surveillance first. I'm reasonably sure he will be contacting Selene."*

"Why doesn't he just give her the money, take his personal cut and be done with it? Who's going to tell the Professor that the terms of his will weren't satisfied?"

Watson agreed.

Holmes said, *"That's the way rational villains would behave but this woman has a vendetta in mind. She wants vengeance as well as the hoard. A streak of criminal insanity runs in the family. We're dealing with a madwoman and two men who are afraid of her. The Assassin, the Banker and the Witch. That sounds like a title for one of your adventures, Watson. Follow Worthy, Baroness. They'll meet somewhere nondescript and out-of-the-way. His office is on 12 Threadneedle Street next to the Bank. Worthy and Sons. He's Jonathan, the last surviving son."*

"Off we go, Pookie. A London flit."

*****

Miss Warburn couldn't see the scarlet clad beauty or her curly white dog when they sailed through the substantial walnut paneled door of Worthy and Sons. She didn't react as they flew into the office of Jonathan who was packing his briefcase. "Miss Warburn, I am leaving for the evening. I shall be in as usual tomorrow morning. We have a full schedule."

"Yes, Mr. Worthy. I hope we have a less exciting day than we had today. Those three detectives were certainly disruptive. What did they want?"

"It was case of mistaken identity. They thought I was someone else but kept insisting they were correct. I had no choice but to challenge them and throw them out. They won't be returning."

The Baroness giggled. *"No, Jonathan! Someone else is here instead. Well, Pookie, let's see where our banker friend is off to."*

The secretary called after him. "Oh, Miss Caruthers called to confirm her appointment. I didn't have her on our schedule."

"My fault. I neglected to tell you. Good evening, Miss Warburn."

"What do you think, Pookie. Is Miss Caruthers his homicidal associate? A coded assignation? Let's see!"

They descended to Threadneedle Street where the banker summoned a cab with some difficulty. Quitting time in the City. He was joined by two specters, unsure whether they were going to some kind of murderous tryst, a gentlemen's club or his home, a scene of domestic tranquility.

After working through the crowded streets, they set off toward the Embankment and crossed over the river into Lambeth. *"Pookie, I don't think there's a banker's club here and I doubt Mr. Worthy lives in Lambeth. That leaves our original alternative. He's meeting Miss Caruthers or Soames or Moriarty."*

The dog growled. *"Yes, dear. This should be interesting."*

The cab stopped at a row of warehouses and Worthy descended. He walked briskly down the road until he came to a building with the sign, Caruthers, Traders of Quality Coffee and Tea.

"Ah ha, Pookie. The mysterious Miss Caruthers is revealed. Probably one of many meeting sites."

The storehouse was closed. He took a key from a chain at his waist and undid a substantial padlock, opened the door and stepped into the dark expanse. The two ghosts passed him and not requiring light, maneuvered their way into a small unlit workplace. Worthy clearly knew his way around the location. In the dark, he entered the office, reached into a drawer, retrieved and lit two candles revealing a desk, several chairs and two wooden file cabinets. The bare essentials.

The unlocked warehouse door swung open revealing a woman clothed in a long dark coat and a floppy hat that shadowed her features. She strode confidently toward the office and said, "Well, Mr. Worthy, here we are as planned. I assume we have news for each other. I'm ready to complete my side of our bargain. What about you?"

"Yes, Mrs. Soames or Miss Moriarty. Which are you today?"

"Since we're dealing with me uncle's bequest, I'm Selene Moriarty. To Jackie, I'm the widow Soames."

"Who is Jackie?"

"Someone you don't need to know. It's him what's going to do the dirty."

"That's what we need to discuss. I don't think we should go ahead with the plan. I can just arrange to deliver the bearer bonds to you without your having to fulfill the Professor's stipulation. Taking my appropriate commission, of course, heh, heh."

"Getting cold feet, are you, Mr. Worthy? Oh.no! I swore I would avenge my uncle as he wanted me to. I'm the only one to do it. Me father and other uncle are both dead and that swine Moran is stuck in the nick for the rest of his life. Don't you understand, Mr. Banker? It's an affair of honor. The Professor's honor and my honor."

The Baroness whistled, *"Well Pookie! Holmes was right. This little lady is bent on revenge. She could have the money, no questions asked but she wants blood. Let's listen in to the rest of this conversation. Maybe we can find out how this is going to take place."*

Jonathan Worthy frowned, " I had a visit this afternoon from your three victims, Holmes, Watson and Lestrade. They're on to the plot. I don't think they know the particulars. By Jove, I don't know the particulars."

She laughed, "And you won't and neither will they until they're dead. They visited me too. Acted as if they were aware of everything. Arrogant fools! I have it fixed so that nothing gets back to me and nothing will splash on your shiny Oxfords. Stop worrying."

"I do worry. They're closing in. Holmes and Watson are no fools and Lestrade is one of the few Yard Inspectors worth being concerned about. If you're going to do it, do it quickly before they get a chance to learn anything more and fight back. Delays are dangerous."

"Well, I guess you're right. I'll speed it up. I kind of enjoyed the idea of those three living in fear for a while but we probably should get it over with. You do your part. I expect those bonds to be in my hands in the next twenty-four hours. I'll do my part. Three deaths that will shock London. Maybe even the world. Uncle would be pleased. Ooh, delicious!"

Worthy shuddered. "Are we finished here?"

"Yeah, go home to your straight-laced wife. Meet me at Caruthers tomorrer with the bonds and watch the newspapers. You wouldn't think of disappointing or betraying me, would you, Jonathan?"

"Of course not! I just want to be free of any suspicions by the authorities. I'm a respectable member of the financial community."

This struck Selene as hilarious. She laughed heartily, nearly choked and waved him off.

"Goodbye, Mr. Worthy. "

The Baroness winced, *"I'm going to follow her, Pookie. You flit back to Mr. Holmes. Here, I'll give you a note to give him. I'll be back as soon as I know what's going on."*

She reached into her reticule, pulled out a piece of Angelic Postal Service paper and scrawled a brief report of what they had learned and what she planned to do. She gave it to the dog who got out just before Selene left, locking the warehouse door. Pookie was off to Baker Street.

Selene waved at the cab that was waiting for her. She laughed again. "Yes, Good bye, Mr. Worthy. Don't worry about the authorities. Worry about me. Enjoy your last few days on earth."

Lady Juliet flitted up to the cab and floated in next to the pub owner. She needed to find this Jackie and discover what he and Selene had in mind for the law enforcement trio.

The cab made its way back to the no-man's land between Covent Garden and Seven Dials. Selene got down in front of the French Bottle and stared at the pub. Soon to be history. She'd burn the place down before she disappeared to the continent with her riches.

The Baroness tracked along behind her as they entered the smoke-filled, noise ridden bar. A pair of toughs were threatening each other and at least one drunk was stretched out on a table top. Ah, yes! London refinement at its peak. Selene waved at Louie, the bartender. "Anything I should know?"

He shook his head. "No, only the usual rubbish."

She looked across the room, getting the attention of a large, blocky bruiser with a set of facial scars and a scruffy black beard. She nodded her head in the direction of a set of curtains behind the bar. He rose and lumbered off in that direction. Selene removed her floppy black hat and long coat and hung them on a rack next to a stool and the till. She filled an order or two for the swill posing as ale and then slowly sashayed behind the curtain. Juliet sashayed right along with her.

"Yeah, Miss Selene. What can I fer ya?"

"You know what you can do, Jackie. It's time to launch our little project. Are you up fer it?"

"Didn't expect it so soon. I'll be ready tomorrer night. Got all the parts. A little bit of puttin' together and Bob's yer uncle. A nice big boom and bye-bye 221B Baker Street. How you gonna get the rozzer and those two snoops together? Be a shame to blow the place up if they're not there. Understand there's a landlady too."

"Sorry about that. She's just going to be in the wrong place at the wrong time. Don't worry. Yer victims will be there. Make sure yer bomb does the trick. You do yer part. I'll do mine."

"Yeah, well, I expect payment up front. Twenty quid, like we agreed."

"You'll get it tomorrer like I promised." She frowned. "Do you take me for a cheat?"

The big hulk stammered. "Course not. Miss Selene. It's always a pleasure to do business with yer."

"Good! Keep that in mind. Now get crackin'. When you're ready, come by tomorrer afternoon to get paid. Then you go to Baker Street and do the deed. Good bye, Sherlock Holmes. Ha! Now get out, Jackie! I have another note to write and deliver."

Juliet was listening to all of this with a sense of horror. She had to get this information to Holmes, Watson and Lestrade. But first, she needed to follow Jackie to his lair. Hopefully, they can trap him before he builds his infernal machine.

Unnoticed by Louie or the gin-soaked drunks but being trailed by the Baroness, Jackie shambled out of the pub, turned down several alleys and proceeded through a set of underground tunnels to his workshop of destruction. He had been a sapper with the Royal Engineers. Demobbed from the Army he was at loose ends until he did a couple of explosive jobs for the Fenians and blew up a bank safe or two for a gang of yeggs. He had developed a reputation in the underworld and was known to the police. They were never able to pin the blame on him. His 'associates' were always ready with an airtight alibi. This job for Selene would be a classic. Sherlock Holmes, the doctor and that Yard Inspector. It would make him famous with certain people. He could raise his prices. Shame about the landlady but that's life. He snorted in laughter. He lit several lanterns, uncovered an empty whiskey vat full of parts and explosive materials and began the tricky job of bomb assembly.

*****

Pookie flitted into 221B with Juliet's note in her mouth. She dropped it on Holmes' lap and headed for a pillow in the corner of the room. Watson was on the chesterfield. Lestrade was down at the Yard offices. The detective unfolded the Angelic Postal Service paper. "She's on Selene Moriarty's trail. The attack is scheduled for tomorrow night. Worthy is getting the bearer bonds together and will deliver them at Caruthers tomorrow afternoon. We need more information on this strike."

No sooner spoken than… Juliet swept into the room. *"A bomb! She has a confederate named Jackie building one in his underground lair. He's going to set it off here tomorrow night.*

225

She's sending you another threatening note designed to get the three of you together. I'll take Martha Hudson out for the evening. It'll be tricky since Pookie and I can't become physical. Maybe a show. Got any money, Holmes? Enough to pay for her ticket? We'll be gone while you deal with your attacker."

"Yes, Baroness. It seems the game is truly afoot. Watson, get your trusty service revolver at the ready. We'll have to notify Lestrade. Tell me about this Jackie."

"I don't know anything more than I've told you. I assume he's an explosives expert. Probably a discharged Army munitions specialist. If you want, I can take you to his underground shop."

"No, let him come here. We need to catch him staging his attack. Watson, can you provide Mrs. Hudson with money for an evening out with the Baroness? I'll send a wire to Lestrade and bring him here. Where's Billy when you need him?"

A knock on the door and Chief Inspector Lestrade appeared.

"Amazing, Lestrade. I was just about to summon you."

"I'm on my way to a serious disaster in Seven Dials. Explosion, building collapse. Could be gas or could be deliberate. I need to talk to the Fire Marshall. Thought you'd want to come."

"Seven Dials? A coincidence? I doubt it. Let's go. Watson!"

Juliet shouted silently, *"I'm coming with you, Holmes. If it's the place I think it is, it could be my friend Jackie. Probably had one drink too many and made a serious mistake putting his bomb together. I won't have to take Martha out after all."*

Of course, Lestrade heard none of this. Just as they were leaving, the page, Billy arrived with a note on the silver tray. "For you, the doctor and Chief Inspector, Mr. Holmes."

Holmes took the envelope, cut it open and read. "It's from S.M. but no signature this time. It reads 'Get together and say your

226

prayers. It'll be your last time.' She wants us in the same spot. Sounds like an invitation to be blown up."

Watson, Lestrade and Holmes raced down the stairs and out to a police wagon waiting by the curb. The late afternoon traffic was heavy and slow. Watson grumped. "We should have taken the Underground."

Lady Juliet was perched on top of the wagon with Pookie at her side. *"Miss Dog, I'll bet Jackie made a misstep. That certainly puts a crimp in Miss Moriarty's grand scheme. But she still needs to get the bonds from Jonathan Worthy. Tomorrow afternoon at Caruthers Warehouse. She may own it. I'll have to alert Holmes. He can get Scotland Yard involved. Finally, here we are. Yes, it's Jackie's hideout."*

The streets were blocked off. Members of the Fire Brigade were moving gingerly through the wreckage. Constables from the local police were controlling the crowd of gawkers who were watching the process.

"Anybody killed? Yeah, they found parts of one body. Blown to bits, he was. The building was empty, thank God!"

Juliet said a short prayer of thanks and thought. *"Well, he's not going to reach the Pearly Gates or Purgatory for that matter. Sorry, Jackie."*

Standing on the side of the crowd was Selene Moriarty. When she saw the police wagon pull up, she faded away back to the French Bottle. "That damn fool. Thought he was the best in the business. Never trust a heavy drinker. So Holmes etc. are here. Things are getting a bit too warm. Have to change my plans. Tomorrow afternoon, I'll get the bearer bonds from Worthy and do him in. No witnesses or informers. Then destroy the pub and disappear. I still have to work out a new plan to eliminate those three worms. Sorry, Uncle James. I'll get to it. A promise is a promise."

She stepped into the pub, looked around in disgust at the room and its inhabitants and sighed. "Oh, well. Paris will be delightful this time of year. I'll need a new name and I'll buy myself new identity papers. Shouldn't take me long to get looped up with some of those French bozoes. Maybe open a bistro. First things first. Caruthers. Tomorrow afternoon."

Chapter Ten

The Baroness had indeed taken Mrs. Hudson to a musical after all. Martha felt a little bit uncomfortable sitting by herself but was wildly entertained by the antics of Juliet and Pookie who had joined the unaware chorus and cavorted through several numbers. The people around her were puzzled when she laughed at what seemed to be inappropriate places. She didn't care. She was having fun and the ghosts were providing it. Lord knows, the show itself was a turkey.

Next morning, she delivered breakfast to Holmes and Watson who had stayed over. His wife was once again away at her relatives. Giggling, she gave a report of the theatrical mischief the two wraiths had concocted. Juliet and the dog who were seated in the dining room rose and demonstrated. Watson guffawed. Holmes exuded a trace of a smile.

He looked at the Baroness. *"What time are Worthy and Moriarty supposed to meet?"*

"Two o'clock. I assume you'll have Lestrade arrest them."

"On what charge? Exchanging inheritance funds is not illegal unless we can determine that she was behind an abortive attempt to blow us to kingdom come. She has covered her tracks rather well up to now. So has Worthy. Nevertheless, we will be hidden inside the warehouse before they arrive, Perhaps she or he will do something stupid."

228

*****

At one-thirty, Holmes and Watson had broken into the Caruthers Warehouse. Lestrade had looked the other way as the consulting detective practiced his lock picking talents. Two constables were on hand to support the Chief Inspector. They were hidden in the darkness behind stacks of coffee beans but close enough to the office to listen, observe and if necessary interrupt the transactions. Watson and Holmes were similarly hidden. The doctor had his service revolver at the ready. This was a dangerous woman. You never could tell what she'd do.

Lady Juliet and Pookie were sitting in the darkened office, ready to warn Holmes who was about twenty feet away.

At two, a side door swung on its creaky hinges, admitting Jonathan Worthy. He crept through the dark into the tiny office and lit a pair of candles. He put down his bulging briefcase and sat waiting for the she-devil to arrive.

Several minutes later, Selene Moriarty/Soames strode through the door, across the now dimly lit warehouse floor and into the office. She said nothing, nodded in the banker's direction, took up the briefcase and spilled its contents on the desk. She examined the bonds, fluttering them in her fingers.

Worthy spoke up. "One million pounds minus my ten percent commission. Your uncle amassed quite a fortune in his lifetime and the bonds have significantly increased in value. You should have quite a comfortable life, Miss Soames."

"Yes, I will be a poor widow left an unexpectedly large inheritance by a recluse aunt. It will be even more comfortable when there is no one to tell where the money came from, Mr. Worthy."

"Well, you will have no worries on that score from me, Miss Moriarty. I am the soul of discretion."

229

"Yes, but you know who I really am. You just said my real name. No, I'm sorry, Mr. Worthy. That just won't do."

She reached into her coat pocket, pulled out a revolver and shot him several times before Juliet screamed. Holmes, Watson and Lestrade raced to restrain Selene. Surprised but still self-possessed, she fired again, hitting Holmes beneath the shoulder. Watson shot at her, hitting her squarely in the chest and face. As she fell over dying, she murmured, "I got him, Uncle, You're avenged."

Watson tended to the unconscious Sherlock Holmes. The bullet had entered above the heart and lungs and exited. The constables called for an ambulance. Lestrade ensured that both Worthy and Selene were dead. Juliet and Pookie were horrified. She called out. "Ezrafel, where are you? Is Holmes dying?"

The guardian angel appeared to her. "I think not, milady although it may be a near thing. Of course, we will keep careful watch over him. Come, let us follow the ambulance."

The emergency vehicle from St. Thomas Hospital arrived and Holmes was gently but speedily taken on board. Watson came along. Lestrade stayed behind to initiate the investigation and to claim the bearer bonds in the name of the Crown.

As they set off toward the Embankment, Ezrafel and Armadel turned to Juliet and said. "Perhaps this will convince the two of them to retire. Caradel is almost certain the Chief Inspector is going to buy that property in Sheffield and settle with his wife into the role of innkeepers."

The Baroness replied. "Let's not get ahead of ourselves. In order to retire he has to live."

Epilogue

Nine earth months later. Miracle of miracles! Holmes recovered from his wounds and after long discussions with Watson

230

and Mycroft, retired to a small farm in Sussex on the Downs, five miles from Eastbourne where he was "living the life of a hermit" among his bees and books. Needless to say, Ezrafel was delighted.

Mr. Raymond came upon the Baroness as she was returning from rehearsals with the Lipizzaners and Pookie. The troupe was a celestial sensation. Ephemeral angels, honored saints and common folk alike 'filled' celestial stadiums to see their performances. The Almighty and Committee had shown their approval and several cosmic composers including Handel had created musical suites to enhance their shows. Need we point out how delighted the dyed in the wool thespian Lady Juliet was with her new show business endeavors.

The Director floated his usual few inches off the ground, patting Pookie and several of the horses. Der Alte snuffled affectionately at him. The Baroness stared. "Well, Raymond, what is it this time? Have the dog or I committed some offense that has the Committee in a galactic snit? Did the horses offend? I can't imagine my parents are at fault. Is my brother a problem?"

"None of the above, dear Baroness. I come with an opportunity. The Guardian Angels have requested that I look in on Sherlock Holmes. I don't do this often but he and I have developed a relationship of sorts because of you. He and I can communicate directly. I plan a one 'earth hour' visit to his retirement establishment just to check up on him. Would you care to accompany me? No obligation, of course."

"As the French say, absolutement! Pookie and I would love to go, wouldn't we dear?" The Bichon barked happily.

Raymond continued. "I understand Doctor Watson is staying with him for a few days. Mrs. Hudson, unfortunately is back at Baker Street. He hasn't been able to persuade her to join him in the countryside. Are you ready to go?"

The Director, Baroness and Dog flitted through the Pearly Gates and descended to the English Channel and the highlands of Sussex.

Located along South Downs Way, in the tiny village of East Dean, his modest home, clothes and manner did nothing to declare that this indeed was the famous and only consulting detective in England, nay perhaps the entire world. Celebrity was packed away.

As they stopped in front of the cottage door draped in English Ivy, a tall, slim figure emerged. He was hatless and wore a set of vintage tweeds that fit him well. His face was tanned and his eyes, surrounded by crow's feet, were bright and sharp. His hair was grey bordering on white, but his brows were still an intense black. His clean-shaven face retained the sharp-etched features for which he was famous. No doubt. This was Sherlock Holmes.

He greeted them cordially as he reached down to pet Pookie. "Mr. Raymond, Lady Juliet, Miss Dog. What a welcome surprise! What brings you to my seaside abode? Surely not some problem in Heaven!"

The Baroness laughed. "No, Holmes! Nothing for you to solve."

Raymond smiled, "Just checking up on a wounded comrade. Your Guardian Angel Ezrafel requested it. He's here, by the way."

"I am quite well and fully recovered from my little incident. The Sussex weather has a great curative influence."

Another figure appeared in the doorway. Watson! A tiny bit older and just a tad greyer but still the same doctor who saved his colleague from death by *(contrary to his medical oath)* shooting the mad woman, Selene Moriarty/Soames. He joined in the greetings.

"Baroness, Pookie, how wonderful to see you again. And you sir, I'm afraid we are not acquainted."

232

Holmes turned to Watson and said, "May I introduce the Angelic Director of Heaven's Operations, Mr. Raymond. Raymond, meet my colleague, Doctor John Watson. Raymond, Lady Juliet and of course, Pookie are looking in on me to assure I am still alive and well. We can't see him but I am told my Guardian Angel Ezrafel is here as well."

Seen by the other ephemerals, Ezrafel bowed his head and fluttered his wings.

Holmes waved his hand, "Come in! Come in! I'd order up some tea or glasses of mead but I know you don't partake of earthly sustenance. We've just returned from my hives. I'm trying unsuccessfully to interest Watson in beekeeping."

Watson shook his head. "No thank you! I'll stick to medicine and writing stories for the masses."

(As with most of his endeavors, Holmes poured what energy he had into his adopted profession as a beekeeper. Not only was he the resident Sussex apiculture expert but his hives supplied honey and beeswax throughout the area including the shoppes, restaurants and hotels of Brighton and its surroundings. His flagons of mead were treasured in many a pub and high toned drinks emporium.)

Holmes laughed. "When I criticized his overly sensational tales, Watson challenged me to write a book of my own. I did."

The detective reached for a bookshelf and withdrew a small blue covered volume. "Behold 'A Practical Handbook of Bee Culture with some Observations upon the Segregation of the Queen.' It's in the spirit of some of my early monographs.'

"Not exactly what I had in mind, Holmes."

"I know, Watson, but it's what I felt motivated to do. I say, do you heavenly denizens house bees in your precincts?"

Raymond responded. "Oh yes! Quite a population of them. They are deeply honored, highly valued and greatly respected. Their honey is one of the major ingredients of our nectar and ambrosia. Lovely stuff."

Juliet looked at Watson. Nodding toward Holmes, she whispered, "I hope you are watching over him, Doctor. I know his Guardian Angel is."

Watson blew out his cheeks. "As much as his persnickety nature will allow. We have just been arguing about his coming out of retirement."

Ezrafel winced. Raymond shook his head. The Baroness looked at him. "Holmes, you're a weary war horse. We all know you're still superior to all of those London hacks who purport to be enquiry agents and consulting detectives and Lord knows *(Sorry, Raymond!)* Scotland Yard is at a loss now that Lestrade is a Sheffield innkeeper. But you were at death's door and you are not getting any younger. Baker Street is no longer available. You've established yourself here and live a fine and worthwhile life. What could get you back to your old haunts and practices?"

"A request from His Majesty!"

She groaned, "Oh Holmes!" and the dog whined.

The End (*or Is It?*)

Angels We Have Heard on High - A Novella

Conclusion of The Adventures of Sherlock Holmes and the Glamorous Ghost

Book Three

234

About the Author

Harry DeMaio is a nom de plume of Harry B. DeMaio, successful author of several books on Information Security and Business Networks as well as the eighteen-volume Casebooks of Octavius Bear and the three volume Glamorous Ghost collection. He is also a published author of short detective stories (pastiches) for Belanger Books and the MX Sherlock Holmes series.

A retired business executive, former consultant, information security specialist, elected official, private pilot, disk jockey and graduate school adjunct professor, he whiles away his time traveling and writing preposterous books, articles and stories. He has appeared on many radio and TV shows and is an accomplished, frequent public speaker.

Former New York City natives, he and his extremely patient and helpful wife, Virginia, live in Cincinnati (and several other parallel universes.) They have two sons, Mark, living in Scottsdale, Arizona and Andrew, in Cortlandt Manor, New York, both of whom are quite successful and quite normal, thus putting the lie to the theory that insanity is hereditary.

Please visit his Website/Blog at www.tavighostbooks.com
His e-mail is hdemaio@zoomtown.com
You can also find him on Facebook.

His books are available on Amazon, Barnes and Noble, Book Depository and other fine bookstores as well as directly from MX Publishing and Belanger Books.

Ingram Content Group UK Ltd.
Milton Keynes UK
UKHW051022150523
421749UK00010B/65